*H*orses
*into the N*ight

T0325488

Horses into the Night

Baltasar
Porcel

Translated from the Catalan
and with an Introduction by
John L. Getman

The University of Arkansas Press   Fayetteville   1995

First published by Edicions 62 S/A, Provença
278, Barcelona-8 as *Cavalls Cap a la Fosca*
Copyright © by Baltasar Porcel, 1975
Translation © 1995 by the Board of Trustees
of the University of Arkansas

All rights reserved
Manufactured in the United States of America

99   98   97   96   95   5   4   3   2   1

Designed by Gail Carter

Porcel, Baltasar,
  [Cavalls cap a la fosca. English]
  Horses into the night / Baltasar Porcel ;
translated by John L. Getman.
     p. cm.
  ISBN 1-55728-332-X (cloth : alk. paper). —
  ISBN 1-55728-333-8 (pbk. : alk. paper)
  I. Getman, John L. II. Title.
PC3941.P63C313   1995
849'.9354—dc20   94-41275
                                        CIP

☺ The paper used in this publication meets
the minimum requirements of the American
National Standard for Permanence of Paper
for Printed Library Materials Z39.48-1984.

The two stanzas of Pierre de Ronsard's
"Sonnets pour Hélène: Quand vous serez bien
vielle" appearing on page 106 are used with the
permission of the translator, David Sanders.

The English translation was made with the
help of a grant from the Institució de les Lletres
Catalanes.

To Maria Angels,
who heard the gallop
of all these horses

*A*cknowledgments

I would like to acknowledge the cooperation, encouragement, and grant support I have received for this project from Oriol Pi de Cabanyas and Iolanda Pelegrí of the Institució de les Lletres Catalanes. The advice and assistance of Miller Williams and Dr. John DuVal of the translation program at the University of Arkansas, Fayetteville, have been invaluable. Critical readings of the manuscript by Dr. Charles Adams, chairman of the English department at the University of Arkansas, and Dr. Margaret Sayers Peden at the University of Missouri were insightful and helpful in setting the work in perspective. Finally, this translation would not have been born without the enduring patience and support of my Catalan wife, Pilar Eraso. My deepest gratitude to all of you.

Introduction

C atalan is an ancient Latin language, kin to Provençal, dating from the time of the Marca Hispanica in the ninth century A.D. The Catalan-speaking peoples originated in the eastern Pyrenees and came to inhabit the southeastern part of France (the Roussillon), the northeastern Spanish coast (including Barcelona, Tarragona, and Valencia), inland to the west of Lerida, then north to the Principality of Andorra, as well as the Balearic Islands of Majorca, Menorca, Ibiza, and Formentera, lying just to the east of Valencia.

Majorca became part of Catalonia by conquest in 1229. An island people located on the crossroads between southern Europe and North Africa and ruled from afar, the Majorcans were left alone to do pretty much as they pleased, including piracy, smuggling, and other seafaring enterprises. Andratch (spelled Andratx in Catalan), located on the western end of Majorca, was home to all of these activities and their protagonists until relatively recent times.

Baltasar Porcel was born in Andratch in 1937, heir to the rich traditions of the region's people. The persistent poverty and insular mentality of Andratch did not match Porcel's aspirations for a literary life, so in 1960 he set off on his first adventure by moving to Barcelona. He survived the first six months by working in a furniture store, at the same time writing articles and stories about his native Majorca, which were published in *Destino* and *Serra d'Or,* two Barcelona literary magazines.

His first novel, *Black Sun,* was published in 1961, to critical acclaim, and received the City of Palma Prize. Both ambitious and prodigious, Porcel's production since then includes twenty books and many short stories and essays. Through these works he attempted to free himself from the weight of the past and deal with an agonizing present, that of the declining Franco regime.

The more critical his outlook became, the more demanding he became of himself and his writing. He progressed from polemic essays in the sixties to a leftist-oriented existentialism, which was based on the realism of the man in the street. He sought his historical roots and Catalonia's reality by exploring the collective memory of his people. A thorough reading of Proust was invaluable to him at that stage. The Paris student revolt of 1968 deeply affected his course of action; it forced him to form a clearer definition of himself in the dichotomy of individual versus tradition, and to a reexamination of the value of individual freedom as opposed to the collective good. Porcel involved himself in the growing crescendo of voices favoring Catalan independence as he did research and traveled widely in Europe, the Middle East, and Asia. He absorbed new insights along with the adventure these travels provided.

In 1975, Porcel brought the results of his search into focus in *Horses into the Night* (*Cavalls Cap a la Fosca*). It was received by the public and critics alike as perhaps the most incisive Catalan novel since the Spanish Civil War. The novel was honored with four prestigious literary awards: the Prudenci Bertrana Award in 1975, the Spanish Literary Critics' Award, the Serra d'Or Critics' Award in 1976, and the Internazionale Mediterraneo d'Italia.

Horses into the Night leads the reader through three thematic levels as seen through the eyes of the narrator-protagonist: the search for his family roots in Andratch; the search for his father, who disappeared from his life during the civil war, never to appear directly again; and his search for a validating self-identity, which he discovers in the vitality of the present.

Porcel's alter ego has no first name in the novel, and his surname is only alluded to, which indicates his underlying identity crisis. The similarity in the sound of the surnames Porcel-Vadell is significant: it is as much the author's as the protagonist's search through the transient, ephemeral past that he discovers in courthouse records, family letters, and oral narratives of his uncle, the town priest, and his grandmother. The past comes to signify rot and decay for him, and dwelling on it causes his present state of mind to disintegrate. This is the critical moment of awareness for the protagonist, and perhaps a message to the reader, who will note that the novel begins and ends in the present tense.

Porcel shows us the transient nature of the reality we know, the mind's attempt to give order, structure, and meaning to universal chaos. Once the human condition is recognized for what it is—simultaneously weak, fragile, violent, fearful, tender, perverse, and loving—then we can fathom its existential nature. It is in *Horses into the Night* that the author begins his statement on the moral and amoral qualities of "the Good," a statement he concludes in a later novel, *Immortal Days,* published in 1984.

Porcel's prose style is often lyrical. His ability to describe what he sees and feels in his reality is astonishing in its evocative power and richness of metaphor. His landscapes often become prose poems in which he casts his characters. The moon, the sea, and the flowering of the magnolias become recurrent mood themes. In order to increase the weight of a mood, he sometimes loads a sentence with adjectives.

Porcel often extends the length of a sentence by adding appositives and subordinate clauses one after the other, thereby slowing the pace of the narrative. When he wants to pick up the pace or contribute a coda to a scene, he uses short, unmodified sentences or clauses. He frequently uses ellipses to indicate transitions from one thought or period in time to another.

Place names are quite descriptive and often ironic: Puig d'en Farineta = Porridge Hill; Pou de la Morta = Dead Woman's Well (one of the characters commits suicide in the well); Coll de l'Aire = Gap of the Air (where the mystic Sleeping Woman lived); En Caliu = The Embers; Puig de l'Espart = Alfa Grass Peak; Coll dels Cairats = Gap of the Beams; Vall dels Moros = Valley of the Moors. The prefix *Son* in the names of estates, such as Son Vadell and Son Farriol, indicates a large, well-to-do manor, while the prefix *Can,* as in Can Balaguer, indicates a more modest farmhouse.

Through these and other stylistic resources, Porcel has instilled in his hometown of Andratch enduring mythical qualities. His visual imagery runs the gamut from musical to violent to pastoral, surviving in the reader's imagination long after the book is put down. It is my hope that this translation faithfully conveys the author's poetic vitality and imagery to the English reader, for Porcel's work deserves a broader audience.

—JOHN L. GETMAN
June 1993

His very body was an empty hall
echoing with sonorous defeated names.

—WILLIAM FAULKNER,
Absalom, Absalom!

Was it the spell of autumn with its luxuriant, rusty foliage, Notre Dame rising in the distance, each stone so precisely cut and self-contained, its spire outlined sharply against the bleak gray sky? I don't know. . . .

I always get up late, toward midday. The heating system has created a stuffy atmosphere in the apartment, which makes me drowsy. I fix some orange juice and coffee. I open the window and sip the coffee slowly, then light a cigarette. And I invariably ask myself how I would describe the huge gargoyles perched on the cathedral I see in front of me just across the river. It's sort of an obsession, maybe tied to the dream that plagues me. Every night the dream traps me in its exhausting and vicious underground existence that I know nothing about, but carry inside me and have to relive . . . where vague, unidentified threats lurk. . . .

I think the gargoyles come from a similar world. They have animal bodies with the sleekness of birds, perverted by beastly, sardonic human grimaces. The Seine flows by, smooth, stoic, and leaden.

I usually drop by the Shakespeare and Company bookstore. It's right beside my apartment building on Bûcherie Square. The books, posters, and other unique objects, such as a balalaika or shabby postcards from the twenties, fill the decrepit bookstore to overflowing and exude a heavy dankness. The man with the goatee always nods off behind the little counter. It moves me somehow to think of the shadows of Joyce, Gertrude Stein, and Hemingway haunting this place from the time when Sylvia Beach had this shop on Odeón Street. It's as if in that remote air, in the eroded neglect floating among those piled-up shelves, an echo of their time remains. Among the corners stuffed with books—most of them used—I find a trace of peacefulness.

And every once in a while I discover a book that fascinates me: *The Art of War* by Sun Tzu, *The Treatise on Buildings* by Procopius, *The Book of John, Archbishop of Thesalonica* (an apocryphal, evangelical assumption), or a tiny volume just edited in Wales that contains unusual lines by Dylan that begin with "And when the last swallow of autumn looks at you. . . ."

Today, however, while a fine rain begins to fog the windows and Notre-Dame and the chestnut trees outside, those who burst forth within me like fireworks in the night are Jaume Vadell, Lord Escolàstic de Capovara, Gabriel Jovera; they are the voracity of the fire in the night, the galliots crossing the Mediterranean . . . yes, they burst forth from the pages of a book. It's as if they had freed themselves from the aseptic print, dancing their last pirouette, contorted and absurd in the late afternoon silence.

It's curious how these old, forgotten books have the power, as decayed as they are, to sharpen my senses and turn me into a conduit for the rescue of fleeting lives already sunken into the past. It's as if the dead, forlorn in the distance, endure as ghostly wretches. They still have a wisp of breath in them, until an arbitrary magic breeze brings them back to life again, even if ever so briefly. . . . I don't know. Maybe it's a premonition I have.

I found the book by accident when I picked up *The Shadow over Innsmouth* (reeking of fish) by Lovecraft, published by Arkham House. Under it was *The Contribution to the Relations of the Order of Mercy with the Slave Markets of North Africa and the Redemptions Carried Out by It* by Father Joaquim Santaló Baratech. It was printed in 1871 in Barcelona in the shop of Jaume Jepús at 9 Petrixol Street, the same publisher who edited *The Ruins of My Convent* by Fernando Patxot. I had been looking for it a long, long time—as long a time as I've been poking around through the dusty and ragged archives, through the worm-eaten family dressers of my hometown. I've been filling up notebooks with what I find, carrying them around with me all the time as if they were an extravagant urn containing the ashes of all my dead relatives. For years now, I have been toying obsessively with the idea of setting up a genealogy of my ancestors, a motley procession of figures lost in the savage obscurity of the centuries, but over which brilliant bolts of lightning quite often flash, or so it seems.

I was interested in the volume by Father Santaló because it was due to attacks by the Turkish and Barbary pirates along the coast of the town of Andratch—located on the western end of the island of Majorca—that several of my ancestors had been forced to sail in chains and leg irons. Jaume Vadell, who has now appeared to me out of the gray midday of Paris, was the first of them; the last of them turned out to be the apelike Arnau. My grandmother told me her mother had known him as an old man. At the end of the eighteenth century the pirates captured him when he was only fourteen. In 1827 he was freed by the very same Order of Our Lady of Mercy. When he returned to Andratch, his arms were long and thick, making him look bent over as he shuffled along. The children would run away scared when they saw him. He used to rock back and forth constantly when he slept, as if he were still seated on the rowing bench, tied to his titanic oar.

I was looking through Father Joaquim's chronicle in the bookstore, skimming over the disasters and rescues, when I suddenly discovered a fantastic piece of information. I paid for the book and hurried back to my apartment. It was crazy to think that it all began in such an improbable way . . . but wait, first of all I'd better tell the whole story. I'll have to go back to the summer of 1678. . . .

A warm wind was blowing out of the southwest one day as two Moorish sloops at full sail steered their half-moon bows toward the island of Dragonera. The island was long and sharp-cliffed, with the vegetation stripped from its peaks, its ridgeline in saw-toothed profile before the coast of Andratch. The sun burned radiantly, turning the sea into shimmering splashes of light. I have sailed these waters many times on days like this, and it's as if fantastic splendors had transfigured the sea.

Pere Papa and Gabriel Jovera were the two villagers posted as sentinels in the conical solid-stone watchtower on the island. Jovera and Papa lit a greenwood fire when they first sighted the ships skipping along at a heavy list to catch the eye of the wind and move in rapidly. With a blanket, Jovera and Papa sent out smoke signals to warn the people in the town. Above the town on the peak of Puig Cornador, the lookout blew his conch horn in warning when he saw the smoke. The somber wailing of his horn spread out over the valley, arousing the people to feverish activity. They closed up the portals in the wall around the town, set cauldrons of oil to boil, loaded their small cannon with shot, and goaded their great mastiffs to fever pitch in preparation for the attack.

But the ships didn't head for the beach of Sant Telm in order to reach Andratch. Instead, they headed for the island of Dragonera, where they dropped anchor. While the Moors clambered up the side of the hill covered with gorse and mastic trees, Papa and Jovera scrambled down through the crags on the other side to escape. The pirates were probably attempting to take control of the watchtower so they could attack the town without warning a few days later. In the chronicles of the times, these actions repeated themselves with terrifying regularity. Every summer panic descended on the town when the Moors came.

Like a lynx, Pere Papa escaped down the precipice, causing an uproar among the nesting sea gulls that flapped and shrieked to the higher peaks, as the wild goats watched them with annoyance. But Jovera, a flabby potbellied man, was only able to hide himself in a cave. The Saracens found him there and dragged him out through a thistle patch to the shore.

The sloop weighed anchor with the badly scratched-up Jovera tied to the mainmast on deck. I can imagine the sense of emptiness bordering on insanity that must have welled up inside of him as he watched the coastline disappear, the song of the cicadas fading among the pines, everything dimming in the glorious light of late afternoon.

The University—as the town council of Andratch was called—awarded the vacancy in the watchtower to Jaume Vadell who was described in the records of that year as "married with two children, owner of a hunting dog, no special occupation, twice sentenced for battery and robbery, and known as a drunk and a troublemaker." Based on those files, I know the episode well: Jaume Vadell is the beginning of our family's genealogical tree. Before him there is no trace, only the common clay of the masses.

After Vadell had served half a year as watchtower lookout, the unexpected news arrived that the Order of Our Lady of Mercy had obtained the release of Jovera. *The History of the Barony* by the Reverend Ensenyat from the House of Joanillo (that profuse and confused local historian), reports the news with emphasis: ". . . and it pleased God that in the course of that year, three captives from Andratch were rescued: the nun Emerenciana de la Trinidad Gilberta from a harem in Bugia; Gabriel Jovera, watchtower lookout from Dragonera, ransomed by a perfume

— 4 —

merchant when he was about to be shipped to Alexandria; and Tofol Claramunt, youngest son of the miller by the same name, who was being used to deliver water by burro." This last prisoner isn't mentioned in the book by Father Santaló. The other two, however, were listed among those ransomed in Algiers in the seventeenth century.

Then the town council notified Vadell that he would have to give back his position to its previous occupant. Jaume appealed their decision through a lawyer, claiming "grave damages, since I am a head-of-household and a devout Christian." But the custom was to return jobs to those liberated from Moorish captivity. The council, however, offered Vadell the first watchtower vacancy that might open up in the town. He finally accepted, declaring that he would personally hand over the job to Jovera "with great pleasure."

It was a stormy day at the beginning of March, the sea chiseled by whitecaps, the sky layered with low steely-gray clouds, when Jovera arrived on Dragonera. He was cold and hungry, and soaked from the bashing of the waves as he crossed the Freu, the channel between Dragonera and Majorca. Jaume Vadell was waiting for him beside a roaring fire, the gale lashing swirls of smoke into the infinite desolation of the place. Vadell, partially hidden by the smoke as if he were an apparition, smiled and offered Jovera some of the sea urchins broiling on the coals.

They sat down to eat. Gabriel Jovera picked up the first urchin, toothsome and crunchy, and peeled it. After he gulped it down, he cried out and began to roll around on the ground with frenetic stomach cramps. He died within half an hour, his mouth frothing and his belly bloated as tight as a wineskin. Had Jaume Vadell decided to provoke an immediate vacancy for the job of lookout? Or was it a question of pure vengeance, one of the many brutalities that this violent, angry man had committed? In any case, Pere Papa, who was crouched behind a wild olive tree, spying on them, began to run toward the boat on shore. Vadell chased after him, but Papa was able to launch the boat before Vadell could reach him. When Papa arrived in town, he told the authorities what he had seen. But when they reached Dragonera, Jaume Vadell was gone.

Vadell must have either swum across the strait or used a crude raft to get to the beach at Sant Telm. They searched for him for weeks in the mountains and valleys, from the foggy and deserted peaks of Galatzó to the abrupt gorges of S'Evangèica. They were always accompanied by the mysterious voices that echoed around the place as evening came on, always with the memory of the abominable bloody stories of roaming, batlike men. All the searchers found was a trace here and there: ashes still warm in a fern-filled hollow, a farmer who reported the theft of a basket of radishes, a furtive shadow reportedly drinking from the well at La Morta.

Finally, using dogs, they found him over by Plana d'en Verd, a high, desolate plain, and they began hot pursuit of the fugitive. Jaume Vadell threw the dogs off his track by walking through the glacial mountain streams for hours until his feet became numb, almost frozen. Vadell was near the edge of town one morning, bone weary, when he heard the yelping of the dogs nearby. He climbed to the top of Cemetery Hill and suddenly saw three huge, hairy mastiffs running toward him and barking furiously, the constables shouting right behind them. Dizzy with exhaustion and and weakness, Vadell stumbled up the long stairs leading to the church. When he reached the last landing, the dogs were nipping at his heels and the shouts of the police were drawing nearer. Just at that moment, Father Gregori Seguí opened the door to the temple and Vadell lurched inside. He had reached sanctuary.

Everything started off well for him there. A royal guard was posted outside the church and Vadell stayed put inside. The parishioners would observe him as he strolled, brows knit, up and down the immense naves of the temple, the sveltness of the Gothic architecture stifled by the shadows in which it lay. Or, they would find him asleep in a chapel, curled up against the reclining figure of one of the anonymous and indomitable gentlemen of the Conquest crudely cut in stone. These worn statues covered the niches that held only a scattered handful of bones and cobwebs.

Sometimes his family—his wife and two children, a boy and a girl— would visit him there. It seems there was a third child who had gone crazy and was mysteriously and brutally clubbed to death, according to the municipal records.

They ate together, onions and bread dripping with olive oil, under the severe gaze of Jesus Christ Crucified or of Santa Lucía Martyr, who held a small plate in her hand with two eyeballs in it, round and shiny in the feeble light of the chapel.

What did Jaume Vadell look like? Not a single bit of information has survived about his person, only the acts he committed and their consequences, reminiscent of hurried silhouettes outlined in sharp profile, like shadows in a Chinese play. And it is in that pragmatic tracing, so clear at the beginning, but in the end so insidiously ambiguous, that a sort of portrait of him can be guessed at, although *certainly* arbitrary and perhaps too archetypal. Could he have been a tall man, broad-faced and rough-cut, with the sharp eyes of a fox? The way I *imagine* him is full-shouldered and hairy, with tight biceps, calculating and audacious: a bloody-minded individual, as slippery as he is violent. After a while in this refuge he probably started roaming around in the church with increasing vexation. Forced to inactivity, he was all the more subject to the demands of the imagination and the flesh. By nature he was a vagabond with the habits of a predator.

Thus, the first conflict arose. Between the church and the rectory there was a little garden cared for by the rector's mother, a skinny old lady with a large goiter. It was summertime, with hot starry nights and the valley filled with chirping crickets and the interminable, liturgical chant of the owls. Since she slept nearby, one night the old woman heard muffled grunts and snorts mixed with clumsy thumping movements among her vegetables. She went out on the roof terrace to see what the noise was, and there among her dignified cabbages and delicate parsley, in the diaphanous bluish light of the moon, she saw Jaume Vadell and his wife, naked and intertwined. They were sighing and giggling, her thick white thighs lofted into the air; he was hunched between them like a menacing beast of the dark. The old lady screeched out in fright.

That was the beginning of a complex battle of insults. The rector tried to keep the peace between the lovers and his mother, but the quarrel reignited every time the old lady found the couple tangled up in her cabbages. Indignation consumed her, and her goiter grew. It wasn't long before her neck looked fatter than her head, and the town surgeon—who was also the barber—cut the enormous protuberance open and gangrene killed her outright.

Rector Seguí wrote in his register with a trembling hand: "Today we have given Christian burial to my mother, dead as the result of the goiter and the curse the Lord has sent us in the form of the watchman Jaume Vadell. She has confessed and received the Holy Sacraments and has requested that perpetual mass be said for her soul on the days of San Joaquim and Santa Ana. May she reside with God in Glory, amen."

After that, rumors spread that Jaume Vadell used to leave the church at night and break into houses on the outskirts of town and waylay travelers in the night. He demanded that they give him—according to a piece of paper later taken from him—"bread, oil, and game birds in order to feed myself, my wife and children, and the mastiff we take care of." One day when Father Gregori harshly warned him to mend his ways, Jaume Vadell attacked him and tried to drown him in the great baptismal font shaped like a monumental marble conch.

But the supreme disaster took place in mid-October. One afternoon when the church was deserted, a widower—a furrier by trade—came to pray with his fourteen-year-old daughter, Paula, mentioned in the police report as "blonde." I imagine her as a quiet little girl with long thick braids and blue eyes. . . .

But back to the facts—Jaume Vadell jumped the furrier and beat him senseless. Then, right there in the San Antonio chapel, he raped the girl.

About half an hour later, another parishioner came in to pray. The furrier was still unconscious and Paula lay disheveled and sobbing in a corner with blood running down her thighs. And the door to the stairway that winds up to the belfry was locked from the inside.

I often think about this episode. I remember reading it one afternoon in the courthouse—where the official had left me alone. He was that myopic Albert Balaguer, an old friend of my father, always dressed in black, his shoulders laden with dandruff. It was a dilapidated office that opened onto a steep alleyway, brutally cold in winter, where once in a while some old man could be seen bent into the wind, his face crackling from the cold, making the effort to get up the hill. I felt a subtle anguish at the time, with a nauseating, bittersweet aftertaste . . . and it comes back to me now when I recall that time and that document. I have never found any other documents that referred to Paula, not a marriage certificate or even a death certificate, and I have looked for them, believe me. Paula passes through this story almost as a sigh—adolescent, precious, and destroyed, melting into the black nothingness of history.

When night had fallen the judge appeared in the church, and under the magnificent portal of the Twelve Apostles—a wide semicircle of bearded reliefs—he called out in a sonorous voice to Jaume Vadell, insisting that he abandon the sanctuary of the church and turn himself over to the secular authorities. From the window high up in the belfry, Vadell guffawed and let loose a shot from his blunderbuss, splitting the judge's head open like a melon.

In view of the gravity of the situation the civil and church authorities came to an understanding, and on Friday at midday a group of them entered the church, including the mayor, a notary, the rector, a scribe, the king's representative, and two guards. In the empty nave of the church, his voice resounding with a deep and solemn echo, the scribe read out the sentence that stated the bishop was to hand over Jaume Vadell to the viceroy. No one answered. The scribe repeated the sentence three times. Silence. They then set about searching the temple. I made a copy of the case history from the archives of the Protocols of the Archbishopric, which reads:

> I hereby declare that in the chapel of the Sweet Name of Jesus, behind and beneath the altar, we did find the person of Jaume Vadell, watchtower guard, dressed only in shirt and undershorts, who did then come out of there, together with his shepherd's pouch, a bag of gunpowder, a gourd filled with olives, a moth-eaten cape, a dress coat in good condition, a rope ladder, and a blunderbuss he declared to love more than his own life. When the gun was unloaded, it was found to contain not only gunpowder, but birdshot and an iron die. In another little bag were found twenty-five more iron dice, six powder loads, and four cartridges without powder, but with just an iron die in each. Vadell declared that these cartridges were kept at the ready so he would not have to rummage through his pouch to find them. He added that he always loaded his gun with dice and shot because the die, apart from its effectiveness on contact with the human body, also spread out the birdshot better, making it a surer hit. Also, when it emerged from the person, it tore up the flesh, making a better wound.

Vadell was jailed—"enclaved" was the church's word for it—in the Sant Miguel Church's prison dungeon in the Bufera Tower in Palma. He saw before him the specter of the noose when he was turned over to the secular authorities by the church, because the latter had acted only in the name of the former.

Thus began an overlapping competition for jurisdiction. The Curia of the Bishopric, after having used the civil authorities, advised Vadell to admit his guilt so that there would be no trial. This would avoid the precedent of secular interference in the prerogatives of the Church, in exchange for which the prisoner's life would be saved. The prisoner then requested that "while the contention continues between the two authorities as to whether the supplicant enjoys the immunity of the Holy

Mother Church, Catholic, Apostolic, and Roman, the supplicant understands that such immunity does still apply to him, and to avoid the other contingency, does accept the punishment of perpetual galley slavery, and only in that case will he renounce such immunity."

And that's just what happened: "The 27th day of the month of August in the year of Our Lord 1689," the court accepted the petition, condemning Jaume Vadell to "go and serve as oarsman in the galleys of His Majesty—may God protect him—for the rest of his life."

On a day when the sea was lightly roiled, Jaume Vadell, linked to a chain of prisoners, was led aboard a launch that would take him out to the galley where he would be clapped in irons. He saw the galley far off, large and slender, rocking to the rhythm of the waves near the tower of Porto Pi in Palma. It was the *Santa Eulària Catalana* whose characteristics were logged into the records of the Admiralty thus: "one hundred twenty feet in length, fitted out with lateen sail, five men per oar. . . ." As they drew nearer, Jaume Vadell could make out the captain's flag waving from the poop deck: three small horses in gold on a field of black.

Jaume Vadell had always seen "the flag with the little horses," as they called it in town, raised atop the tower of Son Capovara. The flag fluttered in the breeze as if in sign of victory, and as it moved, it seemed that the tiny intrepid horses were galloping through the wide open sky. The captain of the *Santa Eulària Catalana* was Escolàstic de Capovara. As a child, Jaume Vadell, whose father worked as a shepherd at Son Capovara, had often played with Escolàstic. Later, Escolàstic left to sign on with the king's fleet. The Capovara family, descended from a Neapolitan who had been an artillery quartermaster in the court of Alfonso the Magnanimous, included themselves among the rachitic local aristocracy.

The estate of Son Capovara was large: it started out in the Andratch valley, passed through the low areas of Galdana and La Santa mountains, then turned back toward Vall dels Marts. Pleasant woods of live oak, endless pine forests, and unirrigated fields—good for raising carob trees and legumes—made up the better part of the estate.

The family house was square with high earth-colored walls. Windows and balconies were distributed capriciously, with a crenelated tower crowning the roof. At the entrance, a deep gloomy arch led to a cobblestoned inner courtyard where the high smooth walls never let the sun touch the cobbles. The façade of the house gave off an air of monastic seclusion, a medieval fortress isolated in the middle of the plain.

The inside of the house was a labyrinth of stairs and floors, of vast halls. As I write these notes, I often make mention of the corridors and rooms at Son Capovara, of its remote silence, of the courtyard with dark ugly moss clinging to its cobbles.

In the rear, a broad terrace lay before the garden filled with begonias, bougainvillaea, gigantic palmettos, cacti, and a central fountain. The lemon grove sloped down to the creek bed, lined with tall trembling elms, covered in springtime by those red and black butterflies with a touch of greenish gold. . . . While Lord Escolàstic was at sea, the rest of the family inhabited Son Capovara: his wife, Lady Elena, thin and fragile, had hair the color of corn, and was toothless from a typhus attack; her daughters, Ursula and Maciana; and the only son, Alexandre, a large man with a soft putty-like appearance. If the weather was good, the family would go out in the afternoon and walk down to the creek to watch the water stream by and listen to its playful murmurings under the tangled bridge of blackberry briars.

In the courtyard of Son Capovara in 1692, coughing and gravely clearing his throat, the mayor announced that the *Santa Eulària Catalana* had been seized by Barbary pirates in the course of a heated boarding near Gibraltar. The crew had been either killed or captured and taken to some unknown place in North Africa, since the Order of Our Lady of Mercy had learned that none of the possible survivors had been put on the auction block in any of the slave markets to which they had access.

Lady Elena fainted; the son proclaimed that he would avenge his father; the daughters embraced each other, blinded by tears. A flock of sheep grazed around the carob trees, munching slowly. . . .

Thirty years faded away. . . . Lady Elena had died in the meantime. Alexandre had not married, and I suspect there were whispers that he had unnatural tendencies, because in the book *Flower of Andratch Romances*, published in 1803 by Dr. Bonaventura Montmeló, there is a couplet that goes:

Of the Capovara, the first is Alexandre,
and toward the rear, he likes to meander.

The last surviving male of the family was also their firstborn, Alexandre, who will now concern us.

He was the one who took care of the estate, where his sister Ursula also lived at the time. Ursula had been widowed some seven years earlier by a notary from Palma, who died in the famous cholera epidemic that scourged Majorca. Maciana, the other daughter, lived in Palma, married to a cavalry lieutenant. They had twins.

At the Vadell house—a hut that was built into the hillside like a cave near Clot de l'Argila—the walls oozed moisture when it rained. In that hovel Jaume's wife had also given up her soul to God. Their son Onofre was a silent, churlish man, probably short of wits. He worked as a black-smith at the village forge. The daughter Margarideta, after giving birth to a stillborn child by an unknown father, was swallowed up by the brothels in town.

And no further news had arrived concerning the luck of the galley crew, by now considered definitely lost. . . .

Until one April morning when a rented carriage, its wheels crackling through the thin cap of frost on the ground, pulled up with Lord Escolàstic de Capovara in it. He had aged tremendously and looked very tired. His skin was wrinkled and burned a deep brown from the African sun. His beard was black and fan-shaped. He wore a large gray cape, and about him hung an air of somber estrangement. Only in his eyes did there remain a trace of the old arrogance: an intense look from the depths of his sockets, inquisitorial, always the same, devoid of any emotion.

The Order of Our Lady of Mercy had paid his ransom near an oasis in Tripoli where the Moors had him harnessed to a water wheel that he had to drag around in circles like a burro, accompanied by the creaking music of the water buckets as they emptied. The water was steely clear, very cool and fresh.

Dr. Santmartí's diary mentions parties and a mass that was organized as a gesture of gratitude to celebrate the return of the old captain. There were dances in the town square, an open invitation to the public to share sugar-water drinks and pastries at Son Capovara. "The illustrious seaman presided over all these acts, barely opening his mouth, demonstrating, thus, the terrible exhaustion and pain gnawing away at him from within."

The old gentleman walked about the estate absorbed in a meditative silence—broken only by passionate mutterings no one dared interrupt— as he recalled the horrible incidents of the African episode: the battle at Gibraltar with the shouting, the smoke and blood, the deafening roar of the cannonades, the boarding, the brandishing of swords and scimitars, and the slave markets, with slaves standing half-naked under the sun, a blanket of sticky flies covering their sweat-slathered bodies. The slave buyers felt the slaves' biceps and checked their teeth. Then came months and months of trudging through the broiling desert in caravans laden with intoxicating bundles of spices. The sullen camels were led by halters, and they bit the men from behind if they didn't watch out.

For years he had to clean out the stinking outhouses of a Moslem judge in the Atlas Mountains; then a vegetable garden near Tunis, where he worked and was whipped from sunrise to sunset for two years. . . . "And you don't die, because man is like a mangy beast who continues to try to survive, to live, eat, and shit, even though they spit on you and stone you, even though your body rots," growled Escolàstic de Capovara, his eyes unusually intense and bright.

A terrible aura of tragedy surrounded the wasted and noble figure miraculously returned from the far ends of the earth. The family and the local notables who went to visit him listened with respect. And when he had finished, the old man became absolutely mute and melancholy. Not even the twin grandchildren were able to shake him out of his mood when his daughter Maciana brought them to Son Capovara to spend a few weeks.

Captain Escolàstic stopped one day in front of the forge. There among the other workers, Onofre Vadell stuck an iron into the forge, pulled it out red-hot, and began to hammer it into the shape of a pickax. The aristocrat watched him for a long time and then asked Onofre what had become of his family. Afraid that the sins of his father were about to fall upon his own shoulders, he stuttered out what their fate had been. The captain listened with his head tilted to one side. Onofre finished. Lord Escolàstic remained silent. The other workers stood nearby, bewildered.

Finally, Escolàstic de Capovara slowly began to speak, explaining to young Vadell that his father had been an authentic model of abnegation and companionship with his fellow slaves during his Moorish captivity, always willing to make any sacrifice for them in order to keep the flame of courage burning. A little over a year ago he had died to save the life of another slave who was about to be punished for letting an ox get too close to a cliff, where it fell into the ravine below. Many things were tolerated in the younger slaves, but the older ones were eliminated under any pretext. Jaume Vadell admitted his guilt in the case, and they split his head open with one swift ax blow. The other slave, who was the real guilty party, was Escolàstic de Capovara himself. Everyone stood listening and looking at him with their mouths agape.

After that the captain went to the owner of the forge and asked him to set whatever price he wanted for the business, because he wanted to buy it for Onofre in memory of his father, the galley slave Jaume Vadell. "An august gesture from a pious heart, praised by all the people in town," said Santmartí, rounding out his narrative. Afterward, Captain Capovara charged Onofre with finding his missing sister Margarideta, stating that he, the captain, would provide a generous dowry so that she could marry "an honorable man."

That same night a turbulent fire broke out in Son Capovara. No one knew how it had started. It was first noticed when the warm sirocco wind lifted the fire to life, as if monstrous flowers were blossoming forth in the darkness, billowing out, liquefying, then shredding themselves back into the blackness. The roaring of the wind died down at dawn, and the ravenous crackling of the fire could be heard throughout the valley, as if a huge beast were grazing.

A whole wing of Son Capovara was left in ruins. Ursula, the notary's widow, succumbed and was roasted alive. Her panicked shouts were heard through the hungry red heat, but it was impossible even to get near her, much less save her. After that, the townspeople observed the man who had suffered every form of adversity as he walked through the back streets of the town, crestfallen and defeated.

Adversity repeated itself eight months later. The other daughter, Maciana, had spent the summer at Son Capovara visiting her father. The twins ran about playing and laughing on the terrace. They put straw hats on the marble figures at the end of the stairway, imagining them to be bearded warriors. Their grandfather would sit on the stone bench in the shade of the cedar tree, its green branches imperiously dark and somber. The children would come up to him and stroke his curly hair as he looked absently off down the valley where the stubbled fields and almond groves lay baking in the sun.

In September, Maciana and the children left for Palma accompanied by a servant. While the coachman grumbled at the horses, the children waved goodbye to their grandfather, who stood unmoving before the solid heavy archway of Son Capovara until the carriage disappeared behind the last turn in the road. Near Camp de Mar, on the hill leading to Font dels Eucaliptus, with the intense aroma of those immense trees in the air, a group of masked men suddenly appeared, firing off their blunderbusses at the carriage. The children, Maciana, and the servant were killed outright. Only the coachman, seriously wounded, survived. The bandits were never found.

At the church, as he presided over the unctuous chanting of the funeral service, Lord Escolàstic de Capovara seemed absent as he knelt at the prie dieu. He did not even respond to the condolences offered him by those in attendance.

"But yet another sponge soaked in bile would be offered that saintly gentleman," as Father Bosch i Mas would later say at the funeral of the captain himself. The priest had come expressly from the bishopric of Palma to give the funeral oration of the eminent gentleman, a résumé of which I found in the parish book of *Efemèrides*. The facts read like this: Lord Escolàstic's son Alexandre, who was fond of hunting, set out at dawn one day and did not return home that night. A search party was organized, then spread out over the mountain paths with resin torches, shouting until the echoes rebounded through the hills and valleys, infusing the abysmal gloom with a singular sprightliness.

At midmorning on the next day they found him at the bottom of an abyss, where he must have fallen. He lay crushed atop a rosemary bush, a flock of crows pecking at his guts and face. His eyes had already been converted into two bloody cavities. One of the ugly carrion crows flapped away with a swollen piece of intestine in its beak. . . .

Escolàstic never left the house again during his lifetime. He requested—and it was granted—that the office of the dead for the soul of Alexandre be celebrated in the chapel at Son Capovara. The old man followed the service standing up, with frozen firmness, the trace of a strange smile on his lips.

From then on news of his life reached the outside world only through the servants. He declined in health, silently and alone. . . . All the townspeople were present at his burial. They wept as they listened to the stentorian voice of Father Bosch i Mas extolling the illustrious memory of the deceased, who was wearing a mask of exalted lividity, stretched out in his coffin, flanked by tall thick candles.

Once the will was read (it is located in the Civil Registry of Andratch, bundle number eighteen on the fourth shelf), the relatives of the second degree—the only presumed heirs, since all those of the first degree had died—looked at each other greatly surprised, for Lord Escolàstic de Capovara had left them only crumbs.

The major part of his fortune was willed to Margarideta and Onofre Vadell, to be shared equally during their lifetimes, and to be mutually inherited in the case of the death or disappearance of either one of them. "Thus I thank and reward," the captain had instructed the notary to write, "the extraordinary service rendered me by the father of Margarideta and Onofre, Jaume Vadell, exemplary Christian."

Onofre moved into Son Capovara, which came to be known as Son Vadell some fifty years later. At about that same time, the family began to use the "de" before their surname. This was the work of that ferocious, vengeful woman, Elionor de Vadell, the heroic Duchess of Pantaleu who is mentioned in the annual Festival of the Valorous Dukes Against the Infidel. This branch of the family is the one of which I am, at the moment, the only living representative.

Outside it is raining heavily. I can barely make out Notre Dame. I pick up the book of Father Joaquim Santaló i Baratech again. When I was reading it a while ago I ran onto a note that has raised a minuscule constellation of shadows from the past. The note was dated May 1732. The Mercedarian from Barcelona had picked it up from a brother priest, the famous monk Anibal de Benavente, who returned to Spain blind after serving twenty years in Africa. He resided in Cadiz at the time he dictated his unpublished memoirs, located in the National Library in Madrid, according to Santaló. The diary says in part:

> A notable case occurred in Bongasik, Tripoli, according to rumor among the Christian slaves. They tell of two Christians born in the archipelago called the Balearic Islands, in a town where the Catalan language was spoken. They had been held captive for many years when finally the freedom of one of them was negotiated. His name was Cap de Tara or Capo y Bara. He had been a captain of a Spanish galleon and was knifed and buried in the desert by a fellow slave who then passed himself off as the dead captain, saying that he, the survivor, had escaped. He was thus able to return to the motherland, bluffing the Infidel, God, and mankind; but in the Final Judgment all will be known and judged. The sinner was known by the name of Badel or Bedello, and, according to rumor, had been captured by the same Moorish boarding party as was

the captain. I received this information as I was about to return to Spain, but I was unable to verify it due to my blindness, a reward given to me by the Lord so that I might mortify myself the more and thus reach Heavenly Glory.

What happened then, in the first third of the eighteenth century in that hermetic estate of Son Capovara? Nobody will ever know for sure. Who was that silent, gloomy old man under whose eye the Capovaras began to disappear, one by one, and the Vadells began to rise? What did he really do? Of all that happened during that time, the only traces are faint; the only answers are more questions. The details struggle in vain in these yellowing manuscripts loaded with unfathomable night. With the past astride those three horses, the banner of Son Capovara came to be ours as well, rebaptized as Son Vadell. By inertia perhaps, because it just stayed up there atop the tower, flapping in the wind.

I, however, never saw it there. The Son Vadell that was my fate to experience was that of its slow, lamentable decline. As for the banner with the three golden horses, my grandmother kept it carefully folded and mothballed in a dresser drawer in the room where they say Leandre Antoni de Vadell had spent his last years, crazed with love and loneliness until he died there. In a corner of that room stood an enormous violoncello, white with dust that had sifted down from the whitewashed walls. Half its strings were broken. They say it belonged to Leandre, who had played it in that room, awaiting his last breath. I liked to give it a furtive pluck whenever I passed by: it gave off a twang that reverberated and faded slowly through the corridors, as if a crazy beast were howling as it escaped the place.

My grandmother used to take the flag out of the drawer and hold it out in front of her, absent-mindedly. It was threadbare, the golden horses discolored, the black silk background ragged, a vague relic of a faded time and people. Everything in the place seemed to have fallen deeper and deeper into the slough of decay. I remember perfectly the last time I saw the house, as if the image were before me now on one of those postcards with the exaggerated colors—reds like freshly cut meat—that still manage to retain an unseeing, mindless vitality.

It was an autumn day then, just like today. Somber and imposing, the old house stood out against the splendid twilight, surrounded to the west by a distant purple glow, like the premonition of a solemn apocalypse. The house had been devoured by the relentless invasion of creeping ivy—unpruned for years—since long before the death of my grandmother, when I left Andratch. More than a building, Son Vadell looked like a mountain of brush, a bundle of thick bristling vegetation from which sagging clumps of sickly little blue flowers bloomed. The tower, the windows, and the courtyard archway had acquired bizarre shapes, absorbed by the relentless advance of the vines. The house looked as if it had retreated to a prehuman state, where the insatiably chaotic plant kingdom had triumphed over man.

Grandmother and I lived in only a small part of the house. The kitchen, dark and full of soot, resembled a long cellar; the bedrooms had canopy beds whose rotten damask coverings hung in shreds. An acute, almost palpable chill floated in these rooms, like a dense and repugnant substance. The large hall . . . it was in the hall that we spent most of our time, seated before a charcoal brazier on that sofa, ashen-colored from all the dust encrusted in its plush. The shabby, faded velvet drapes barely hung there, and the window curtains were so thin from many washings that they disintegrated if you touched them. The minute stitches of the mends followed arbitrary tears, sketching intricate abstractions against the window light. A copper pot and a silver platter were spotted with dark oily stains and had lost their original patina years ago. A sense of silent surrender floated amid the vast space of the hall, full of rancid shadows and the subtle odor of musty decay.

On the small marquetry table, its pieces of inlay separating in places, there stood a music box shaped like a drum, its paint blistered and peeling, with two ballet dancers on top. If you wound up the box, the figures would execute a slow mechanical dance, as though they were prisoners of an extravagant magic spell. The melody was subtle and weak, as lively as a feigned and frayed delight. It reminded me of my sister Cristina, smiling and pale at the edge of death. . . . In the winter we used to spend entire afternoons in that room, the rain falling ceaselessly outside. The brazier only gave off an echo of heat; the cold seemed to squeeze my temples. I would listen to the music box, always churning out the same tune, while Grandmother either dozed or sewed, muttering unintelligibly or obsessively retelling tales of death and her dead kin.

The walls of Son Vadell were covered with oil paintings in baroque frames, along with photographs of dead family members in bamboo frames. There they hung, all the heirs of this house and all those that Grandmother had been able to gather up from other houses where relatives had died. And if I asked her who that man was with the waxed moustache and the homburg over on the right, she would look at the photograph quizzically, doubtfully, and answer, "I don't know . . . maybe Antoni, or your father when he was young and shipped out and sailed around the world . . . or maybe my brother-in-law Pere Jordi before he went broke. . . ." And then she would mechanically move a little glass crocodile or a little lacquered box full of buttons to another spot on the wobbly table.

Like the individuals they had been in life—many of whom she had known—the dead left her indifferent. They were her tribe, like an infinitely remote kingdom that held her in thrall. The past—neither hers nor any other—barely existed for Grandmother Brigida. It was all reduced to a useless, boring labyrinth of confusing reminiscences: "Yes, of course your grandfather was a great hunter . . ." or "I don't know whether it was him or that Pau, the one they called the trapper—not the one who's still alive, but the one your grandfather used to talk about who lived so many years. Then of course we wouldn't have known him. No . . . or maybe it was the crippled one, before he got that way—Amàlia's husband. But we must never speak of Amàlia, nor should you ever look her in the eye. We have had serious quarrels, very serious quarrels . . ." She was devastatingly voluble in her meandering recollections.

In her barely audible voice she would recall facts and people who had no emotional dimensions for her, as if they were disordered slides in a projector tray. Only one thing—the wearisome weight of death—filled her existence, as if life were only a point of transition, a memory between two realities. She believed we were not only headed toward the shadows of nothingness, but that we had also come from there.

Grandmother Brigida wore a striped smock, faded from the many washings she had given it, using whole bottles of bleach each time. Shielded by that penetrating odor of cleanliness, she walked about stiffly, her head slightly tilted, her clear blue metallic eyes motionless and absorbed in the distance, as if she were always harking to something, something that was about to be said to her from the infinite, overpowering regions of the dead.

Mounted over a console table topped with a vase full of thick, immaculately stiff wax flowers, an immense mirror reflected the vast hall. In that huge mirror everything appeared magnificent; the room took on a magical depth, as if time and the reality of the room were different from that reflected in the mirror. I used to look into it, and would be overcome by the uneasy sensation of finding myself on the threshold of an ill-defined space, teetering on the verge of a concrete revelation. This space was carefully profiled and also ambivalent, as if the silvered glass harbored a danger. . . . Not a sound came from the rest of the house.

As the time for All Saints' Day approached, Son Vadell ceased to be that house of complex, unsuspected depths into which no one dared to tread, for that was the time when Grandmother concentrated all her cloudy and confused anticipation. She would launch into a clean-up from top to bottom, her mouth open, breathing heavily between her pink and toothless gums: ramshackle rooms with worm-eaten bedsteads, dark and narrow stairways, doors with rusted locks, parlors whose mildewed walls made them look like vast fields of cotton . . . she submitted it all to a feverish transformation that began with a furious pretense at cleaning. She would flick a rag over the surfaces of the furniture, just enough for them to look like a long ox tongue had licked them. The stirred-up dust formed a cloud that moved shapelessly from room to room, each time settling a little lower, until the particles again came to rest on surfaces identical to those from which they had just been dusted.

She would splash Zotal from a bucket—a potent disinfectant that ate into what little varnish was left on the floor tiles—stinking up the house with such a violent stench that it stuck in my head for days and days, as if someone had injected it into me. The windows, locked in the clutches of the ivy roots and vines, would open only a little bit. Even so, the fog of disinfectant managed to spread out to the courtyard. It gave the impression that we were keeping putrefied things all over the house.

And on Halloween, the eve of All Saints' Day, Grandmother would begin the most careful and delicate part of her ritual: from cardboard boxes and straw-wrapped bundles she would take out some little glass vessels. She would place various vials of oil on the table, then set about filling the vessels with the oils and placing a little piece of wick on a cork into each vessel; the butterflies, as she called them, were ready. The aroma of the oils spread through the room. I used to watch her, curled up at her side, hypnotized, while I listened to the frightening sounds of the evening and the night coming from the deserted fields, from the depths of the courtyard. A little breeze would whisper friendly and gloomy suggestions from the dark. That was when the long ceremonious troupe of the dead began to rise, their feet barely touching the stones. Up they came through the lemon grove, gliding through the courtyard; I couldn't see them, but my intuition felt them coming nearer, in silence, in their Sunday best, looking sorrowful, exhausted, and discouraged. I had only known a few of them in their lifetimes, but I had looked at all of them in the sepia-colored photographs with the flamboyant signature of the photographer at an angle in the corner, or in the blackened and cracked oil paintings. I was frightened by the mere idea of looking outside, of opening the door to the vestibule with its armor and weapons collection hanging on the walls covered with spider webs.

Grandmother would light the butterflies one by one, observing with minute attention whether the wicks caught fire or not, whether the corks floated level or not. I would listen for the inaudible arrival of the specters, each one of them imagined in hair-raising detail: Leandre Antoni, his lips a sickly red, as if he had just sucked on something bloody; Françesc Joan de Vadell, the elegance of the naval uniform enlivening the darkness of the picture; my sister Joana, in a photo that caught her in profile, looking at Mt. Galatzó in the background (I remembered her face contorted with anger, just as I remembered her some months before her death); my grandfather, his thumbs in his vest pockets, with a thick gold chain crossing his bloated abdomen; a group of distant relatives whose faces and names I always mixed up, all of them wearing straw boaters at a deserted beach whose name I never knew; a young woman with a prominent bust; Grandmother said it was "Cousin Eulària" wearing an Astrakhan coat with the collar turned up and a vivacious look on her face . . . and then the image of Joana would come to mind, or that of Cristina and Marteta. They would all smile sweetly; they wanted to caress me. I pushed them away, horrified. It was as if they were stretching out their arms, calling me to their side. . . . I jumped over beside my grandmother; I was trembling as she took me into her lap. She continued to play with the butterflies without paying any attention to me. Now they were ready, lined up on the table and on the chairs, their meager flames burning straight up, a laconic gathering of tender helpless spirits.

Then the phantom procession began. The house was dark, still full of the choking odor of disinfectant. Grandmother hurried from room to room with short shuffling steps, the little vessels bobbing in her hands, the wretched little yellowish-orange lights trailing behind her, and me clutching at her skirt. I didn't know exactly where those corridors of dense, fetid air led, nor where those ravaged rooms were, with their locks rusted shut. We left tiny flaming butterflies on the dressers and corner tables, on the window sills, and on the stairway landings. Little by little the blackness became populated by fireflies . . . tenuous lights that marvelously magnified the volume of the rooms. Everything seemed immense, inscrutable, mysterious. If you came near the fragile circle of light, unusual things appeared: the reflection from a mirror, like a puddle of water at dawn; a white vase full of flowers, all wrinkled and dried, the residue of centuries past; the face in a photo whose grimace of satisfaction or severity seemed expressly aimed at me; a section of the stair banister, converted into abstractly suspended whorls; a part of a painting with the head of a child, the eyes glazed; half a clock face with Roman numerals, like a harsh warning. . . .

Only the objects remained, for the dead were no longer there. Their imaginary individuality, their elegant poses had melted into the darkness surrounding the fragile flames. They were now like a seething shapeless mass, limited by the reach of the halos of light, a frenetic dough struggling to assume a visible, corporeal form. I thought if all the lights were blown out at once, hordes of the dead would overpower the house. And I almost imagined formless hands and faces surging from the dark with bony desperation, in a vain and wild attempt to put out the shimmering threatening lights.

The smell of the oil and the burnt wicks of the butterflies mixed with the disinfectant, weakening it and creating a new odor, less incisive, duller but more tenacious than the one before it. Wasn't it like the juices of the dead as they decomposed? It made my head spin.

We returned to the great hall. Grandmother thumbed her way through her rosary beads with a fervid obstinacy, while we each ate a piece of bread with sausage and olives, almost as if she could better perceive the presence of the dead with all her senses fully awakened. Grandmother Brigida was a different person then, actively interested in things, constantly watching the subtle incandescence, the rosy breath that came from the house and invaded parts of the great hall, as if to announce a startling arrival. My bread stuck in my throat, and I said to Grandmother, "What about my father, Grandmother, where is my father?" She thought for a moment and then said, "Your father . . . studied to be a ship's captain and he became one, and he traveled, but not much. . . . You had not been born yet . . . he laughed a lot, sometimes like a lunatic, and when I heard him laugh like that it made me want to dance. . . . Afterwards . . . look, the sea is very big and it opens and it closes . . . ." She was quiet again, praying to herself. And I thought about my father, taking form then fading away, as if I were seeing him through layers of moving liquid.

Grandmother Brigida, after finishing her bread and sausage, invariably recalled her first love, for the food had soothed her viscera enough to mellow her and make her more cordial. She acted like a spirited adolescent, for a while at least, her joy crowding out the forlorn atmosphere of death that usually gripped her. I never knew whether that first love was my grandfather or another man, because she would only tell me this much: "I was wearing a sky-blue dress, quite full in the skirts, with a lilac-colored ribbon at the waist and a broad-brimmed straw hat, white as chalk. I was just coming out of the mass for the Month of Mary, where I had sung to the Virgin—had sung quite a lot, in fact—and admired the bouquets of May roses that almost completely covered Her. And then there he was. He dismounted from his horse; he was in the military and often appeared on horseback. It seemed as if my breast would burst when he greeted me. The horse was a sorrel, slick as varnish, and in front of the church there was a palm tree. 'Brigida,' he said, 'have you noticed the sun's not so hot today? I've galloped down to the elms by the creek and they're full of huge butterflies.' I nodded my head, without saying a word and touched the golden cords of his uniform with my fingertips." And then she fell silent, returning mechanically to her rosary.

But the vision of her knight remained there suspended in the air. I could see the horse and the Virgin among the flowers, the timid damsel and the brave soldier. Every year on the eve of All Saints' Day they all returned from oblivion and played out the same scene, like the dancers on her music box who stiffly repeated their awkward dance steps.

*O*n the other hand, the memory (I was about to say the presence) of Leandre Antoni de Vadell for me was almost constant through his portrait, so strangely soft and alive. It hung in the vestibule between the portly grandfather clock—whose pendulum looked like an elaborate bunch of grapes—and a panoply of battle axes, blunderbusses, and crossed fencing foils entwined in a thick, fluffy net of cobwebs. The vaulted high-ceilinged vestibule was drafty. The entry door was sieved with cracks between its old oaken planks. The air from the courtyard blew in impetuously, loaded with an almost opaque, fermented humidity. Perhaps it was this air that had given an extravagant patina to the picture of Leandre Antoni: in spite of its age, instead of darkening, it had preserved a cloying aura of rosy clarity, as if someone had varnished it with a coat of egg yolk.

The man in the picture was thin, middle-aged, bony, and angular, with thinning red hair. His Adam's apple stood out prominently under a weak chin. The small eyes seemed obliquely focused, as if he were cross-eyed. The curious thing, however, was the hint of emotion that seemed to emanate from the picture, as if it were about to explode in a sudden bloody outburst. As a child, whenever I went through the vestibule I avoided looking at the picture of Leandre Antoni, afraid that it might burst open and spray me with some sticky-warm repugnant stuff. When I think of him now, I feel absurdly relieved knowing that he is safely far away. Even so, I still feel his presence as if he were alive. There he hangs, with serpentlike cunning, always watching, always dangerous.

But the letters seduce me, clamoring feverishly for my attention. Leandre Antoni died in 1795, at forty years of age. The painting must have been made shortly before his death, to judge from the cruelty with which time has gnawed away at each of his features, accentuating them, creating this brutal caricature of fleshly glory we are all in the process of becoming.

The letters—enthusiastic and blissful songs of love—reflect a still-majestic glory, like birdcalls in mating season, urgent and sure of themselves. There are nearly two hundred letters stuffed in a bag with an embroidered bouquet of royal lilies on it, like those that flowered in July in the garden at Son Vadell—long, white, and bell-shaped, with yellow pistils. The petals felt clean and cold and exuded an intense fragrance. The dates on the letters are from 1787 to 1795. And the only theme throughout the lot of them is the love of Leandre Antoni for Plàcida Sol de Cartanyà.

However, it is impossible to get a coherent idea of this correspondence, for the pages of every letter that the moths and humidity had not eaten away are completely out of order, and not a single one numbered. Paradoxically, this fact adds a certain delirious force to the expressions of Leandre Antoni's sentiments, the scenes transfigured by the adoration he feels for Plàcida. Not one of the pages seems to connect with the next, and thus the broken, zigzag reading of a group of them leads with crazed confusion from one topic to another, each of them hiding in a vertiginous tangle for the better part of the narration, constantly throwing the reader suddenly and impetuously right into the heart of new and exciting tales of the spirit. It's like dazzling fragments of a dream, or the hazy memories of a long drinking bout. And atop all the hyperbole, like a monument built stone by stone, stands the figure of Plàcida, magnificent and exultant.

Plàcida was the only daughter of Alfons, Baron of Cartanyà. In the volume *Chronicle of the Years of God in the Century Now Ending* by the Franciscan Anicet Marimon, we can gather quite a bit of information about the family, although the Franciscan Third Order denies public access to the second and third volumes of the manuscript, since they are often embarrassingly frank about the internal religious matters of the province.

In about 1790, the baron was a fat, old, weak-willed tippler, who vegetated in his dilapidated mansion out on the flatlands far from Andratch. His wife, Baroness Irene, was a crusty, dry-humored character who often argued with her neighbors, had had it out with the rector over which pew was theirs in church, and was unwilling to pay debts promptly. In all the local archives referring to that period, we continuously find the name of Baroness Irene de Cartanyà involved in some conflict or other. And sometimes her declarations and attitudes contradict those of the baron, who always seemed willing to compromise.

Today nothing remains of Son Cartanyà except some tumbled-down walls and a surprisingly well-preserved chapel dedicated to San Pancracio, the child martyr. But the fig grove thrives: luxuriant fig trees loaded with fruit surround what was once a house in the middle of the flatlands.

The Cartanyà family was practically ruined ". . . for Sir Alfons had busied himself in his youth more with soirées, hunts organized by the Viceroy González Alcorcón, and the company of *ladies* (the mere mention of their true names would offend Christian morals) than with preserving the health of his estate," according to the elliptical admonitions of Father Marimon. This profligacy must have been the motive for their moving from the city to the Andratch estate, where they made their living raising pigs.

In the summer, a great herd of swine grazed under the dense cool shade of the fig trees. The figs ripened and fell. They became food for the beasts, together with the fledgling birds that took their first flights and landed, a little disoriented, right in the midst of the hungry hogs. Swarms of flies and the stench of pig manure and rotten fruit hung in the air about Son Cartanyà, forcing its desperate inhabitants to close all of the doors and windows.

During the day the house appeared deserted. When night fell, the inhabitants opened the house and surrounded it with piles of rosemary, which they set afire. The sweet-smelling fires formed a wall against the mosquitos and the stench, as well as against the pigs circling around just beyond the light of the flames, grunting nervously, rooting about, fighting among themselves, and squealing outrageously.

Dame Irene died around 1800. The baron survived her, probably crippled and made an idiot by an attack of gout, but that detail is not clear in the papers I consulted. Plàcida joined the convent of the Clarissas in Palma. She was forty years old, eight years younger than Leandre Antoni would have been, had he lived. Because she became the Mother Abbess of the convent, a painting of her has come down to us. It can still be seen in the auditorium of the old convent, just off the little square by the seminary. It's the picture hanging beside the third column on the right, the one crowned with a baroque angel.

I don't know whether that round, glowing moon-face, inquisitively alert, has much to do with the real Plàcida from age twenty-seven to thirty-five, the time when Leandre Antoni presents us with his adoring vision of her. But of course when they painted her picture, a quarter century could easily have gone by; it's impossible to guess the age of the model from the face the painter captured. No, body and spirit don't come together until the grave. With the passing of each little fragment of time, we are transformed a bit: an old man would never recognize the youth he had been, even if he were to find himself suddenly face to face with that youth, smiling, powerful, and muscular, his skin tight and lustrous.

But Leandre Antoni immortalized Plàcida, at least in his imagination, making her the ideal woman unscathed by time. Through her sweetness and splendid flesh she became a triumphant creature, devoted and engrossing. It's as if he had carried on a tenacious, imperious struggle against decay and nothingness. I'll transcribe some fragments of the letters here:

*A*s I look at the bridge, I don't see what is before me. Instead, I see it through your words. Do you remember that afternoon on the way to church when you turned to your mother and said, "Look at the bridge, so dark this sunless afternoon, and look at all the swallows in the air." Maybe you have forgotten the incident, but I have not.

It was spring and the tenuous darkness of dusk was settling to earth, blackening everything. But the sky still retained a limpid, opaline phosphorescence, through which the swallows dived and swooped as if crazed, crossing back and forth endlessly, letting out an almost inaudible, nervous chirping, lost up there in the great void. . . . Every time I go by that bridge, whether at midday in August or at night in winter, I see it just as you admired it that day, immersed in the incipient darkness and crowned with the shrieking birds. That is the bridge I will always see from now on, the landscape sinking into the soft, diminishing evening.

⁌⁘⁋

I like it when you are naked and you get on top of me. It's not enough that I penetrate you, I need to be under the weight of your body so that you dominate me and possess me. It's as if it were you penetrating me, possessing me. . . .

⁌⁘⁋

You haven't come. I've been waiting for hours or days, I don't know. I don't know because I've ceased to be me. I've become a shapeless lump, sensitive only to your absence, as if an abundance of pain and anxiety might rush into the void, as if nothingness had a life of its own.

⁌⁘⁋

We both ate from the same plate today. We shared the cherries and the meat, the rim of the glass was marked with two sets of lips, one over the other. Kissing you seemed but the continuation of the meal; eating but the continuation of the kiss. The attention, the looks, our viscera, our acts, all converging on the same, our love. As if the whole universe were within us, as if we had shaped it ourselves.

Could it be that the world is made up of just one matter before creation, like the sea with its waters and fishes and waves? All one, a fusion: all your beauty, your bursts of laughter, and your teeth biting the fruit. . . .

✦I✦

I tremble with pleasure as my fingers run over your body, as I squeeze your tight buttocks, as I cup your toothsome breasts to my mouth, as I soak my every pore with the stuff you're made of. It's as if Mother Nature were in every part of you—as if the earth, crumbly and hot from the sun, and the trees with their solid wood, and the deep permanence of the rocks, as if all that had become softness and throbbing tenderness, as if the world had taken on your form and was mine, all of it.

✦I✦

The path to the pond only exists when I walk at your side. When you are not with me, it is just a place I pass by without noticing. But with you it is as if the daisies had just burst into flower, as if the stones had brilliant and suggestive forms, as if the feathers and the colors of the goldfinch had burst forth all at once. I take you by the waist, I feel your body under my hand, your warm body, and. . . .

I could go on quoting forever. But first I feel obligated to explain that everything in Leandre Antoni de Vadell's letters is false. In 1786, the year before he began to write the letters, Leandre Antoni had asked for the hand of Plàcida Sol de Cartanyà in marriage, but he was refused by the baron and baroness. Although Plàcida's better days had by then slipped away from her, it's probable that the parents were still waiting for a suitor of higher rank, at least higher than that of a local farmer, however well-off he might have been, as my relative Leandre Antoni surely was. Or maybe his sickly appearance didn't please Plàcida. . . .

It is also possible that Leandre Antoni, when he asked for Plàcida's hand, had only seen her from afar, or if he had spoken to her at all it would have been the most superficial of conversations. Apart from the rigid customs of that place and time, there was the fact that the Cartanyà family, proud of its nobility, didn't have friends in Andratch. And Son Vadell and Son Cartanyà are very far from each other . . . maybe the bridge scene was typical in this case: the man would be crossing it at the same time as the two women, whom he would greet obsequiously while they talked distractedly about the swallows. . . .

He must have loved her with a crazed ardor. After the rejection by the Cartanyàs, Leandre Antoni secluded himself in Son Vadell, and it seems that he barely left his solitary rooms. Like those blind clumsy insects flying toward the flame and death, Leandre Antoni limited his movements to the zone of light around a lantern, where he would write more and more vehement letters, imagining that through this mad and miserable self-punishment he could convert his pain into happiness, his inexistence into life. With his back to reality, he shrank little by little into an underground world saturated with aberrations and love . . . accumulating letters instead of sending them to Plàcida, stuffing them into the bag with the royal lilies embroidered on it.

It was my uncle Dionís, the vicar of the town, who unexpectedly explained to me what I suppose were the last days of Leandre Antoni. My uncle lived surrounded by documents, books, and archeological tidbits. It was as if his already exhausted life fed only upon the secular dregs he extracted from endless hours of poring over manuscripts, of being absorbed by archaic readings. Since he was nearsighted, he had to stick his head right down into the book to read. He was the cousin of my grandfather, and for a while he gave me unenthusiastic classes in Latin, history, and literature. . . .

It was wintertime. Hints of light filtered through the balcony's dirty windows that looked out on the cemetery wall. Marble crosses and untrimmed cypresses rose above the wall, as if they had been piled up there haphazardly. The vicar sat hunched down in an enormous wing-backed chair. Fearful of the cold that seemed to stick to his bones, he had wrapped himself up to his neck in a tattered red blanket. Only his bald head stuck out, as if he had no body.

One afternoon he was speaking to me of Shakespeare, of Macbeth and the hunger for power, of Hamlet and the craziness of revenge. . . . He went on describing these passions with distracted monotony until he got to Romeo and Juliet, where he stopped pensively. Slightly inspired, he began to talk of "one of our ancestors" who had died of love, "of a love not returned," I remember him saying. He then told a tale that in general terms corresponded to the story of Leandre Antoni, and which I was able to reconstruct years later. The priest finished a bit rhetorically by saying that "his death was due to unknown causes, although for months the symptoms had been apparent: the patient never left his room; he was consumed by a great weakness that finally left him bedridden, where he lay with his eyes closed for three weeks before he died, eating only bread and milk and mumbling nonsense."

During those perfumed summer nights, Leandre Antoni must have remained in his room writing feverishly, the heat of the oil lamp making the sweat drip into his eyes, blurring them. When he paused in his writing he would look out the window onto the plain, where the huge mansion at the fig plantation would appear to him, enveloped in its fantastic dance of smoke and fire, suspended in that foggy light that made it all seem an illusion, full of fabulous apparitions. It must have been in moments like these that he would take the violoncello and embrace it, saying through its unintelligible, harmonious musical language that which he could not say in words and which would remain muted forever.

Could some part of all that have possibly stuck to the portrait? It's stupid of me to think so, but in any case a vestige of that tremendously sick passion is what I did feel so many times in the shadowy vestibule, under that staring portrait with its motionless, swollen lips, long before I knew anything about Leandre Antoni.

*T*he white altar was illuminated by two very tall crimson candles that seemed to float in the middle of the church overflowing with shadows, like a phantom ship sailing serenely through the calm, oily waters of a nocturnal sea. Dressed in a stiff purple chasuble, Father Dionís sluggishly officiated the mass, murmuring unintelligible prayers in a hoarse singsong voice. Sudden coughing fits that ended in muffled rattles racked his stooped and gangling frame. "*Ite missa est,*" he spelled out in a cracked voice, his back to the altar. Then he raised his arms lethargically, like a huge somber bird about to lift off into the night. We all knelt; the vicar sketched an emphatic, absent-minded benediction in the air. Everything appeared to dissolve into mysterious, bottomless depths.

A butterfly, trapped in a thread of yellow light, fluttered in front of the golden miniature of the chapel. The air was freezing, and in some far corner a winged beast squawked and flapped about in outrage. It sounded like a solitary, violent agony: its echoes rebounded off the geometric ribs of the high arches and then were lost, resembling the muffled rumblings of a distant thunderstorm.

The vicar wavered as he came down from the presbytery. He pressed the chalice close to his sunken chest, his toothless mouth hanging agape; his pale thin lips made him look like some gelatinous, aquatic creature. He tottered toward the sacristy, his stumbling steps resounding through the pregnant desolation of the temple. Intermittent burps rose in his throat, giving off the sickly rancid odor of communion wine.

Not many of us attended that first mass; the townspeople were still locked in their slumber. I sat curled up beside my grandmother, who prayed hurriedly and without pause; she followed the mass from a distance with vague mechanical gestures, as if she needed to recover something soon, something urgent and decisive from the past. A few nuns from the convent—kneeling, murmuring hulks—were squeezed together near us, huddled inside their habits and wimples, locked within a clammy viscous world of their own.

A thin young man with a shaved head, an ex-seminarian whose tuberculosis had forced him to give up his studies, repeatedly ran through the Stations of the Cross hanging on the two rows of sturdy mossy columns, mere blemishes in the dark. One morning he decided he wanted to play the monumental organ again. Nobody could remember the last time it had filled the temple with the solemn fiction of its music. The organ stood above the choir, infested with cobwebs, unserviceable. With the imperious fan of its tubes pointed upward in the direction of the walled-up rose window, the seminarian sat down before the keyboard; then the altar boy pumped on the bellows. All it let out was a monstrously long asthmatic wheeze, while a heavy majestic cloud of dust rose from within it.

My mother sat in front of the carving of the Sacred Heart of Jesus His face looked down at her with perverse severity. She was absorbed by Him, her pupils dilated, her face waxen. Occasionally, my grandmother would look over at her out of the corner of her eye. My mother never noticed us; we never spoke to her. Barely outlined in the depths of the nave beyond her, some indecipherable silhouettes loomed, as if they were emerging from undefined regions where substance had not yet completely taken form.

The sacristy walls were whitewashed and covered to the ceiling with old images of saints, their mutilated nimbuses long lost to decay. It was a warehouse of debris, a nest of worm-eaten wood, the paint peeling from their antique and solemn visages, all of them tipping slightly forward, grotesquely staring at the floor, their features frozen in mute expressions of madness. In winter, on foggy days when the town seemed to rise up and poke through the smoky billows, ragged streaks of fog would seep through the unhinged windows, making it look like a last sighing breath overtaking the sterile saints. The figures bloomed and then disappeared within the grim dance of bearded faces, cloaks with rounded pleats, pointed wings, breasts wounded with arrows, the crosses inscribed *Jesus of Nazareth, King of the Jews*—their crowns radiant, their eyes wide open, all in silent, crazed mockery of the resurrection. . . .

Outside, I remember the silvery surface of the puddles reflecting the timid beginnings of the day. They also captured and reflected the huge volume of the temple, making it look like an enormous steel engraving. The church was the ambitious work of egos and prides long since vanished, that seemed never to have been remembered centuries later by the silent imperturbable stone. This titanic edifice had continued to decline, constantly undermined by the rot of time. The sterile fig tree trunks and the shrubby mastic trees had broken through the ashlars of what had been the airy flying buttresses. The rains and the humidity had converted the Twelve Apostles stationed about the tympanum of the portal into fetal freaks, an amputated, noseless, pathetic display of lepers. Cracks where the pigeons cooed and nested distorted the front rose window.

In the belfry, where the blue banner of the fleeting miter and the black banner of the duke fluttered on the peak, only bits and pieces of the sculpted cornice and one lone gargoyle remained—a beast, half-dog, half-monkey, with the wings of a bat. Could it be the memory of those many times I had stared at this ugly demon, intrigued and frightened by it, that has created the fixation I have with the gargoyles of Notre Dame? Those sculptures are like a blasphemy in material form, the appearance of the abomination I sometimes feel lies in wait for me. . . .

The last time I went to Andratch, I returned to the church. A memory from the past had drawn me there. I was walking on tiptoes, crossing the dark spacious enclosure, when I realized how on guard I was, as if a trap were about to snap shut on me: The tumult of memories had pulled me back with a brusque jerk to the anguished helplessness of my childhood. It seemed as though all those years in between had not existed, as if, as I crossed through the surrounding gloom, all my accumulated experience had been relegated to a useless struggle around an unbeatable central redoubt. It was this terrifying foreboding that so dominated my childhood, that foul and destructive tentacles, a slimy enslaving whip, might snap at me from out of the dark.

In front of the temple, descending toward the town, the proud stairway stood triumphantly deserted, serving only as a pathway to the void. It was bordered by luxuriant plane trees and delicate lindens that in autumn appeared damasklike, their foliage tinged with the color of molasses. . . . A scene comes back to me from memory: on the stairway landing, the Vicar Dionís de Vadell was standing, his legs spread, looking at the horizon without really seeing it, his neck twisted and his fetid breath escaping in boiling white clouds . . . a dog passed by, head down and determined. Drops of rain dripped solemnly, intermittently, from the trees. Then the priest strode off, a bizarre and obscure silhouette, murmuring the name of God breathlessly.

*I*t was there in the church on Sundays where I most often saw Aunt Amàlia, either entering or leaving mass. Rather, I didn't see the real Amàlia, but only the harsh personification of evil and hate, the image of Amàlia my grandmother had instilled in me. Her invariable warnings were bereft of any real ill will toward Amàlia, due to the passage of time and Grandmother's forgetfulness. They were simply irrevocable facts, irrevocable because of their aseptic lack of emotion: "We will not speak of Amàlia, nor will you ever look her straight in the eye. We have quarreled, quarreled mightily." So I saw her and I didn't. I felt her presence intensely: it didn't matter whether she defied or evaded me as she passed by, for she radiated both triumph and shame.

Then summer came, the summer of my sixteenth birthday. . . . We were riding our bicycles, some friends and I, to Les Dunes, the long beach to the west of the old abandoned port. We crossed through the estate of Ses Veles, loaded with intricate shades of green, the polished colors of the fruit shining secretly through the leaves.

The path wound between thick stone walls. Branches of the fruit trees from the orchards on either side hung down over the walls—apples, peaches, grapes—forming cool patches of shade scented with celery and mint. The frogs croaked in the canebrake, which bowed ceremoniously to the slightest breeze. Only an irregular slit of sunlight reached the center of the path and followed its course between the two walled curtains of brilliant green.

After the suffocating heat of the flatlands on the way to and from the beach, all of us were parched by the sun and rubbed raw by the sand in our clothes. Arriving at the welcoming shade of Ses Veles was like being rocked in a delicious caressing softness. We usually left our bicycles hidden in the first spot we found and made our way into the orchards; we looked cautiously for a ripe plum, or got a drink, or took a swim at the waterwheel. . . .

That morning we were at Son Farriol. We drank clear cool water out of the buckets at the waterwheel. We didn't see anybody around; it looked as if the garden and house beyond the nursery were abandoned. We put on our bathing trunks again and jumped into the big pond—the biggest in town—and tried to catch fish in the deep part: freshwater fish, red and fat and slow, that glided through the long tremulous strands of soft and slippery moss. . . .

I was coming up for air, my lungs about to burst, when I saw her standing at the edge of the pond, her hair tangled in the wind, her eyes boiling with anger. She scolded my friends, who ran off with their clothes under their arms. From just that brief glimpse of her standing there, I can still remember every detail of her body—each part of it, like a sector of a map. She was tall and thin, with her hips aggressively poised, outlined by a yellow silk skirt with many pleats that caressed her skin as it was billowed out by the wind and her ample thighs. The tendons in her neck stood out, tensed. Her small, full breasts strained against her brown blouse. She held her arms akimbo, her legs spread defiantly. She was the flaming image of fury itself, framed by the wind-lashed trees, the windy summer morning flooded with a deluge of sun that fused with the multitudinous chirping of the cicadas. It seemed as if the intense brilliance of the sun were making the day, the earth, the trees creak in anguish, monstrously.

Like lightning needling the night with its sulphurous brilliance, that moment overwhelmed my sense of time and anchored it to some point in eternity: a simple, unsurrendered permanence, one of those enduring memories everyone has, surviving all of life's vicissitudes and the process of decay. I got out of the water dripping wet, my mouth agape, trying to catch my breath. A boy of sixteen and Aunt Amàlia, a woman of forty-one, to whom I had never spoken, whose eyes I had never met, and who now stood facing me in a rage, a rage against one of the many boys who had invaded her garden.

She suddenly stood stock-still as she looked at me, her arm raised, her lips rolled back, teeth firmly clenched, suffocating the exclamation she had been about to let loose at me. Then a smile broke out on her face, a smile of dramatic surprise, suffused with dark pleasure. It resembled the emphatic fixation in the portraits under dirty glass hanging in the hall at Son Vadell that represented tragic scenes from Racine: Ifigenia, Esther, Phaedra, all caught and frozen in the ecstasy of their moment of pain.

Aunt Amàlia came over to where I had gotten out of the water, its opacity furrowed by the vague, reddish movements of the fish. The first thing I noticed about the woman of flesh and blood standing there before me was that she was not the archetypal, frozen and timeless figure I had seen only seconds before. It was her heavy, invasive perfume, artificially out of place here among the other odors all mixed together: the saltiness of the sea breeze, the manure in the garden, the soft clean aroma of the plants. I still remember that perfume; I can smell it even now, as if it were a part of me.

Later it mixed with the depraved, disturbing fragrance of the magnolia blossoms that lay open like decadent offerings, making me dizzy. The odor almost reached the windows of Aunt Amàlia's bedroom, which is where we went. "They have run off with your clothes," she said. "Come on and I'll find you some others." I followed her in silence. She had green eyes, moist and turbid as if she had been drinking. She smiled uncertainly, ironically. I followed that head of lustrous red hair, her lips parted, her elongated face with that green-eyed languid, yet incisive look that took me in and soaked me like a waterfall.

She walked nervously, yet with agility, each movement of her body outlined beneath her skirt. I felt the wind overhead, thrashing and whistling through the trees. We walked up the wide stairway to Son Farriol: I, silent and still wet from the pond, climbed step by step past the flower pots filled with dwarf palms, basil, geraniums, and flowering cacti; Aunt Amàlia, as she mounted the stairs, was outlined against the gallery of prodigiously rounded arches. One thing was certain: I felt I had broken with my past, and now life was about to begin anew for me, free and vibrating with lusty power, in a new place faraway from here.

Once in her bedroom she turned toward me. We stood there face to face, motionless and silent, the room saturated with perfumes, the magnolias agitated by the wind outside. She stretched out her arms and rested her hands on my shoulders. She lowered her arms slowly, sliding them down my body, pressing herself against me, panting like an animal. Her eyes were almost popping out of their sockets, as though I had suddenly grown larger beyond her field of vision, and she wanted to engulf all of me within her gaze. Then her hands reached my bathing trunks and continued downward, peeling them off me. I felt my penis give a spastic jerk, and my whole being concentrated on that exasperating exclamation of flesh.

She slid down to her knees but I grabbed her by the hair, pulling her back up with a tug. That long, lush red hair. . . . I pressed her close to me, clawing and ripping at her blouse. Her breasts lay tanned and bare in their abundant softness. I sank my face into them, nuzzled them, rubbed and licked them, while I grabbed her by the haunches, my fingers tensed over that proud rump. A frenzy welled up in me that felt like prickly bee stings all over my body. She was by then standing absolutely stiff before me, her mouth open, her eyes closed, not making a sound. I bent down and pressed my head furiously against her belly.

I threw her on the bed, a warm mixture of linen and soft feather-filled comforters. The headboard was a protuberant baroque carving of stars and leaves. She slowly spread her robust thighs. The nettle of her sex was ripe and rigid, the roar of the wind spewing wisps of magnolia through the room.

Son Farriol was the ancient property of the ephemeral and tragic ducal house of Pantaleu, with our terrible Elionor de Vadell as consort to the duke. She and the duke lived and died to feed their own demented arrogance. Aunt Amàlia's father, Daniel de Vadell, the brother of my grandfather, had bought the estate when he returned to Andratch after many years of absence.

I have since come to learn a lot about him through fragments I have gathered from various sources, including Father Dionís and another relative, Onofre Capllonc. But on that summer day when I went to Son Farriol for the first time, I knew nothing about him. I went back only once. Up to that point I had been living in a glass cage. I saw the world outside the cage, without being able to feel it or interpret it. I was isolated by my grandmother, and by the abysmal seclusion of Son Vadell. We existed only through words and ideas that expressed old fixations: judgments formed years and years ago, then converted into prejudices, as if the universe and its people were frozen in time, having found their definitive form in a past I had never known.

In 1894 Daniel de Vadell was twenty years old, five years younger than his brother Jacint, my grandfather. The latter, even in his old age, was a large man, presumptuous-looking in those Prince of Wales suits that made him look stiff in the photographs—a heavy gold chain crossing his vest, shiny spats, a large flabby face, his cheeks sagging in puffy bags above his double chin. He died before I was born.

I haven't been able to find a painting of Daniel. But Capllonc, who in the two periods of the younger Vadell's life in Andratch had spent a lot of time with him, described him as "a very jolly fellow, who could talk your ear off. On Sunday afternoons he would go to the Republican Center and play the guitar for the dance." The vicar, with a nasal twang, described him as "tall, rather thin, and often wore white rope-soled shoes and a kerchief tied round his neck. Later, when I looked at your father, I always thought he had something in common with Daniel."

I remembered clearly as a child what that busy little woman said as she presided over the elephantine Sleeping Woman at Coll de l'Aire, interpreting to my grandmother the abstractions that appeared in the clairvoyant's dreams. The Sleeper was seated with her eyes closed, exuding an acrid sweat. The small woman said that the Sleeping Woman, through her, would answer my grandmother's questions: "If your brother-in-law behaved in that way, it's because he was that way. There are men who go through life feeling the things that happen around them. Today they want something and tomorrow they forget what they wanted, and the next day they laugh, because as the years pile up, they feel that things have changed, just as their lives and bodies have changed. But not so with other men. To them things are like a house or a mountain—always the same as the first time they saw it. That's why nothing made him change in all those years, from the day when he thought he had to change things around at Son Vadell. Those people with ideas. . . ."

*P*erhaps there was a similarity between Uncle Daniel and my father, physical as well as moral. If my uncle was quite able to make his own terrifying decisions, my father, from what I have been able to learn and guess about him, was also a man of firm, solitary decisions that often seemed to be made without any consideration for anyone else, because in his world there was no one else but himself. . . . Is it possible that in this obsession of mine to dig down to the very roots of the family, what I'm really looking for is an understanding of my father, or at least a way to discover him in my imagination?

That forsaken, torturous influence of Son Vadell, with so much death and decay that lasted so long and reached so deeply within me. . . . Only the memory of my father—a tenuous but permanent image in my mind—seemed to carry with it an air of nobility, details of which I was unable to interpret, but intuitively grasped in my attempt to break through that seemingly impenetrable shell of time.

Yes, perhaps I *was* searching for him and didn't know it. And maybe I'm still searching for him today, even with everything solidly in its place, converted into a mental landscape that is irreversibly burned into my being, like the cadaverous montage of a Christmas manger scene. What I'm looking for could be the audacious resurrection of one of those figures, so that it would turn everything upside down, at least in my mind. Then I could get free from this impasse and transform everything into a lively allegory, since turning back time and beginning anew is impossible.

And wasn't that what I fantasized, many mornings during mass, with my eager eyes painfully dilated, trying to bore through the darkness and the hardened, exhausting reality around me? As I sat beside my grandmother, my eyes wandered over to one of the bare chapels with its thin Gothic arch. It was the chapel of St. John the Baptist, with its lavish marble baptismal font full of stagnant water, populated by larvae swimming nervously about. In one of its dark nooks stood the large sepulcher of the duke. There the gentleman lay, fitted out in helmet and suit of mail, carved in worn, beige stone, his hands crossed over the hilt of his enormous sword, and eternally asleep at his feet lay his little dog.

"The duke, Grandmother, who was the duke?" I asked, during those frozen hours of the afternoon in the great hall of Son Vadell. She continued to sew, seated close to the balcony, making the most of the fading light that seemed to drain everything away, as if nothing would ever return from the tangible world of things.

Her head bent over her sewing, her scant white hair askew like a fistful of cotton, Grandmother answered mechanically with a complicated tale in which she mixed historical detail with apocalyptic visions, respecting and distorting at the same time Father Dionís' annual sermons on the Feast Day of the Valorous Dukes Against the Infidel:

"The duke was the duke, and the duchess was our relative, and the bishop as well. They resisted, died, and were resurrected in their red diamond-studded tunics, so that all of us, the whole town, might be saved. The duke and duchess were like the king and queen of Andratch, and the bishop, Marc Maria de Vadell, was like the pope. 'The Infidel are coming!' they warned, and then the Moors swooped in on horseback with their machines from Hell, that is to say from the kingdom of the Turks, which you should know is way over there where the earth and the sea come together in an endless waterfall, dropping straight into the other world of the Devil, and the Infidel came up the waterfall, guided by the crescent moon, which is night and darkness, and that's why they come by sea, which is as we'd say, up the waterfall. And the bishop, his staff encrusted with emeralds, blessed everything and they were able to kill the duke, but the duchess triumphed and the dead piled up higher than Mt. Galatzó and Elionor the Duchess laughed, raising the flag high and the people praised her in their joy and Christ Our Lord smiled, that Day of the Faith."

I listened, trembling with fear and happiness, for I knew her story by heart. I followed her, recreating the spell of each of Grandmother's words, correcting her automatically, fleshing it out, for I had heard the vicar's sermon many times, and I would build imaginary mental castles with colossal battlements, and imagine bloody battles amid a deafening trumpetry.

I was moved deeply as I sat there in the church, looking at the funereal monument of the duke, feeling as if it were invading me, as if armies of the duke were advancing over a vast, shining horizon. And his image . . . the duke, buried there a few feet away . . . maybe he got up every Night of the Faithful Dead, stiffly dragging his rusty armor and his rust-encrusted sword around with him. Through the visor of his helmet I could see the empty sockets in his skull. Why did the dead rot? Why did only bones remain, covered with a layer of white and crumbly dust?

And suddenly the stained-glass windows of the apse began to change colors. The blue and the violet, the white and the yellow and the green, all the particles of color began to light up as the sun rose, passing from one stained-glass window to the other, weaving the story of the escape of the Holy Family from Egypt. The refraction from each piece of glass as it caught the new light began to tint the presbytery with capricious flourishes. Within my head the duke continued his stiff creaking walk, when suddenly I noticed two rose-colored circles of light rays passing through two camels from the Sinai Desert in the upper window, focusing with increasing intensity on the face of the duke's little dog.

Was the dog about to come back from the dead to join his risen master? I watched, bewitched, as two colored spots blossomed forth on the tomb. Yes, the dog would also awake from his stony sleep; then he would jump up and down around the duke in his steely promenade, and then take off after a flushed partridge among the lemon trees in the garden at Son Vadell . . . and with his heart beating, alive again, he would banish the gloominess from his master, the Noble Victor, who would suddenly acquire flesh and a short blond goatee and would put his foot in his horse's stirrup and would smile—even break out in crisp laughter—as he galloped off toward a distant land to combat the Infidel. And the dog would follow him, barking happily, running after the loud, galloping hoofbeats. . . .

My father's beard was short and honey-colored that evening in August when he left. He smiled as he told me the story of "The Love of the Three Oranges," as he sat on the terrace behind Son Vadell. "Well, it's time for me to go now," he said. He chuckled as he ruffled my hair, then walked off through the lemon grove. I remained there, standing beside the dry fountain, and it seemed that in his laughter there was an iridescence, like sunlight shining through the leaves of a windblown tree.

*B*ut I was back in Son Farriol and the people who surfaced and resurfaced in my memory were Grandfather Jacint and Great-Uncle Daniel . . . . My great-grandfather Bernardí, their father, had been a justice of the peace, as well as a useless pawn in a fruitless Carlist uprising when Amadeo of Savoy abdicated. He had that strange streak of stubbornness common to many other members of the family. If everything didn't work out just as he thought it should, then it was the fault of the rest of the world. The only measure of what was right lay exclusively in his heart.

It seems that Jacint constantly argued with Daniel about his always hanging out at the Republican Center. Jacint was also displeased with Daniel's girlfriend, the daughter of the lamplighter in the Port. Onofre Capllonc vaguely remembered it this way, "I was digging for crabs among the rocks when I noticed the two of them walking along the beach holding hands. I think she had brown hair and usually went barefoot. With the noise of the waves dashing against the breakwater, I doubt they could hear themselves talk, but they did smile at each other. . . ."

After many of the arguments that must have taken place in the then-sumptuous hall of Son Vadell, my great-grandmother would sit suffocating in a corner, fanning herself with a mother-of-pearl fan decorated with Japanese girls. Then, Daniel would appear later at night under his parents' window, accompanied by the euphoric little orchestra from the center—with guitars, a drum, a warbling trumpet, and a melodious mandolin—and would mockingly dedicate a parodied serenade to Bernardí de Vadell, his father.

A bit of his joy and charm from those years has survived in his portrait, a youth with a kerchief round his neck and white rope-soled shoes. However, what survived in the face of his brother, Jacint, my grandfather, was arrogance and pride. Jacint always kept horses, and he even rode them through town. As a young man, he would parade around town, mounted atop the most elegant horse of all.

The relationship between the two brothers was reserved, if not often bitter. I can imagine the practical jokes that Daniel must have played on Jacint, who probably treated his brother with a twisted condescension. At least that's what I gather from what happened during the last hours of Bernardí de Vadell's life. Although he was at death's door that night, the old man was clearheaded and calm. Jacint told Daniel that he would stay up and watch over the old man. So Daniel went off to bed. They woke him at dawn and told him his father had died in the night. He rushed to his father's bedside, and it must have been then that Jacint announced it would be a good idea for them to have the will read, since their father had changed it just before he died, while Daniel was asleep.

They went to the lawyer's office. It turned out that Bernardí had only left Daniel the minimum the law required; the rest of the estate went to Jacint. Shaken, Daniel looked around at those present, one by one. Years later the lawyer's secretary told Father Dionís de Vadell what had happened. Daniel looked at them all; nobody said a word until the lawyer ventured, "I don't know what to say. . . . The only thing I know for sure is that your brother called me to the house and I found your father angrily shouting insults about you. . . ." Jacint was looking down at the floor and was about to say something when Daniel abruptly got up and left.

Nothing was heard from him again until twenty-seven years later, in 1921. All they knew in 1894 was that after leaving the lawyer's office he was seen on the streets of Andratch striding along rapidly, as if possessed, and that shortly after that he had bought tickets on the stage to Palma. From there they supposed he must have embarked for the peninsula or some other place. He did not show up for the funeral.

It seems likely that Jacint influenced the old man against Daniel in those last hours before he died. Did he perhaps tell him Daniel was about to marry the lamplighter's daughter? Or that he had joined the Republican Party? I doubt that Daniel ever found out what was really said, though he must have been terribly sure of what had happened.

As sole heir, Jacint ruled over Son Vadell. The estate was nothing like what it had been during the times of the Capovara. Whole wings of the house had been demolished and new ones raised in their place. Almost all the woods had been sold, and the greatest part of the tillable land was now devoted to truck farming. The unfortunate Felip de Vadell—a real workhorse—had, at the beginning of the nineteenth century under the idealistic influence of the Royal Society of Friends of the Country, drained marshes and dug wells, converting the dry land into the greenest truck farm in all Andratch. It stood at the edge of Ses Veles, crowded with trees and nurseries, and was practically Son Vadell's only source of income when Jacint inherited it. However, he did have the stables that he himself had built, and in which he raised more than a dozen fine horses. He bred them to sell to race enthusiasts or to be coach horses for the gentry in town. And expensive horses they were indeed, requiring special care. They became their owner's obsession.

The truck farm at Son Vadell made the family one of the more influential in town. It set the prices at market. By 1921 Jacint was already white-haired, and always dressed by the best tailors from Palma. He rode little on horseback by then, although he still kept his stables. During the racing season he was often seen in town riding about in a cabriolet. It was so light and airy that it seemed almost a toy, pulled by his favorite horse, a powerful and brilliant black with a white star on its forehead. It seemed that Jacint couldn't go anywhere unless he was seated high upon that throne, his horse trotting proudly down the road, as if in a ballet.

He didn't take much of a personal interest in the land, occupied as he was with his horses. Didn't the harvests come forth predictably, almost automatically? Didn't the farmhands come and go regularly with baskets overflowing with fruit, vegetables, cartons of eggs, and cans of milk? One day, however, he suddenly had reason to worry. It was when he found out that another neighbor, in this case Biel Vergés, had sold his holdings to that lady whom he had only heard about vaguely, but who was now the owner of all the land that surrounded Son Vadell.

Perplexed, he made inquiries. It seemed that a real-estate agent in Palma had made all the purchases in the name of Lola Blázquez. She lived in Tijuana, Mexico, and she always paid the asking price. No one had ever seen her.

Until she arrived in town. First an automobile appeared, coming down Sa Carretera, raising a huge cloud of dust. Its wheels were thin and very high. It advanced down the street amid loud reports and a deafening clatter of sheet metal. The three people seated inside looked like ghosts wearing caps, goggles, and long dusters, covering them from head to foot. The townspeople, who had scarcely ever seen a horseless carriage, milled around the contraption.

The three occupants, two women and a man, emerged from the vehicle and began to peel off their goggles and dusters. One of the women was fat and very blond, her hair plaited in two thick braids that fell over her plump bosom. Her dress was like a cascade of purple gauzes. Rings and bracelets sparkled all over her and tinkled as she moved. The other woman was a green-eyed redhead, her face lightly freckled. The man was stoop-shouldered and stocky, with black circles under his eyes, his forehead deeply wrinkled and his eyebrows knitted together in a permanent frown, halfway between distrust and contempt. It was Daniel de Vadell, his wife, Lola Blázquez, and his daughter Amàlia. The surprise of the townspeople grew when several hours later the newcomers set themselves up in Son Farriol. The estate evidently also belonged to them. They made contact with no one except the hired help. Little by little, bits and pieces of their lives became known in town; a mixture, I suppose, of truth and fantasies which, diluted by the passage of time and the disappearance of those who shared their lives with Daniel and his legend, is all that has come down to me. Daniel de Vadell did not give out any details of his past, not even when he went to see the vicar at the end, when everything was finished.

Some said his money came from his wife, the daughter of a pharmacist in Tijuana. Others said it came from running contraband between Mexico and the United States. Yet another group claimed that Daniel, with money from his father-in-law, had bought land in the shanty town of Tijuana, which became a quagmire in winter, as well as other mountainous land on the outskirts, where he had built rental shacks for Mexican immigrants who were waiting to be smuggled across the border to California. The only sure thing in the rumors was that he had become a wealthy man.

The day after his arrival, Daniel started his projects. A gang of laborers plowed the rocky fields, while others planted trees; a group of masons fixed up the house and converted the old crypt of the dukes of Pantaleu—by then a pestilent sinkhole—into a huge pond. The broken gravestones had sunken into a black muck and were overgrown with prickly brambles. It was the same pond where I went swimming years later that summer morning. . . . Aunt Amàlia and the fragrant, wind-tossed magnolias, and the perfume. . . . And then came the wells: Daniel de Vadell searched for water with vehement energy. Dynamite was being set off constantly—one charge blew off Onofre Capllonc's hand as he was blasting. Sometimes they found water early, but Daniel de Vadell would impatiently shout "Deeper! Deeper!" to his crew.

Discouraged and worried, Jacint watched all his brother's activities from his cabriolet. But he still couldn't fathom how these activities could affect him, until the two water wheels in the gardens of Son Vadell began to dry up. Daniel had kept digging new wells until he tapped the vein that fed Jacint's water wheels, and then he dug even deeper so that the wells would draw off all the water from Son Vadell.

Jacint hurriedly deepened the wells that fed his water wheels, while Daniel kept doing the same with his. Then Jacint started digging new wells to increase his water supply and to offset Daniel's new wells. Those were months of anguish. Jacint had to give up his pastimes, his horses and cabriolet. He now spent the entire day in the fields, staring fixedly at the earth, as if he wanted to bore through it with his eyes until he reached the humid subsoil, where the invisible water veins and sudden gushers played out their mysterious games.

Jacint had never worried very much about money. Everything had always turned out well for him until the dynamite and the digging drank up his reserves. At the same time, the truck farm was able to produce only so much, what with the lack of water and the mess with the digging. My grandfather had to ask for loans from the bank and from some friends. Finally, he regained and secured his water supply. He had won, or at least tied, in the water war.

Then Daniel suddenly opened up another front. Now that his gardens were producing, he sent his men to the shops and markets in town that were until then supplied by Son Vadell. His men offered the same produce at much lower prices. Jacint became alarmed: if he lowered his prices, his brother would lower his even more. And he needed that income to pay back the loans. Grandfather, according to those who knew him well, began to dress more sloppily, to walk around with a stoop-shouldered, hang-dog look. He set himself up in the truck garden and absent-mindedly hoed and pruned by himself to save the wages of a farmhand and to watch more closely over his truck farm. He became his own gardener, he who had never lifted a finger to physical labor before. His black horse grazed nearby, neighing contentedly, frolicking in the moist, silky alfalfa.

Daniel, on the other side of the thick green hedge, busied himself with running between the rows, taking care that the work was done well, and all the time chomping on a large cigar that gave off a dizzying thick blue smoke. He never relented except occasionally when he would cast a furtive eye in the direction of his brother's garden, as if afraid it would somehow get away or reveal some miraculous new abundance.

Often neither one of the brothers was able to sleep at night. From behind closed shutters each contemplated the same inert and fertile blackness; each would imagine the same fields; each would even imagine himself out there guarding the fields, stripped of all the complex emotions inherent in the normal mind and spirit of man, hungering only for the other's destruction, becoming amorphous lumps of fear, subhuman lunatics, mental defectives. Their reactions became as instinctive as those of a snake or a tiger.

My grandfather finally had to give up. The bank took over his truck gardens. Later, Daniel bought them from the bank and added them to his holdings. Even today the garden at Son Farriol, Aunt Amàlia's place, is the largest one in Andratch.

Jacint let the rest of his hired hands go and took over the stables himself. He spent all day and part of the night with the animals, taking care of them, exercising them, and mucking out their stalls. On the south side of Son Vadell the remains of Grandfather's stables still stand, with their long, low doors and windows, their bars thick with flakes of rust. They lead down to a half-basement that is almost inaccessible today due to the heavy cobwebs blocking the way. These ghostly webs look like ripped, ragged blankets, remnants of a celebration centuries ago. Everything to do with the horses is still there: collars, saddles, harnesses, and even the cabriolet. It all hangs from the walls or lies abandoned and rotten in the corners, crumbling to dust at a touch.

Even after the foreclosure on the truck farm, Grandfather still couldn't get out from under his tormenting debts. Alas, the horses. . . . One day good fortune knocked at his door. A horse-trader from Palma made him an exceptionally good offer for his stable of horses. It would be almost enough to settle his debts, according to Uncle Dionís. But then he would be left alone, without those proud animals that had been the joy of more than half his lifetime.

Jacint thought it over. Pensively, he patted the hindquarters and the necks of his animals. He felt their hides ripple as their flanks shivered; he felt their deep panting; he felt the power flow through their bodies. He finally accepted the offer, but under the condition that he could keep the black horse, his favorite. But that could not be. The horse-trader's client wanted to start his own stable and he would only buy the lot of them if every horse, especially the black one, was included.

Grandfather had no other choice but to accept the offer. One morning in early spring the horse-trader and a couple of his stable hands came to Son Vadell, paid for and took the horses. Grandfather watched his animals go, his arms hanging limply, his eyes filled with tears, his face a loose, shapeless lump of skin. Then Grandmother went to consult with the Sleeper at Coll de l'Aire and mentioned the episode several times. Why? It's strange that this episode would impress her more than any other, unless, I sometimes thought, it had to do with that other dark and dear presence, always fresh in the depths of her memory—the incident with the young soldier on horseback, that day she came out of church in her billowy sky blue dress.

"I was frightened because it was as if they had taken a piece of him away; he looked so wrinkled up and wasted. I don't know what he said to me afterward because even his voice had weakened and faded. He spent day after day walking from one end of the stable to another, as if he were lost, and then he would stop suddenly and listen. He thought he had heard neighing and kicking, as if the horses were still in the stable."

"There they are, Brigida!" he exclaimed suddenly in the middle of lunch. He got up quickly and went outside, but the courtyard and the stables were completely empty; he continued to hear the noises of the horses: whinnying would cut through the silence like a whip, horseshoes would echo on the cobbles in the courtyard, a stable boy would shout at a horse that had backed up and kicked the stall door. . . . Jacint de Vadell, who was still in bed that morning, awake but in a daydream, got up and ran to the window and threw it open. There were all his horses: the black one, the two sorrels, the white one, the three dapple grays, the two mares, and the four little colts. Several men were holding them by their bridles. Jacint rubbed his eyes and looked again. Yes, *they were really there!*

Jacint dressed in a flash and ran downstairs. He threw the door wide open. On the other side of the courtyard, under the entry arch, he saw his brother Daniel de Vadell on horseback, sitting motionless, looking at him.

It was barely daybreak. A weak, leaden light hung over the courtyard of Son Vadell, where the snorted breath of the restless horses lingered in the air like ghosts drifting slowly apart, weaving a fantasy of frosty incandescence, as if a mythological transfiguration were about to take place. Astonished, Jacint took two steps forward . . . well, I'm not sure of this, but it was like watching a movie in slow motion. Jacint stepped forward with one leg, then the other, raised his arm and pointed with his index finger at his brother, whom he had not seen for thirty years, then opened his mouth to say something. Neither he nor anyone else will ever know what the words might have been, had he had time to speak—which he didn't—for suddenly two men grabbed him and brutally threw him to the ground in front of the horses, who were nervously pawing and stomping the cobbles.

The blood from the black horse came first, like the rush of a nightmare or an explosion of overwhelming blows to the head that leave a person rattled and groggy. They violently forced the beast to the ground in front of Jacint and held it there tightly while the ax flashed like a bolt of silver lightning. The surge of blood, flaming red, hot and steaming, hit Jacint and splashed in rivulets between the courtyard cobbles, now plump and shiny, bathed in blood, taking on the shape of a monstrous starfish.

The neighing of the other horses gathered momentum, as if the courtyard were filled with many other invisible beasts jumping around in confusion, their nostrils dilated by the thick odor of blood and fear. One by one, as the ax blows fell, the rest of the horses collapsed in front of Jacint's eyes. He twisted and struggled as he cried out, crazed by the agony within and before him. The young colts, sleek and long-legged, were the last to be beheaded. They barely moved, as if anticipating the ax blows, and then they dropped with slow humility, as though genuflecting on their way down.

Daniel and his men left. Jacint lay on the ground soaked in the horses' blood, at one with those huge bodies piled up around him, some with their legs sticking stiffly in the air, others still pulsing blood from their wounds, creating a mingled flow of blood and heavy clouds of steam. The eyes of the beasts, large and open and glassy, reflected a hallucinated and murky serenity, distant now from what had just happened moments before, far from their moment of death and the terror of each huge swift slash of steel.

Grandmother had to put Grandfather to bed, where he lay for many days as if in a coma. She didn't dare go out through the courtyard, what with all that butchery scattered about, so she used the door to the terrace, where she watched the corpses, slowly bloating and oozing and stinking, sucked at by shiny green bloat flies that gathered in tight swarms, terrifyingly still, hour after hour, getting fatter and fatter, until they could no longer fly. Soon the rats arrived, curious and suspicious. And on the second day, the crows, alert and severe, sat poised on the cornices of the courtyard. Then they descended with an unholy clatter of wings, cawing raucously in the fetid wind.

It was the townspeople who next discovered the disaster. The town council sent men and wagons to cart off and bury the carcasses. They fined Uncle Daniel heavily. And as for Grandfather, when he finally got up, he never spoke another word again, nor did he appear to hear anything. He sat all day in the great hall, hands crossed on his knees, like someone visiting somewhere, waiting to be called to go somewhere else. Death found him sitting just that way.

The whole town attended the funeral except those from Son Farriol, who were ordered by the police to stay indoors for several days, otherwise their safety could not be guaranteed. The day after the funeral Daniel went to visit Father Dionís. The priest told me about it, racked by his violent, hacking cough, as if it weren't that weak, worn body coughing, but the echo of another one, distant and gigantic:

"He came, and I hadn't seen him since before he left town . . . we were cousins, he and your grandfather and I, as you know. He looked at me as he sat down, without opening his mouth. And no, it wasn't as I had thought at first, that he would feel consumed with remorse, for he then spat out that he hated Jacint even more now than before, because he had been beaten by him twice: first, thirty years ago by persuading his father to convert Daniel into a bastard; the second time was just now, by dying before Daniel could exact his full vengeance. 'When I was young, just a child,' said Daniel, 'I had thought—no, hadn't even thought—about always living closely tied to Son Vadell. I just assumed it. I was *I-and-the-property*. I was one with the house; we formed a unit. And Jacint, when he threw me out, he threw me out of my house, out of my land, and out of myself. I thought I would go crazy. And if I worked and made money,' Daniel continued, chewing the words without looking at me, 'it was only so that I could get my revenge. For years and years I thought about only that, working out my plan detail by detail. Everything in my life was provisional, all the time waiting to return here and annihilate Jacint, him and his property. It didn't matter to me that I had to feed off stinking carcasses like a hyena; I had become this hate, this maniacal desire to do him harm, to enjoy watching him crumbling in my hands. As fire is to wood, everything I did my whole life, the properties I bought and built up, everything

— 49 —

was related to Jacint. Never, never in my life did I ever consider that he might die, or that I might kill him, for that matter. Never. Maybe it was because I had never thought about my own death. And now he's gone. He's stolen everything from me again, thrown me out again from the world I had made for myself. I'll leave for I don't know where, to work, to do whatever it takes to get me going again. If I stay here I'll die.' And he got up and left. I don't think I said a single word to him all the time he was there. Nor did he expect me to. A couple of years later, just after he had married off his daughter, I heard rumors that he was no longer around here. I have never heard another word about Daniel de Vadell."

The vicar fell silent, adding after a while, pensively, "They say that when he left he took the Vadell flag. I don't know whether you knew that he had one put up at his house when he bought the truck gardens . . . the three horses on the black background. It's silly, I know, but I thought it was as if the horses had come out of the flaming gold and had galloped off into the night, crushing everyone in their path . . . I didn't see the dead horses in the courtyard; no, not I. I still don't picture them that way . . . they should gallop on forever, riderless through the night . . . and leave destruction behind."

*I*t was through the flag with the three horses on it that I got to know the story of Felip de Vadell, the father of Admiral Françesc Juan de Vadell. I was walking along Palla Street in Barcelona one day when a window display of books on sailing and old maps in a used bookstore caught my attention. As I came closer, one of the books leapt out at me. It carried our family coat of arms embossed on the cover. It was titled *The Lonely Times of Felip de Vadell* and was printed in Morella in 1944. Its author, Eduard Albert, was unknown to me, but I bought it anyway.

A matter never cleared up by the historians is how Françesc Joan de Vadell managed to come into his inheritance in 1813 and at such a young age, since the death certificate of his father, Felip, was dated 1830. It's probably because the researchers had concentrated their efforts—and rightly so—on the two great achievements of that mariner, leaving family and economic matters aside, even though they played an important part in the maritime career of Françesc Joan.

On the first of these occasions, the omission was less important, since it was a daring mixture of intuition and skill that permitted Françesc Joan to come and go as he pleased from Mahon to any point on the northwest peninsular coast as captain of the ship *Son of God*. He did this from 1808 to about 1810 while he was a young officer of twenty-two. He worked as liaison between Lord Collingwood, then commander of the British Fleet in the Mediterranean, and General Wellesley, the future Duke of Wellington and supreme commander of the English Expeditionary Force in Spain and Portugal. Wellesley was in command of the mobile forces, and Collingwood commanded the base at Mahon, Menorca. The French sailed the waters between them. Françesc Joan de Vadell even transported the personal aide of Castlereagh, minister of war under the Portland cabinet, from Galicia to Menorca. He was the courier who carried the British strategic war plans against Napoleon. The famous *History of the Royal Armada* by Sir Robert Crossen and staff devotes about five lines of praise to him.

But the struggle he carried on against the Algerians, then part of the Ottoman Empire, is another thing entirely. As the Napoleonic war enveloped Europe, the Maghreb pirates acted with enormous impunity in the upper Mediterranean. From about 1814 until 1830 (the year of the French conquest of Algiers) Françesc Joan fought against the depredations of the Algerian pirate ships as commander of two successive ships of his own, *Valor* and *Principe de Asturias*. The results were bloody and highly effective. He personally equipped and armed the ships at his own expense, although they sailed under the flag and direct authority of His Majesty, he did not operate as a privateer.

Noam Ventury, Pierre Saint Suplice, Josep Moliner Udina, and Esteban Pérez de Castro—to name only four specialists from various countries—all recognized the constant peace-keeping efforts of Commander de Vadell. The battle off the coast of Djidjelli was fought on a day in 1818 when the north wind turned the air clear and icy sharp, and the sea was roiled with greenish-white waves roughly curled by the crisp wind. The battle is noted by both the Catalan and the French writers. Vadell sank two Algerian ships and captured three others, one of which had the son of the Sultan of Constantinople on board.

In spite of the captured enemy property, such a campaign would have been very difficult to sustain or even to initiate without the fortune Felip de Vadell had passed on to his son while still alive himself. It was the author of the work published in Morella who provided the key to this previously neglected question.

Eduard Albert was born in Valencia and spent many years as secretary of the town council in San Miguel, capital of the Maestrazgo. Isolated from the rest of the world, he published at his own expense some pamphlets dealing with strange themes overlooked by the major historians, such as *News of Gil Mocoso, Spanish Military Observer in the Crimean War* (1885), and *On the Excessive Use of Salt on the Berber Galleys of the Eighteenth Century. The Lonely Times of Felip de Vadell* is only thirty-seven pages in a quarto edition. It carried the seal of ecclesiastic approval from the bishopric of Segorbe, and under the date on the colophon page, it states that it was published in the fourth year of victory.

The prologue is picturesque. Albert relates that in July of 1936 he bought more than eighty kilos of assorted books and papers from a junk dealer in Valencia, most of which was dated before 1914. The dealer got it from a wealthy family who had fled during the early days of the Popular Front, leaving everything behind. Albert paid very little for the lot, and set about examining it carefully, "since in those bitter days of struggle and impiety it was consoling to immerse oneself in papers from a time that could do no harm to anyone," he explained. He didn't find much of interest: some banal religious literature, legislative tracts, some geography and physics books. Many of the books had been bound in parchment, no doubt from older folio volumes. Eduard Albert decided to take apart the least interesting ones and save the parchment to bind better works of his own.

That was how he came across a long document he couldn't find a good use for at the time. In it, a woman named Benvinguda Clapés tells the notary of the town of Andratch a disconcerting story. . . . It was not until three years later while working on the project of the salt and Berber galleys that he discovered Admiral de Vadell's full name was Vadell Clapés, and that Benvinguda Clapés was his mother.

I'll give a brief résumé of Albert's study. It begins by explaining that the marriage of Felip (the son of the youngest brother and the heir to Leandre Antoni de Vadell, Plàcida Sol de Cartanyà's lover) and

Benvinguda produced one son, Françesc Joan, and three daughters, Adelaida, Rosa, and Maria Mercè.

They lived at Son Vadell, where Felip—the friend of a Palma banker named Baltasar Suan, who was also a member of the Board of Governors of the Royal Society of Friends of the Country—carried on an agricultural program that was "intelligent and effective," according to the norms of that society. The truck gardens at Son Vadell, as I explained earlier, were the fruit of his efforts. Reforesting, digging wells, and draining wetlands were his goals. In the course of a dozen years he changed the appearance of his estate substantially.

I don't know whether the picture the erudite Valencian author paints of Felip is too commonplace or not, but there's no reason to doubt it. He describes a very plump Benvinguda, kneading honey-tart dough and setting crocks on the fire copiously laden with pork, chick peas, and cabbage. . . . Two of her daughters were already engaged, one to the owner of a couple of flour mills and an olive oil press, and the other to a law student from Andratch studying at the University of Cervera. Françesc Joan was the youngest of the children, and he was placed with a local priest who taught him the elements of reading and writing. The boy, according to Albert, had "from his earliest childhood shown an interest in the sea, obeying the call of Destiny."

Nobody paid much attention when some brownish spots appeared and later became more prominent on Felip's face and hands. "He must be working too hard" and "a temporary eczema," said the family. Soon the spots became red, running sores that scabbed over. The doctor advised treatment with salves, but the sores didn't go away; they grew larger instead.

Until one day they decided to go to Palma. They hitched up the wagon, and, well-provisioned with food, Felip, Benvinguda, Françesc Joan, and a servant set out to cover the seven leagues between Andratch and the city. The doctor was either Pou Villalonga or Dr. Martí y Montcada, who were the best known at the time according to what I was able to gather from the files of the Association of Pharmacists. Such a long trip wasn't meant to be just any everyday consultation.

The diagnosis was diabolically simple, leprosy. Felip fainted, and in the wagon on the way home he wept silently as they trundled up and down the hills, through the pine forest, and around the tight curves that followed the coves licked by the sea. He sat beside his wife, who was piously pensive and kept to herself, as Benvinguda later narrated to the notary. The son "had cut a branch of wild olive and was smacking the mules with it unnecessarily, with an anger not meant for the poor animals."

Eduard Albert transcribed her declaration in its entirety, and it is greatly expressive of the atmosphere at Son Vadell once the wagon reached home: ". . . and my husband sat separate from us in a corner facing the wall, and my children sat together on the other side of the dining room, and I sat in the middle, and nobody said anything because we didn't know how to talk about it, because it was as if a stranger with no resemblance to any of God's creatures had moved in there, separating us and staring at us all."

It was then, presumably under the brutal pressure of the truth, that the family situation changed completely. What had been Felip de Vadell's sustaining force until then? Love for his wife and his children, a desire for their well-being, a deep dedication to his work on the farm, and from what evidence I was able to gather, a certain physical strength and a friendly character. But then suddenly his whole world fell apart. Beyond the physical pain he suffered, Felip realized that he had ceased to be the person he had been up until then. This was a mental—or rather a moral—revelation to him; in the space of a couple of days something had happened: nothing less than the intellectual understanding of a concept, more than a fact. It was a revelation that would change his future from top to bottom, and it meant something more cruel than just an early death as the result of the disease. He saw in the eyes of his children and his wife that he had not only ceased to exist as father and husband, but that they were revolted beyond all comprehension, as much by the illness itself as by the fear of contagion. And it was not possible to change a thing. The new situation was irreversible.

That same night they made him sleep in the hayloft. He left the house crestfallen, a defeated man. The rest of the family argued nearly until dawn, and when the sun came up Benvinguda and Françesc Joan went out to speak with Felip. The son remained at the foot of the ladder to the loft. The mother went up. The daughters watched from a window in the house.

The decision they had taken was that Felip should sign over all his property to the family and the son should become the head of household. Felip should then disappear and set himself up in the hills nearby, where they would bring him food and whatever else he might need. The leper docilely assented to everything they proposed. The feeling of defeat, of despondency, of nearing the end, must have overwhelmed his soul, like being buried under an avalanche. His only thoughts were of his own fall and destruction. The only thing he must have wanted was to stay there, buried in the hay and the dark, for the solitude it gave him: ". . . and until he left on the third day, he did not come out of the loft nor say a word," Benvinguda Clapés recalled.

He left loaded down with a bundle containing a couple of blankets, a water jug, a rope, a little picture of the Virgin . . . and he set himself up in the crypt at Son Farriol, from where he could see, beyond the flatlands of almond trees and truck gardens, the house at Son Vadell rising above the lemon grove. Each week he was supposed to come down to a spot where a carob tree grew, and there they would give him food and water.

The crypt lay at the bottom of a steep hill in a run-down olive grove not far from the house at Son Farriol, abandoned seventy years before in the time of the duke of Pantaleu. The low area was rough and overgrown with brush: furze, gorse, and wild olive. A heavy rotten odor hung over the area, and the sunlight never entered it. The peasants had used the place for some time as a dump for dead animals. Bare bones and long, weathered skeletons and pieces of stinking carcasses stuck out from among the dark green plants. And the crows were always there, watching motionless on a branch, soaring slowly overhead, cawing stridently in the wind.

In the center of the hollow there was a semicircle built of brick. It was the cúpola of the crypt, accessible through a rusty iron gate opening onto a stairway covered with green slime. It seemed to drop down into the bowels of the earth itself. "A humid vapor, smelling of rotten vegetation, arose from that subterranean hole in which a dozen gravestones were lined up, broken and disfigured, all covered with black, dripping lichen. Some of them were simple, enormous geometric cubes, while others were bizarre upraised angels; on one, a bulky stone lady slept, covered with prickly bushes. An uncertain light filtered through the half-blocked skylights. And I saw many sleeping bats hanging from the ceiling, like little soft velvet bags."

The description in quotes is from Claude de Bainville. The scene I am describing is taken from some engravings by Stéphane Corbière, the friend of Doré. Corbière and Bainville took a trip through the islands in 1887, and they published their experiences under the title *A Stay in the Balearic Archipelago*. I suppose they were guided by the latest romantic extremes, since they entertained themselves by visiting places like the crypt at Son Farriol. The writer created a detailed semblance of it, and Corbière, although he carved in boxwood, which left heavy lines in the engraving, managed to create a remarkably gloomy atmosphere in the print.

What Claude de Bainville didn't know was that probably the only human remains left in the crypt were those of Felip de Vadell, already disintegrated in the dirt and mud. The remains of the duke and duchess of Pantaleu and the bishop had been moved to the local churchyard. However, when the leper took refuge in the crypt, the ducal bones were still there. And although the Frenchmen's notes were written more than half a century after Felip de Vadell's time, I suppose few things would have changed in the hollow, which in the course of another huge turn of the wheel of fortune, a new Vadell would convert into a pond where I, still later, would go swimming, would get to know Amàlia, and consequently would move back through time to an unknown side of the distant history of my father, all part of the subtle, hidden web that forms and ensnares us. . . .

Sometimes the shrill croaking of the frogs would echo through the crypt, and a toad would jump into a stagnant, malodorous puddle. Flocks of birds swarmed over the place at dusk. And Felip made himself a bed in a large empty niche. Made of branches, dry grass, and his blankets, that corner—discovered after his death—resembled a giant bird's nest. It was impregnated with a foul putrid odor.

Felip de Vadell was first seen walking furtively among the ruined olive trees. He was wearing worsted wool and a straw hat. He carried a noise-maker in his hand, and he was supposed to twirl it as a warning wherever he went. Sometimes someone would go near the crypt, walking a mule by the bridle or carrying a hunting net. And suddenly he would hear the hollow clicking of the rattle from the bushes. The man would run off quickly, looking back in fear.

Years later, Felip was seen moving around with difficulty; the illness was devouring him rapidly now. And often when the farmhand came close to the carob tree to leave him his food, Felip's weak voice could be heard from behind a rosemary bush, begging the servant boy to stop and talk with him, keep him company for a bit, even if for only a few seconds to talk about his wife and children. But the boy would always leave immediately, mumbling something unintelligible.

Only on rare occasions would the boy speak at a prudent distance, as when the leper asked why they had made that procession the other day from Son Vadell to town. The servant told him that two of his daughters, Maria Mercè and Rosa, had both married at the same time, and that the church overflowed with flowers and an orchestra of strings and woodwinds had played at the reception. . . .

Benvinguda, his wife, continued to spill out her memories, recording her afflictions before the notary as if someone in some all-embracing region in the great beyond could relieve her of her remorse: ". . . and they say that he can't talk anymore, or that he has forgotten how to do it, and to get someone's attention he meows like a cat, and on clear days I see his shadow dragging along out there, far away."

*I*t was not that morning in August when Aunt Amàlia drew me back to my father's past, but a quarter of a century later, the last time I went to Andratch. It was also autumn then, and I was there to clear up some inheritance papers—Grandmother's, whose death went far back in time, and the vicar's, who had died relatively recently—and also to pick through the files again, trying to find some threads, however tenuous, that might lead me to my father and other ghosts.

I decided to go to Son Farriol one afternoon just after sunset. The road to the house was straight and flanked on both sides by pomegranate trees. I stopped to touch a pomegranate, ripe and radiant in its crystalline redness. It seemed to me that I was reenacting things I had done many times before, when in reality I had only set foot on Son Farriol that one time, that summer's day. . . . But perhaps my memory of those brief hours, of that precise and burning reality, unavoidable and unforgettable, had overwhelmed my normal sense of time, walking like a dream through my mind, locked in an endless, fixed, and morbid space within me.

A cool, tenuous vapor arose from the tangle of plants tied up with canes in the garden. However, the dirt road was still hot from the afternoon sun, exceptionally intense that day, as though it had been traveling closer to earth than usual. It seemed as if an enormous beast had just passed by on the road, leaving its still-steaming trail behind. For a moment I thought it could have been that great legendary dragon blowing its fiery breath on the isolated cliffs of the other side of the river, where he guards the garden of the "Love of the Three Oranges" . . . the one from the legend my father had told me just before he left.

The magnolias around the house had already lost almost all their leaves. Dark against the façade, the branches rose practically naked, unusually severe. Some late magnolia blossoms still lingered, spongy-looking, tinged with a swollen white sadness, as if they signaled an exotic mourning. There was no one to be seen anywhere. On the grand stair-case, the potted plants were no longer there—only the stairs and the walls, sun-scalded stone surfaces, plain and rough. I entered the house. It was silent and dusty, the great hall long since abandoned. I think it was the cloying odor of her perfume that reached me and made me sense the pres-ence of Aunt Amàlia even before I saw her.

And I breathed it in, not by means of my senses focusing on a mental image, but quite the opposite, as if I were an irrational being. As I came in contact with that atmosphere a sensory phenomenon arose within me, a scent that existed only in my imagination, since it was not there in reality at all. It was probably a conditioned reflex, because when she started to talk I tried to catch a whiff of her, searching for her like a sniffing dog, not knowing at first what she was saying, just hearing her voice. She had suddenly appeared, tall and blurred in the shadows on the other side of the hall, or had probably already been there before I saw her. She was so far away that it seemed impossible for any aroma of hers or of the magnolias, already past their prime, to reach me. Opaque at first, her voice seemed to rise out of the dusty immobility of the hall:

"I waited for you to come back after that day, and I waited many more days, but you didn't come back, and I couldn't go get you, because outside here, I am as I was then, a frightened cripple. Everything that tears me apart is also the only thing that sustains me, just as everything that tortures me also supports me; it's all here within the walls of this house. . . .

"I'll tell you what it's like to wait, when evening comes on and the land becomes quiet, an hour or maybe a half hour when the waters of a river become still, forming a big backwater with fern fronds and the flight of the praying mantis caressing its surface like a capricious play of friendly colors. That was the backdrop of a party we held at the convent. I was a little girl and appeared in a white tunic with a blue lily in my hand, and I sat at the edge of the still pool in the river, in front of the dragonflies and the long, folded fronds. I recited a poem about the hour of dusk, the meditative and euphoric hour.

"But that's all a lie. The darkness thickens; it comes toward you; it licks you and touches you; you don't feel it but you see it, and you stifle the cry and the fear that gnaws at you and you think about how you and the walls and the trees begin to decompose, to melt down into the terror. Then the world puts on its true face: nothing has a shape, only a nebulous oppressiveness. From out of the night the cataclysm lurking behind everything stalks me; the dark becomes eyes and hands, the murmur of the coming collapse.

"Everything dies before it's born, desire dies before becoming reality, and only its absence remains, and you live with that absence. I waited for you, as I waited for him for years and years, watching the garden path, and I watched more closely as the dusk blurred things together, the shadows and branches turning into apparitions. Ghosts of you, of him—sometimes you were a crack of light, at other times the moving shadow of a palm tree swaying in the breeze, or the song of a nightingale among the leaves, or an apple falling softly, imitating the sound of a cautious footstep. I really wasn't myself; instead, at every moment I became the reflection of anything inside or outside of me. And I peered down the valley beyond the garden where the olives and the carobs and the almonds were at first definite forms, but then became lumps of darkness. Either he or you could have been any one of those sketchy shapes coming toward me.

"Or the blotches would have suddenly become horsemen at a gallop, a cavalry charge, the horses stomping, the armored knights with their helmet plumes in the wind, lances at the ready, the rumble of hoofbeats, and the shouts of battle, the clouds of dust trailing behind like formidable fluffy foxtails, their splendid flags of every color, all galloping wildly toward Son Farriol, invading the garden and the house, tipping over, breaking up, and piercing bodies with sharp lances, arriving at my bedroom to surrender at my feet and free me. A destructive human tumult of fright, flames, and chaos, as when the Moors came in the times of the duke, destroying the estate and turning the duchess over to the men and the dogs, who pummeled her in blood and sperm.

"But not for me, I told you. The knights would bow to me and I would rise and leave, reborn. 'From the tombs of the conquerors, from the sleeping church will arise the knights who will crown you princess,' your father used to say. Only a cataclysm could have made it happen that way, because only through the victory of disaster could I have saved myself from the swamp that was sucking me under; yes, sucking me into it. The olive trees were not knights, nor were the carob trees horses, and the lights of the town rising at the end of the valley accentuated even more the depth of the night and my absolute desolation . . . like the loneliness of a wild animal in its den, like the solitude of my husband, Ferran, already an animal, ringing his bell in his room for me to come to him, sitting there in his wheelchair, a survivor in the antechamber of a death that would not come.

"I concentrated all my hate on my husband, Ferran, that drooling bug-eyed swine, his chest and thighs covered with pig bristle; I would brandish a flaming pine torch that the armored knights had given me, and, amid the shouting, like the Moors laying siege to the duchess, I would set fire to the curtains and drapes, and Ferran and Son Farriol would all burst into flames while I ascended radiantly . . . I was transfixed, as if I could see it all. I saw it, and maybe still see it, since not even the illusion exists anymore, because I'm used to seeing it. I dreamed of a great change, and I knew its shape from a picture he had brought me when I was a young girl, that time when he sailed. Antoni, your father, dressed like an officer . . . that smile. . . . He brought it from Egypt: Isis, the moon goddess, transfigured into firmament; she covered the earth, her very long figure full of stars, a splendorous miracle. A great change, like the curve of the sky that I could join and climb beyond Son Farriol and Andratch, resurfacing in another place, new and unknown.

"Shit! Shit! Shit! Every way I turn I wind up beaten by disgust, tired of constant, useless worries I know by heart, detail by detail . . . you'll know what I mean now: you saw me that morning when you got out of the pond, but I didn't see you, a wet boy with a frightened look in his eyes. What I saw was him, because you were like him, and were about the same age as he was—about seventeen—when he also sprang out of the water naked that summer afternoon, riding bareback on the black horse from Son Vadell, shouting at it and laughing, crazy from doing things that began and ended in and of themselves, as if life, all the energy of life, were concentrated there in that spot where he was and wherever he moved.

"He was different from that moment on, and I was too. The days go by, you do things, and what you do means nothing: the only thing that really *exists* you don't see; it's the path that is being made inside you, leading you somewhere. You feel it, you live it suddenly with a lightness that destroys you; it pierces you and it changes you from top to bottom. Before then, I had been preparing for that only subconsciously. I had only seen your father from a distance. I knew he was my cousin Antoni, two years older than I, son of my uncle at Son Vadell, and that I wasn't supposed to talk with him or any of them because we were enemies. He stayed at the margin of my life, like that hill that's barely visible over there on the horizon. I see it, but it has nothing to do with me. . . .

"I still wore braids that afternoon. I was sixteen and maybe had a premonition that the time of preparation was over and the secret and sacred act was about to happen, just as in the novel I was reading that took place in India or China, and where a monk walked for years and years after the flight of an arrow that someone, maybe a god, had shot. Where the arrow landed was supposed to be where the river of life was born. I read a lot back then, but that afternoon after lunch when everybody else was taking their siesta, I couldn't stay in the swing under the grape arbor, nor in that cool corner of the garden where the banana trees grow.

"I headed off toward Les Dunes, barefoot and exhausted from the heat. My feet sank deeply into the sand and walking was difficult. All I could see around me were the hillocks of sand that went on and on, rising and falling into little hollows full of sun, with the little dwarf tamarind trees eaten away by the sun and the wind and the salt, making them seem more like minerals than trees. I crossed pockets of heat as though I were on a pilgrimage to somewhere, maybe toward the disintegration of the sun: the heat cut off my breathing, I felt I was burning up; I unbuttoned the collar of my dress. Suddenly the beach appeared before me, vast and deserted, pale yellow and bright, white-hot reflections breaking up maddeningly, the apathetic sea rolling in an enchanted spell of steely efflorescence. I felt dazed, parched by the suffocating air.

"I was standing there in the blinding light when I heard the laughter and the splashing. He and the beast were a whirlwind of light and spray and noise coming from the sea, a brilliant apparition of water, a thousand slashes of light. Antoni laughed and laughed as he came closer to me, riding bareback. He laughed and he looked me in the eye and when he got up beside me I was petrified—or incredibly open in anticipation—I don't know which. But he put his hand on my hair, moving me back toward the dunes, I walking like a zombie and he still on horseback. We stopped at a low spot in the dunes. I felt as if I were standing at the open door to an oven. I noticed that he was naked, but I didn't care. He dismounted and put his arms around my shoulders and then began to unbutton my dress. I let him do it, half-closing my eyes, and as he exposed more and more of my body to the sun, the heat that had been choking me escaped, and a kind of burning euphoria overcame me: it was like buried embers bursting forth in flame.

"And suddenly he tugged hard at my braids; they came loose and all my hair fell free, and I felt freed as well. As I dropped on my back, the sand burned me like a red-hot iron. Antoni threw himself on top of me and hot thick juices joined our sexes. He possessed me fully, voraciously, and I would have bitten him and eaten him to sate my hunger for him inside me. . . .

"That was it. I discovered through him that I was a woman. And from then on I would run like crazy to wherever he called me—unkempt, bewitched, my sex so hungry for his. He made me submit and I obeyed until he told me I should marry Ferran. I was his whore and his lover, and I'd still be his until the end of time. Right now if he were here. I twisted under him, howling with pleasure, crying with gratitude. An avalanche of happiness and pleasure cascaded over me. . . . You wrote me telling me you were coming, that you wanted to find out things about your father. Well, now you know. I can see him here right now; I can see him as he lay upon me in my room, where he would sneak in at night, or on the dunes, twisting around under a tamarind tree, the sun dancing all over us, the branches scratching us, the salty sand burning in my bitten skin. . . ."

I had been edging closer to Aunt Amàlia and I looked at her in surprise as she stood there invoking ghosts, first with a neutral voice and then with a desolate, pathetic grotesqueness. This woman had once been a crowning beauty full of desire and energy, a defiance of human decrepitude to all the pulsing vegetation around her; now she could only count on the faded desire within her shriveled frame—not even on that, just the *desire* for the desire, a memory, a reflex, something by now second nature to her.

She knew it too, at least at some moments. But she saw herself as the person she had always been before, or as a consequence of that person, without being aware that there was nothing left of that part of her. The only thing remaining was what had not been, what she had not had, a tumult of dissatisfactions, frustrations, and foiled desires. I looked at her carefully; nothing remained but an echo of what she had been thirty years ago . . . an echo of the habit of her gestures, of her postures, of the inflections of her voice, of everything in a young woman that is graceful, mysterious, the incipient invitation to pleasure, to caresses, to the aggression of the male burning with passion. But all this in an old woman is nothing but a lamentably displaced residue, a shameless and anguished exhibitionism.

Aunt Amàlia in the twilight represented something more than just fleshly rot and decay: she was the moral equivalent of the fermenting pus of physical ruin. She stood there, emaciated, her eyes bloodshot, with a faraway look that did not see, nor was able to reflect the mirages of her self-centered conceit. An aggressive smirk crossed her face, produced by her false teeth that were probably made for her years ago when she still had some flesh on her cheeks. But now her teeth danced about in her mouth, sometimes getting out of place and making a clacking sound, or at other times getting tangled with her tongue, giving a sibilant shrillness to her speech. White as ivory, the teeth looked as if she had just scrubbed them with detergent; they contrasted sharply with her wan complexion, with her wrinkled clothes. A sharp odor of mothballs filtered through the moist, liquescent oriental perfume she had daubed on. Before, she and that fragrance had meant one and the same to me, but not now. It seemed that her body no longer gave off a fragrance of its own, not even when wetted down with scent, regardless of where it came from. Like a piece of stone, she had become impervious to fragrance.

Her teeth, with their surreal perfection, pushed her thin lips out and formed a lump in the lower part of her bloodless cheeks, where she had painted an exaggerated rosette of rouge, accentuating that gaunt, sickly mask even more. Flounces and laces were stitched to her dress like frazzled artificial blooms. The dress was ancient and cumbersome and reached to her feet, obviously rescued from some garret, a piece forgotten and then recovered from a wardrobe of leftovers from the past. It hung to one side on her. It didn't look like it was covering a body, but rather a fragile scaffolding of bones over which the cloth had been hastily and carelessly draped. Aunt Amàlia had become the personification of absolute annihilation. Everything about her spoke failure, time irreversibly spoiled and broken.

I listened to her without recognizing anything about her that resembled the woman whom I had once clutched closely—hot as she was— and whose image had dogged me ever since. But I wasn't looking for that anymore, because all the while I remained at her side, I felt at the same time very, very far away. It seemed as if we were officiating at an ancestral ritual, familiar yet foreign to us both, in which the words and the communication were distant, with only the gestures remaining, our bodies repeating only movements and postures.

No, this woman of the second visit was different, but had always been the same, a scarecrow. The mere idea of comparing this woman to the one who had once embraced me—or my father—disgusted me. I felt a physical rejection, mixed with a humiliating moral repugnance. I imagined the clear, exultant sensations of the lovemaking I had experienced with her, her flesh soft and taut, the restless surge of lust before orgasm. I imagined both hers and mine, because the explanation was more complex: both of us had been fulfilling a ritual, but at the same time both of us, in our exalted inward escape, had been making love, yes: I with just a woman—who happened to be her at that moment—but she had been making love almost certainly with her Antoni, my father, lost by then to both of us. . . . But to join those images of when I was sixteen with the Amàlia who stood before me now, a delirious wretch who at certain moments still seemed to be languidly offering herself to me, was an obscene execration. I could envision her body as if her dress were transparent—her empty, withered dugs; the hanging flaps of skin on her belly and haunches; the reek of her shapeless black sex. . . .

She kept on talking, but impelled now only by the wind that had driven her years ago, like a ship with its sails gone slack but still coasting along on the failing inertia of the last breath of wind. I was thinking how useless everything was, how cruel the years were—"where time leaves its bruises the spirit does not heal." Old age, for one who has not experienced it yet but sees it in others, appears as an abomination, pitiable perhaps, but the object of contempt and rejection. Old people ought to be locked up in a dank secret hiding place and left to vegetate like the leper Felip de Vadell; they should be shut away from laughter, faith, and feelings, for they are reprobates, gross offal, and these cadaverous remains are the coming image of you, a warning for the future. It profanes your desires. I wanted to slap her, but I fled instead.

*A*nd I walked and walked. It was night by then, and tall clouds and a crescent moon dotted the sky. It seemed as if they ran in pursuit of each other; first the jovial yellow slice of moon spread its quiet opaline light; then the clouds reigned, darkening the sky as if a big blanket had covered everything. The spirit of decay that had overwhelmed me in Son Farriol seemed to stick to me. I felt split up inside, as if my inner body parts and the lumps of dough in my brain didn't fit together. They were being subjected to a rapid succession of jolts, attempts to make them fit. Only by exaggeratedly swinging my arms and legs back and forth could I make my body's center of gravity change from inside to outside, and in that way I was able to calm down, little by little.

The town appeared as a black mass on the horizon, over which the chimneys of the houses rose, sending up spirals of sooty smoke as a fleeting warning to me. I wandered down one narrow street after another, sometimes finding myself in a street I knew well, almost as if the walls were a part of me, and sometimes not knowing where I was, as the darkness spread around me. Like the strings of a net, the narrow and tortuous streets clung to the zigzag pattern of centuries past.

Many houses had been abandoned. Their people had emigrated, leaving cracked and caved-in doors and shutters off their hinges, swinging in the wind. From out of the hollow openings dark plants with rough leaves and huge crowns of prickers spied on me. And sometimes a cat's head would peek out, its eyes bright and alert, as if it had just come from committing some crime, or had seen something threatening or dangerous behind me. The wind picked up. All the pieces of wood framing danced and rattled, filling the deserted streets with dissonant clattering noises, as if there were invisible drums and rattles working up a wild concert for Good Friday, when any sound at all that is not muted or made of wood could disturb the death of Jesus Christ, who rested in cerulean calm in a blue glass urn atop the main altar.

The memory of Father Dionís began to overpower me. Often at this same time of night, I used to go with him when he was called out to give last rites to someone near death. He would wear a white cape with gold embroidery in which he wrapped the chalice. I would hold a huge violet umbrella and carry a lantern for him. Our footfalls echoed in the narrow stone streets as if a crowd of people were following us. In the weak lantern light, the decrepit fronts of the buildings followed, one after the other, piecemeal, as if they were sections of a theater set for the Great Wall of China, an incongruous fragmentation of the town and of the night . . . out of which masked figures suddenly arose, only to disappear again, instantly swallowed up by the night. Reverend de Vadell observed all this out of the corner of his eye, perhaps with the irrational premonition that they could be empty cloaks, abominations of nonexistence itself. The little lantern swinging back and forth as we walked created a measured and grotesque rotation of the vicar's, the umbrella's, and my shadows . . . a spectral canopy in a solitary, solemn procession. More than carrying out a ministry for the great beyond, the gloomy presence of the priest seemed a lugubrious confirmation of the irrevocable.

*T*hat was the period when the vicar gave me lessons. Grandmother believed that whatever he taught me would be better than anything I could have learned in the town's public school, so I had to go to the vicarage in the afternoons. The vicar would be waiting for me in his study, a large room overflowing with masses of papers. Books, bundles of documents, parchments, and drawers stuffed with file cards were all piled in disorder on the shelves covering the walls, on the floor, and on top of the furniture, as if a windstorm had just stirred everything up, muddling it completely. The floor was bowed up in spots and trembled with every movement. The bang of a chair or a door slammed shut would provoke the collapse of some of the piles of papers. The priest would then pick them up hurriedly, sticking them roughly back into any hole at hand. Everything flew around, slipped around, seemed to move around all by itself, imbued with a spirit all its own.

Father Dionís had accumulated part of the church registry there, along with documents from the town council, books and file folders and notes, everything that might have had even the vaguest reference to Pope Luna, his formidable, intransigent, and only passion in life. The dust, the cobwebs, and the humidity had taken over that fragile material, and the study exuded an unbearably heavy odor of having been closed up, airless for eons. There was a rat trap set in a corner and baited with cheese. Sometimes the trap would disappear under a pile of paperwork, and the priest would only find out if it had caught a rat when, after a few days, the place began to smell of death.

And in the middle of the room, in an immense cage mended with wires and strings, an ancient parrot snoozed in its sparse plumage that looked as if it had been eaten away by mange. Stiff with age, the old bird would rock back and forth dangerously on its perch, and just as it was about to fall off, it would flap its wings chaotically, amid spasmodic squawks.

But was that the reality of the vicarage, or was it the other, the reality evoked by the restless verbal phantasmagoria the vicar vomited forth during the chilly empty hours we spent together? A lone, weak lightbulb hung from the ceiling, sinking the room into a deathly gloom. Beneath it rocked the face of the priest, seemingly floating there, emerging like a scrawny polyp from his black cassock, his eye sockets two murky circles, as though he had no eyeballs at all. His head and hands made jerky movements, like a clumsy marionette.

I was supposed to have my lesson prepared and then explain it to him, and sometimes I did. But if he had received some book or paper referring to the Great Schism of the West or to Pedro de Luna, his brain would heat up and he would start shuffling documents around, mumbling unintelligible abstractions, then he would turn to me between mutterings and launch into a sometimes abstruse speech. At other times it was as clear and simple as the golden legend:

"I have seen many people near death, and so it must have gone something like this with him: suddenly he sat up in bed, the shock dilating his big eyes, his arms flapping like wings. He began stuttering and shouting things nobody understood. He was wearing a long white nightshirt and the skin on his face sagged, forming two dirty earth-colored folds. He was bereft of teeth and hair, sodden with sweat; he was just able to murmur

'Avignon! Avignon!' Then he spat up blood, soiled his chin and nightshirt with the sinister red stuff, and pointed with his index finger imperiously and frighteningly at the cardinal of Santa Maria of Cosmedín. It was the Holy Father Gregory XI who, nearing death, had pointed out Pedro de Luna! Or was it God who had done it, through his vicar on earth?

"Pedro, the cardinal of Santa Maria of Cosmedín, was surprised. A sort of dizziness made him sway in his alcove among the embroidered beauty of the tapestries, the reliquaries of gold and silver encrusted with gemstones, the iridescent pomp of the pontifical court, the cardinals and prelates, noblemen and domestics. Two men of the purple cloth hovered over Pope Gregory and laid him down. His breathing was now a weak wheeze, and the annoyed cries of the multitude echoed outside. Upset, Cardinal Pedro de Luna walked over to the balcony. It was spring (the seasons pass me by now, and I don't notice them, but the winter cold seems to pursue me), and as a young man Pedro used to spend a lot of time outside on the terrace, bewitched by the view breaking out in colors, the greens in proud exaltation every minute of the spring.

"Those days of the death throes of Pope Gregory XI occurred in the Roman spring of 1376. The tender sun of April, like a caress, spilled over the flowering gardens of the Eternal City; the walls of the palaces acquired the toasted splendor of fresh-baked bread. The cardinal looked out on the plaza. Egged on by the Roman aristocracy, the townspeople roared out that when the French pope died a Roman pope should be elected, and if not, they would make the cardinals take notice that their blood was as red as their bonnets, because Gregory was French. Since 1305, the Holy See had been located in Avignon, France. In fact, at first the pope was a prisoner there, but later, French popes were elected, because Italy was a nest of nobility poisoned by their internecine fights, with bandits ruling the highways. But Holy Father Gregory had managed to return to Rome and die there soon after. And now the aristocrats didn't want to let the Holy See escape them again. They lusted after the money that kings and pilgrims deposited in the papal treasury.

"Pedro de Luna contemplated the agitated crowds from the balcony. I would have spit on them! Pedro *did* spit on them! He had to quickly withdraw inside, because a huge rain of rocks crashed against the balcony and came rolling like a horde of rowdy animals into the dying pope's room. The cardinal knelt on a prie dieu. Now he understood the admonitions of the bedridden Pontiff, now he saw that Rome was the new Babylon, and that the route to salvation lay through Avignon. But what was to be the mission for him, the last surviving sailor on the ship of the Church? Although all the fibers of his being demanded that the supreme powers unleash another universal flood and that only the pontifical palace remain afloat on the dawn of the forty-first day, he bowed his head and must have prayed that the will of God, whatever it was, be imposed upon this house of darkness.

"Once Gregory XI was dead, the Sacred College of Cardinals went into conclave. There were sixteen cardinals present: eleven French, four Italians, and the Aragonese, Pedro de Luna. In the street the rabble brandished pikes, axes, and knives all too menacingly, by the light of bitterly smoking resin torches. The Sacred College of Cardinals trembled; they could barely make themselves understood with the racket of the rebels outside. And so they decided to get out of the difficult situation by showing a fictitious pope—an Italian—to the crowd, so that they could then retire to a safer place and vote for an authentic Holy Father without pressure. But none of the princes dared show his face to the dangerous crowd. One of them, the cardinal of San Pedro, submerged in the slough of his eighty years, could not even utter a sound. The only thing he could do was make the sign of the cross, over and over again.

"Suddenly some of the princes of the church looked at one another, and then turned toward the cardinal of San Pedro. They threw themselves upon him, shoving the tiara firmly onto his head and putting the pontifical cape upon his shoulders. The old man cried out in terror and struggled to escape. The cardinals grabbed him and shut him up by wadding a piece of the Virgin's cloak into a ball and stuffing it in his mouth. Then they seated him on the papal throne and showed him off to the crowd, his eyes bugging out in fear. He struggled under the precious robes, the canticles, the incense, and the cortege of cardinals. But the public caught on to the trick and their fury grew. They broke down the doors with a battering ram and burst in upon the conclave. The cardinals freed the old man from San Pedro, still frozen in fear, and precipitously elected an Italian prelate whom no one knew: the archbishop of Bari. Meanwhile, the crowd ran off, looting deliriously everywhere. And the cardinal of San Pedro lay in the arms of death, looking like a fool wrapped in purple robes, nearly tumbling out of his wobbly throne.

"Five months later, the Sacred College met in Fundi. In the interim, the archbishop of Bari, Bartolomeo Pignani, had taken charge of the Holy See in Rome under the name of Urban VI. The conclave of Fundi declared null and void the election of Archbishop Pignani and voted in a new pope, Robert de Genève, a Frenchman, who took the name of Clement VII. Then all the cardinals followed him back to Avignon. The Great Schism of the West had begun—two visible heads of the church, one in Rome and the other in Avignon, divided consciences and nations. . . . Urban VI was left alone, frenetic and humiliated.

"And he conferred the cardinal's hat upon twenty-six new cardinals, and contracted a troop of mercenaries to defend his rights. Illegal, heretical, and satanic rights! But hate and fear consumed him, and at the slightest indication that his cardinals might betray him, he ordered them tied to the torture rack and watched as their bones popped out of joint and their eyes were blinded by burning irons. He didn't even dare leave them in prison when he traveled, for he feared they might rise up against him, so he sailed off with a ship full of blind cardinals as his prisoners—his court of cripples—who prayed and wailed at his feet.

"But it did him no good. He died of poisoning and his Sacred College hurried to elect a successor, Boniface IX, insatiably rapacious and intransigent, who wouldn't hear of renouncing his office. Meanwhile, in Avignon, Clement VII negotiated with the other nations and named Pedro de Luna as his legate, and the kingdoms of Castile, Aragon, Navarre, France, Brabante, Scotland, England, and Ireland declared themselves loyal to him. But Clement VII died one day in 1394. The French monarch had vexed him that same morning; he then celebrated mass in a fury, drank a tall glass of wine, and dropped dead as if struck by lightning. Apoplexy or poison? We'll never know. . . ."

What happened next? With frightening indecision, I contemplated the old priest and his solitary debates I knew by heart; that's why I could put his exultant confusion of dates and themes back in order. As he became more agitated, his head drew nearer mine to underline an expression or an argument, for him decisive and for me as muddled as the rest of his delirium. Practically the only thing that was clear to me was his breath, those fetid vapors from that huge, flabby mouth, his swollen tongue covered with a white slime, like a slippery cavern. Sometimes I thought he didn't even see me: he seemed to be speaking to himself, focused only on his unique and magnetic center point, his mental edifice, growing fervently as each new memory surfaced.

I never interrupted his crazed chatter, which he only broke off in order to search out some quote in an ancient handwritten document, inevitably destined to demonstrate the authenticity of Pontiff Luna. The vicar's precarious existence fed exclusively on that secular rubbish that recreated facts and personalities from periods long since deeply sunken into the bowels of time, and for many of which not even a gravestone remained. Sometimes the vicar bent over and sobbed, and then it was an effort for him to put his words back together again. More than ever, that was when he referred explicitly to Pedro de Luna, the axis around which he turned and turned with assertive fury.

A strange aversion mixed with fear gripped me at certain moments. I had a premonition that we were about to trespass upon a sinful area . . . but he nattered on, not even noticing the scandalous squawking of the parrot when it dozed and teetered on its perch.

"Conditions that in truth, as if the light were not light . . . human conditions, political conditions. The kingdom of this world wanting to reign over the territory of the Lord. *We will elect you pope and you will resign.* They say those were the conditions they imposed on him. But how can man undo what Jesus Christ has put together? Because Benedict XIII—that is, Pedro de Luna—was named pope by the conclave of Avignon on the death of Clement VII. He obtained all the votes but one, his own. Within a week he was ordained presbyter, consecrated as bishop, and after saying his first mass, was solemnly crowned pope. It was the Spirit who designated him through the Sacred College; it was God with whom he was going to establish physical contact, once he was consecrated.

"Small and thin, his sixty-five years were like those of an oak, stronger as time tempered him. He was chaste and austere. He had been named a canon lawyer by the University of Montpellier. When convinced of an idea, he adhered to it with fervor. And they crowned him with the white and angular tiara of Saint Silvester set with black stones of a unique brilliance. Constantine the Great had given it to Sylvester I as a symbol of the definitive triumph of Christianity over idolatry.

"Why did he have to abdicate? Why? They threw the reasons in his face: Christianity was divided, the winds of heresy had begun to blow in Germany and the Low Countries, so the policy of the kings demanded his resignation. But all that, whatever it was, should not have been directed at him . . . it was Rome that had opened the Great Schism! And Benedict XIII paid no attention to any of them, while at the same time he anathematized the Roman pope, naturally! He refused with proud firmness to renounce his position *via cesionis,* proclaiming, 'I prefer to be flayed alive.' The monarch, the theologians at the University of Paris, the emperor of Austria, even his own cardinals argued with him, attacked him, and abandoned him. Tempted by gold and their own convenience, they turned their backs on the one who knew only the dictates of the Spirit.

"And the French troops threw themselves on Avignon, their impious ladders breaching the battlements of the papal castle defended by the remaining loyalist troops. Pedro de Luna was forced to escape through the sewers; then he left from the Rhone in a Catalan galley with people of our lineage, who were with him to the last. 'For the pure, all things are pure,' said Saint Paul. It didn't matter to him that the sewer was his carriage and the jeering and insults his miter, for he was the representative of Christ on earth!

"I've read a lot on the question, I've searched for years and years through all the books and papers that mention it, and I can affirm that God was with him. I can affirm it in a loud and clear voice! Of what importance are earthly failures, even though they be centuries old? Perhaps the moment has not yet arrived when all the great evidence will come to light; perhaps the ways of the Lord, of eternity, are inscrutable.

"In Rome, the cycle of death and elections continued. Innocence VII replaced Boniface IX, then Gregory XII assumed the throne. And all Christendom boiled in passionate confusion. In 1409, the Council of Pisa met with cardinals from both camps. They deposed Benedict XIII and Gregory XII and named another pontiff, Alexander V, a Greek Franciscan. The other two rejected a Conciliar decree. And thus there were three popes—a three-headed church that would last five years, because at the death of Alexander a successor was named, John XXIII, who was the old pirate Baldassare Cosa.

"The Council of Constanza opened after that, and under the auspices of the German emperor, John XXIII was deposed for being undignified and a simonist. He escaped disguised as a groom. Gregory was also deposed and escaped to Gaeta, where he abdicated and died soon after. Benedict was then deposed; but, alone and obstinate, sure of his investiture as the only authentic representative of Jesus Christ on earth, he ignored the edicts of Constanza.

"In Perpignan in 1415, before the Emperor Segismund, before Ferdinand, king of Castile and nobles and prelates and doctors, before Vicent Ferrer, Pedro de Luna spoke in Latin for seven hours from the pulpit of the cathedral, irrefutably proving his legitimacy. And he said, 'You say that all the popes who have come after the Schism—and in consequence all their cardinals—are doubtful, and I accept that. That being so, then I am the only cardinal still living who was elected prior to the Schism, the only one who can designate a new pope, and nothing says I can't name myself. However, you don't want me to be pope. It's true that you can stop it, that you can deny me and pursue me. But what you can never deny me, for it is my authority from Heaven, is that I—I alone!—am the only one who can name a new pope.'

"They listened to him in silence, and in silence they rejected him, including King Ferdinand and the Valencian Vicent Ferrer, both of whom had been practically created by Pedro de Luna. And so he had to escape again, this time by sea, on the open sea, where he would not be plagued by underhandedness and betrayal, where the solitude of the clouds and the waves would respect his pontificate.

"The Council of Constanza proclaimed a new pope, before whom all Christianity paid homage. He was Martin V, who went to Rome. Meanwhile, in the Castle of Peñíscola on the Valencian coast, Benedict XIII awaited the judgment of God that man had denied him. The Schism was ended. Pedro de Luna was condemned as a Schismatic. He responded that the Schism had been enthroned in Rome and that the purity of the faith resided in Peñíscola. He then anathematized the Roman pope.

"The Roman pope! I'll tell you, for it's as if I were seeing it now. I'll tell you who this pope was and how Benedict XIII was endlessly attacked. One example will suffice. One from a day in 1418, if you like. Gusts of wind from the south tossed up whitecaps, as if milk had been thrown on the sea. Pontifice Pedro de Luna coughed, and shivers ran up and down his shrunken body, by then just skin and bone. His little eyes appeared covered with a thin, oily film. The wind scraped against his dry, numb skin, which looked like these parchments here. It must have been the same as fingernails scratching a plaster wall. His nephew Roderic was at his side. Wearing the dress uniform of a pontifical guard, Roderic's helmet was crowned with a ruffled yellow plume. Gripping the battlement of the last and highest tower of the Castle of Peñíscola, wrapped in a gray, soft and fluffy cape of marmot the czar of Moscow had sent him in the days of glory, the pope urged Roderic to tell him what his eyes could no longer see.

"Roderic must have looked at the isthmus, a white stretch of sand that separated the fortress crowning the protuberant isle of Peñíscola from the pebbled beach and the hills of carob trees. I have been there, the same as I have been to Avignon; I walked in the same places where His Holiness Benedict XIII had lived. Then Roderic looked around and narrated the events he saw as they unfolded: They had tied the friar to a stake and had to hold his head up because it kept flopping over as if it had no spine. Canon Valent came forward and offered him the cross to kiss. The prisoner broke out in tears and suddenly, while the canon was urging him to seek God's pardon for his soul, the friar shuddered and vomited. Thick green mouthfuls of the stuff splattered the canon and the soldiers. Was it fear that had undone his innards or was it the Devil, having possessed him, who offended the holy cross? We will never know.

"And then a soldier came forward with a torch in his hand and bent down before the bundles of firewood piled around the base of the stake. The friar shrieked and screamed and twisted about, drooling his vomit. One, two, then five tongues of flame shot up rapidly, pale in the blazing sun. The crackling fire and the crazed howling of the prisoner filled the air. A penetrating odor of seared roasting flesh reached the Holy Father's nostrils. Perhaps his nose was able to smell more than others'—keep in mind he was nearly blind. . . . Yes, yes, above the blows of the waves against the rocky shore of the island resounded the impetuous crackling of the burning pyre and the raucous contorted cries of the condemned friar. The fire, an instrument of justice, had consumed Friar Peladi Calvet.

"And when the friar had become little more than a charred stick, the pontiff must have felt tired and cold. He was already ninety years old . . . that's a lot of years for a person, though very few for conserving the faith. He went into his bedroom. The fireplace was lit. What I would have done—and I'm not as old as he was, not by any means—would have been to take off my cape, rub my hands together and maybe smile as I watched the wavering tongues of flame . . . because that day something doubly important had occurred. The cardinal of Pisa, legate of the Roman Pope Martin V, had tried to poison Pedro de Luna, using that recently roasted Benedictine friar as his instrument. His Holiness Benedict XIII had a sweet tooth. As was his habit, his quince jam stood on the table from the day before. He tried some of it, but noticed that it had an unusually bitter taste. . . . Not only did God save him, but He showed him what tricks Martin V and his people were up to, how the whole world was conspiring against Pedro de Luna.

"Ninety years . . . ninety-six. . . . It was the longest pontifical reign ever, surpassing even that of Saint Peter. Wasn't this also evidence sent by the Lord to mankind? And the year 1422 arrived, the seventeenth of November. Still absolutely lucid of mind and firm of will, what failed Benedict XIII was his body; he became bedridden. Since he no longer had any cardinals, he named four, so that they could perpetuate his Holy See: the Prior of the Carthusians of Montealegre, Domingo de Bonnefoi; the two Aragonese, Juliano de Loba and Ximeno Dahe; and Jean Carrier—the faithful, ever-faithful Carrier—who wasn't to be found in Peñíscola, but in Armagnac beside his sovereign count, representing Pope Luna.

"And then the Holy Father died, on the afternoon of the twenty-ninth. The chronicles tell how his coffin and his tomb exuded a marvelous fragrance.

"But the stench of hate was more powerful among the living, who had pursued him without mercy. Martin V refused to allow him to be buried in holy ground. Finally, in 1430, they carried the body to Illueca in Aragon, where he had been born and where his family still lived. Almost four centuries later, Napoleon's troops arrived in Illueca and sought out his tomb. The body was well-preserved. So they cut off his head and threw it out the window! Vicent Ferrer, before he died, had prophesied that children would play ball with the head of Benedict XIII. Ferrer, who was a traitor, knew the people of his race. That noble skull, I have held it in these very hands you see here before you, yes! In the palace of Saviñán in Aragon, which belongs to the Count of Argillo, there's a fir box where they keep the skull. It's large, with an aquiline nose. It's been mummified, and there's still an eyeball in one of the sockets, hardened to glass, eternally vigilant."

Whole afternoons of inflamed, labyrinthine chatter . . . that did, however, let me get away with very little studying. That is, it helped me to make very little effort. The fact that I barely ate and the possibility that I might catch a cold or become overtired were horrible nightmares for Grandmother Brigida: the memory of my sisters weighed like a tombstone on her. "We don't know what God or the Devil might send us. But we do know what we ourselves can do. Sit down and don't move," she ordered me endlessly, even though I was often already sitting down.

She repeated it with the same mechanical tone of voice as when she prayed. She didn't pay any real attention to what she said, but she was convinced of the intrinsic value of the words, the mere mention of which worked like an incantation and put into gear the necessary protective devices called down from unknown, omnipotent regions. Sometimes I asked myself if we didn't live more from invisible and probably inexistent things than from the reality that was truly ours. . . .

And I obeyed her and sat down—except when I would run off with a friend to play in the mountains or go for a swim at the beach. From this Parisian afternoon I can see myself now as I was then—a child in short pants, a young boy in knickerbockers, my hands quietly resting on my thighs, not daring to move them in case the ghost of fear should brush close to me. I would sit there looking at my arms, at my legs; I would think about my brain, as well as about possible enemies whose acts were uncontrollable and who might annihilate me. Just like what had happened with Cristina, Joana, and Marteta, exhausted and consumed by tuberculosis. . . .

It's an image of spring that I've never forgotten—an image full of soft, floral exuberance exposed to the fragile warmth of the sun that is pierced by threads of acute cold; butterflies of a bright yellow that look like dissonant splashes of light; honey-colored bees that fly sluggishly, lazily from flower to flower: white marguerites, red poppies, little purple bells of rosemary . . . and cascades of birdsong all around me. . . .

An image of the three girls standing around the fountain, the music of their games falling over the waterlilies and the iridescent-colored fish. Marteta was laughing and watching the ingenuous and clumsy leaps of the puppy, and she pulled on his curly fur. Joana was reading in the shade of the cedar tree. Cristina was looking at the sky, perhaps smiling, her breath coming rapidly. And I, only a year older than Marteta, was way up in the grape arbor watching them. I don't know why. Yes, maybe to be able to remember them better later. . . . The lemon grove lay there in front of me, with its precise and vivid yellow dots among the leafy greenery, giving off a subtle acidic aroma. . . .

An image of the time when no one had any idea about what would soon sprout inside each of them and destroy them. . . . It was a picture of peace and happiness then, but when recalled later it would become something intensely and inexplicably painful, like claws of the great beyond that have power over what has been, power to reach out to the point of even poisoning memories. It was not toward those memories that the steely claws drew near, but toward me, and not then but now. They draw closer to my imagination, the only place in the universe where that picture still lives. . . .

Marteta was blond, her hair a golden fluffiness of curls. Her laugh was a soft gurgle that always seemed just about to become a sigh. Her starched billowy dress had lots of bows and ribbons. She stood and laughed among the marguerites and the poppies near the enchanted fountain. . . . Marteta has remained in my memory as a fragile creature in waiting . . . awaiting death, as if from her first childish babblings she had been destined to lie, diaphanous and cold, in that small snowy white coffin, which one day at noon was carried on a bier across the lemon grove.

Instead of being a body in the process of coming to life, she had been an embryo of death. It's always been difficult for me to remember Marteta playing with excitement and joy, even though I had seen her like that hundreds of times. She appears to me instead as if she were exhausted by the slightest movements, which were like a wounded animal's feeble attempts to heal itself.

And then there was Joana. Tall, big jawed and broad shouldered, she had a surly firmness in her gaze. She would go around wrapped in a warm-toned woolen shawl. She spent a lot of her time standing near the courtyard arch. Women would come to buy lemons and she would follow them with her gaze, immobile and mute, a spark of defiance in her eyes. Little by little they stopped coming. It seemed that Son Vadell was in the clutches of a clammy atmosphere of destruction. And the lemons rotted in the grove, exuding a sickening, sweet fetidness.

One day her fiancé came to see her. In a stuttering voice he told her that they ought to break up because his parents wanted him to get a job in the city for an indefinite time. My sister Joana just stared at him without saying a word. She looked at him with angry cruelty in her eyes, as if his leaving meant victory for her. Having acquired the illness that was gnawing at her by means of a brutal inner extortion, it had turned her into a vengeful symbol of evil that would pit her against others in the same gratuitous and devastating way this evil had been forced upon her.

Of my three sisters, Joana was the one who resisted the disease the longest. She fought each coughing attack furiously, and sometimes, unable to hold back, she would hack and spit and flail her arms against tables, vases, and mirrors, blindly smashing anything in her way. She died without opening her lips, her eyes fixed accusingly on Vicar de Vadell, who, surrounded by candles, held the holy chalice in his hand. He stood in front of her indecisively, without daring to look her in the eye. Dionís stretched out his bony hand, holding a small white wafer between his fingers. Joana didn't even refuse his offer by shaking her head, she just lay there staring at him. He put the host back in the chalice, wrapped himself in his white and golden cape, and left.

A lot of people in Andratch reacted to Joana's death with an inner feeling of relief. They would no longer have to quicken their stride as they walked by Son Vadell, freed now from that harsh figure always standing there in silence. . . .

With her thin neck, her skin unduly pale, her cheeks sunken in with two mystical flaming dabs of rouge on them, Cristina walked feebly among the lemon trees, her silk tunic fluttering languidly in the wind. Each day she became more fragile and more eager to live, her lips parted and transparent. During the last weeks, locked in her bedroom, emaciated and trembling, she appeared on the balcony and looked at the sunny fields. As she stood gazing at the clouds rising over the crest of Mt. Garrafa, she felt no relationship between her and imminent death. Her heart overflowed with pleasure, just as though a miraculous benediction were about to descend from the imperturbable, empty skies. Yes, that's the way I would describe her—tender, fragile, and full of capricious grace, yearning to be pampered, protected. . . .

I would have described her that way if, with the passing of time, I hadn't come in contact with Rafael Bardají, her fiancé, about whom I remember very little from that time. They had kept me away from Son Vadell at that time out of fear that the tuberculosis would crush me as well. I went with Grandmother Brigida to live in the old tower house near the Port. And it was she who described Bardají to me the day of Cristina's burial. The casket was full of flowers; her face protruded sharply from the soft cushion of petals. Rafael stood there immobile for hours on end in front of her in a dark suit, his eyes fixed in an absent stare.

Years later I often went for walks with Rafael Bardají. We used to take the solitary path leading to La Trapa, behind the mountains of En Farineta and La Santa. Sometimes the wind that whistled down through the narrow passes came from the high, deserted mountains surrounding the valley of La Trapa. It shook the arid vegetation, the thistles scratched against each other, emitting a wild, erie sound, like an army of dung beetles or locusts advancing, bashing their shells and antennae together.

"At first, she appeared to me in dreams. . . . Then, it was as if she were at my side, as if she were watching over me," recalled Rafael. It all started toward the end of Cristina's life. The man loved her with a thirst, a restlessness. And the worse she got, the more Bardají was at her side. He came morning and evening to Son Vadell, both before and after school where he was a teacher; he spent as much time as he could close to his fiancé.

"And it was then that she started acting strangely. If at the beginning it seemed to be desperate love, it soon became a disturbing extravagance. As if touched in the head, she would rove through a room, the terrace, or the courtyard with her eyes, mumbling with a shifting smile: 'I'll be back here . . .' or she would run her hand over a dresser, over the gramophone, caress a rose, and whisper with a diaphanous and piercing radiance, 'I'll keep on caressing them, from the other side. . . .'

"I would listen to her and a shiver would run down my spine, but I didn't say anything; I tried not to pay attention. Until I finally understood that Cristina was driven by a truly unusual belief in an unspecified but certain resurrection, like the return of her spirit. . . ." Cristina knew that she was going to die. But she talked and chattered on with a feigned cheerfulness, as if it didn't have to be that way; though thinly veiled, a flash of terror and desperation lurked in her voice and eyes. It was as if she were acting out a play based on an implicit understanding that only provoked real emotions from explicitly false motives.

"She would drag me over to the sofa in the great hall, or we would stay in the courtyard if it were windy outside, so that she could get a little air. And then she would describe the house we were going to live in once we were married, as if we were going to start moving in any minute now. She described the furniture, her wedding dress, and the people we would invite. She described everything in great detail, even an argument about the color of a curtain, and she laughed when she thought that if we had children we would bring them into our bed in the morning so that we could play with them. . . ."

And if Rafael was quiet, if he looked down at the floor with his eyes brimming with tears, she convulsively demanded that he answer her questions of what he thought of this and what he would do with that. "And I had to invent things and talk nonsense, to fake that I was faking, torturing my insides day after day. . . ." And Cristina, still dreaming, would mumble as she listened to him, "Even though it doesn't happen, it will happen. And I'll be there. Don't you ever forget it. You and I will do all this, somewhere we don't even know about yet. . . ." Rafael would look at her out of the corner of his eye in alarm, at the same time commiserating with her, fearing as much for Cristina's sanity as for a kind of dark, ambiguous threat that seemed to hover behind her words.

And if they were alone, she would come up to him and embrace him with trembling sensuality, offering him her mouth and her burning hot tongue, submerging him in a turbid and dizzying lust. Tensed with fear, Bardají thought of the danger of contagion, at the same time overcome by the blistering heat of her mouth, by the excited, hysterical desire rising in Cristina's body, by now just skin and bone. "I am yours and you are mine; I don't want you going with any other woman. You have to promise me that. . . ." And Rafael, his hands running nervously over that hot flesh already destined to rot a few days later in the grave, promised whatever she asked, as he shuddered from a disturbing erection.

After she was buried, Rafael Bardají remained lost in a loneliness watched over by her demanding ghost. "Since then, she has risen from the shadows every night to haunt my dreams. . . ." He would barely close his eyes and Cristina would be there, the image of desolate sweetness. And then they would walk around and talk together, just as when they were engaged. But now they would walk through bizarre places, full of crushed plants, smoking holes in the ground, and birdlike flying eyeballs making human gestures at them. Cristina would begin in a weak childlike voice, talking about everyday things common to them both, but soon her voice would begin to change until she became hoarse and lost it. . . . "And I began to see her during the day as well, or rather to have a premonition of her being somewhere around me, maybe in the shadows or camouflaged in the top branches of a tree. I felt her presence vividly, and then her voice would talk to me . . . and in my imagination we chatted. It seemed as if her spirit were following me practically everywhere," Bardají explained, as we sat close to the Font de la Menta, looking out over the valley of La Trapa and the open sea beyond, with only the whisperings of the wind cutting through those great silent spaces.

But, imperceptibly, everything began to change. The figure of Cristina would burst forth in Bardají's sleep, disconcertingly irritated, a false cutting smile on her lips, her body making subtle lascivious movements. Rafael would look at her, and her lewdness would excite him. He tried to go to the woman, but he couldn't, as if he were glued to the floor. And she would unbutton her dress; she had enormous silky soft breasts, a pair such as Cristina had never had, and the sight of them stirred his desire . . . but nothing ever happened. Rafael would wake up all sweaty and confused, sometimes with his shorts shot full of sperm.

He would swallow hard, moved by repressed desires as he watched other women on the streets. And at first it was like a dream, a warning from Cristina that made him turn his glance away and repeat to himself that *No,* he would not look at another woman again, as if he had been about to commit a sacrilege, as if by doing so he would hurt Cristina, would bury her even deeper than she already, irretrievably was. "At night I would toss in my sleep; Cristina, her splendid breasts almost touching me, made me get all twisted up in the sheets, until I would wake up screaming, my voice strangled. . . ."

Then he unconsciously began to take on an attitude of escape, of rejection toward Cristina. When he felt himself under her influence, he would often make an effort to pay no attention to her. He would stare unabashedly at a passing woman or he would do the opposite of what her voice suggested, as if he hadn't heard it clearly. "But she noticed right away. I swear, it was as if she were attacking me. I would be walking along and I would suddenly turn around, under the impression that a bird was flying at me like a dart, its beak stretched out to strike me . . . and at night, the crazy scenes kept repeating themselves with Cristina running after me.

She might appear crying, or imperiously angry; her face would change horribly . . . and I would run away . . . or I wanted to grab her and strangle her to destroy those nightmare masks."

Did Rafael Bardají come to hate the memory of that girl whom he had loved so much? The neighbors said they had seen him in the court-yard behind his house, talking out loud as if he were arguing violently with someone, when in reality there was nobody else there but him. And he would suddenly grab a knife or a stick and jump around striking out furiously at thin air until he collapsed, exhausted.

*R*afael Bardají had become a prisoner of the tight oppression Cristina's death exercised over him, a state of nonexistence that permeated him and beat him down. . . . At this time some parents began to notice absurd anomalies in what their children were saying in Bardají's class at school. They would hear the children mention a famous monarch whom the parents had never heard of, or the children would talk about a nation their parents didn't know existed. And so they asked their children more questions. The answers were well-informed, extensive, and convincing, except for those initial incongruencies.

The problem grew. One day a boy located a river in one continent, when in reality it flowed through another; or he would explain a chemical reaction with the formula written the opposite of what it should have been; or he would recite names of authors and literary works nobody had ever heard of and that couldn't be found in any encyclopedia. It was as if through the mouths of his students, who continued to be really interested in his games, indications had filtered out about a chaotic collapse of the universe.

I didn't experience that period at school, because throughout all those long months I was stuck in that airtight chamber created by Grandmother and Father Dionís. Only later did I attend school; it was located in an old wine cellar with very low ceilings and thick walls, from the time when there used to be vineyards in Andratch. Arches of exaggerated thickness separated the dark and musty classrooms, with only a few weak lightbulbs coated with grime to alleviate the gloom. In the winter they would stoke up a coke-burning stove, and it would unexpectedly begin to give off a dense and bitter cloud of smoke that choked the room. Then we would have to open all the windows; I remember coughing with tears in my eyes and getting wet from the rain that splashed in. Heavy drops would land on our exercise books and the ink would run.

At the beginning nobody paid much attention to what the students said. The parents thought it must be a joke, or that they didn't know enough about the subject. But finally they decided to take steps. Rafael Bardají was submitted to a discrete investigation.

In class, his lessons were concise and irreproachable. He lectured walking up and down the classroom, hands behind his back, his chin held high. His clothes were an impeccable black and he wore a tie. Four times a day, going to and from the school and his house, he would compare the time on his pocket watch with that of the town hall clock. Those who listened to him in the classroom noted nothing out of the ordinary until his eyes would narrow, almost becoming oriental slits, and a sibilant tone would color his voice. That was when he would introduce an extemporaneous element into his lecture, fruit of his imagination, only to come back immediately to his prepared text.

Taking advantage of a cold that kept Rafael in bed for a week, a school inspector from Palma came and examined the students together with the other two teachers. Seated at their black desks in that crypt-like setting, they answered the questions with absurd tranquility, explaining truth and fiction in an indecipherable mixture.

After that, Bardají himself was severely interrogated. With stiff deference, one leg crossed over the other, smoking with a cigarette holder, he shrugged off every specific concrete question. He imperturbably maintained that reality did not only consist of accepted fact or existence according to the theories by which feelings have been cataloged—all of them definitely conventionalisms. No, reality was also that which could yet be created, could still happen, and even that which never would take place, but would have been formulated—ideally—in a rapture of intuition or will, since ideas and words were as objectively solid as facts and material. The world, he went on to say, is the brain's ordering of chaos, of empty space, and also of dark and capricious laws. Experimental proof is forcibly reduced to a timorous, hurried demonstration of a provisional and deficient quality that we, in our fear, convert into inflexible rules.

Rafael spoke in short sentences, the new one mixing with the echo of the previous one as it resounded between the huge arches of the school.

The sentences didn't seem to have anything to do with him, as if individual pieces of him were breaking loose and floating about in a fog. "Thus for a schoolboy whose mind has not yet been corrupted by the seriousness of established ideas, a country or a personage that is solely the product of the imagination may, and in fact *does,* have as much validity as those that exist geographically or historically."

The investigative commission listened to him with astonishment. "You may condemn me, because you adults are analyzing me from your iron-willed, gridlocked minds. I may appear to be a fake to you. I don't deny it; you're right. But you're only right with respect to yourselves, not with respect to the children, who are still pure and distant from the chains of convention."

They threw him out, and he left, laughing hilariously as if an invisible crowd were carrying him off on their shoulders.

I like Paris. I'm here because I want to be, because it's the place where I feel least tied to the past and its memories, but where at the same time each Gothic façade, each corner of the Seine with the delicate, swooning willows leaning over it, each advertisement for a movie, each bookstore loaded with suggestive letters and colors . . . each of these things speaks to me. And they speak to me in an intimate language that's really mine. I'm here and I'm not here at the same time. Paris for me serves as a set of checks and balances. But now that I have brought up La Trapa, a sudden tangle of converging roots grips me, drawing me closer to it. I would like to submerge myself again, even if for only a moment, in that formidable group of elements . . . they call me, a calling that has little to do with my conscious mind and much to do with the visceral, inner strength that has made me and sustains me.

Two hundred and fifty mountainous acres, with the central valley almost barren of cultivation . . . inaccessible mountains made of huge, flat steely rocks, a rough and deserted terrain exposed to open space and the sea. . . .

It is a rugged imposing headland, broken suddenly by very high red rocks jutting from the sea above the waters of the remote and empty horizon. Cala Sanutges, Cap Grossor, Coma de Campàs, Morro de la

Rajada, Cala En Basset, Puig Blanc, Vall dels Moros, Font de la Menta, Puig d'En Farineta, a list of lost names to the north that many people from town have never been able to tie to their geographic place with any accuracy—they would just point to the gigantic and inaccessible silhouette of a huge peak in the distance. Only the fishermen, the hunters, and the charcoal makers knew the route to La Trapa. They were able to find a path through the proud pines and the lower valley filled with furze and broom. It was the territory of the avid and vigilant kite, the slippery weasel, the voracious wild goat.

The arrival of the monks was still remembered by the old folks, like a supernatural myth of indestructible presence. It happened a century and a half before I was born, but everyone continued to refer to it as if they had themselves seen it, as if it had just recently happened.

This is the way the legend goes: One humid and sticky winter morning, with the weather out of the south, the lugubrious caravan unexpectedly entered Andratch. The hooded brothers were seated motionless on the wagon benches, a silent and dismal scene. The snorting, sweating mules continued to pull the wagons. . . . Their pilgrimage had begun in a corner of Normandy. One day a troop of people assaulted their silent, orderly monastery singing "ça ira," waving the tricolor flag with vociferous joy. Expelled by the French Revolution, the monks had dispersed in disguise and confusion, always followed by the specter of the square-framed guillotine rising rigorously against a leaden sky. They had seen that machine many times as they stood camouflaged on many a street corner in whatever towns they had to pass through during their escape.

The city of Saragossa took them in, allowing them to regroup. And they got under way again out of pure fear when Napoleon's troops advanced. They set sail for Majorca this time. They bought the inhospitable peaks and founded the new La Trapa. Among the peaks they displayed their white habits, billowed out by the cutting wind. They never opened their mouths. They were dreamlike creatures, seemingly hiding something implacable, something shockingly rigid under their masks of iron purity.

They worked with obstinate energy, as if they were building much more than what they seemed to be achieving materially, a mysterious and titanic work whose spirit reached beyond space and time. They cut stepped terraces into the rocky hillsides, separated by enormous stone walls laid out to perfection. A deep well was dug out of the rock, and its water distributed through an intricate subterranean system of canals to irrigate as far as the bottomland, where many splendid ferns grew, and there it ended in a hidden reservoir. They patiently hauled baskets of good brown dirt up the mountain from the flats below and mixed it with their yellow clay soil.

The grafts on the fruit trees took, and the following February the almonds burst into milky white flower; in June the pear trees turned a fluffy green; in October the abundant pomegranates opened their sparkling crowns. The wheat fields in summer took on the color of crisp old gold. And the foliage of the gardens, a labyrinth of light and shadow stirring a kaleidoscope of color, exuded the sensual aroma of flowing sap. Opened by brigades of pickaxes, a path wound up through the heights skirting the peaks until it reached the road between Andratch and Sant Telm. Two mules with pack saddles trudged up the path, one of them ridden by a lay brother, his eyes cast downward, endlessly mumbling the rosary.

The buildings began to take form. The monastery, a large spacious manor house, consisted almost entirely of whitewashed corridors, with fragrant flower pots of basil laid out in rows, as though they were guarding the cell doors. And the church looked as if it had been made of clean white lime, with the blind geometry of its neoclassical arches and a pointed belfry. And on a hill stood the small cemetery, reflected in the surface of the reservoir, with young cypresses among whose branches the roses intertwined.

Brother Pierre du Saint Calvaire was its first client. He broke the sacred rule of silence one starry night in March as he lay lathered in the holy oils of the last rites, bellowing crazily for them to leave him alone and not enter by that door, which didn't open to any mansion, that rectangular arch over the catafalque, the bluish blade high above, waiting to be sprung.

A great deal of the provisions and building materials they needed were brought by sea. High above, on the edge of the precipice, they set up a huge apparatus of giant pulleys, sort of like a water wheel, with a horse harnessed to it. It had a wooden cage at the end of the long rope and served as a rudimentary elevator for that immense cliff. On many occasions only one brother would go up in it. The cage would move slowly toward the sky, and out of holes in the cliff rocks the sea gulls and cormorants would flutter and scatter. The sailors in the catboat below gazed at the scene in complete absorption. It seemed to them that they were seeing a simple and solemn medieval miracle in which a man was fervidly ascending toward heaven, surrounded by doves, just like in church paintings.

When the monarchy returned to power in France, the monks set out for home again. Once more the wagons trundled through the streets of Andratch, the majestic and gravely hooded monks rocked stiffly back and forth at every bump in the road, as if they were made of wood. All they left was a dog suckling her four pups. They turned out to be little straw-colored dogs with very long, thin muzzles, very useful for hunting hedgehogs and jack rabbits. The townspeople called them and their breed "traperos."

La Trapa stood abandoned. The two hundred and fifty acres returned to the grave solitude of nature unaffected by man, exuding the solidity of its veiled mineral and vegetal pulse.

Bardají and I only got as far as Font de la Menta. But many times, hiking alone in the months before I left Andratch, I would get as far as the old Trappist mansion. I preferred not to be seen by anybody; I was sick of everything, and the hike to La Trapa calmed my nerves and relieved my depression. Those hours alone doing physical exercise comforted me. I would get up early in the morning and follow the monks' old path. A single pear tree survived in the garden, its branches thick and unpruned. It still produced huge juicy pears. The roof had fallen in on the monastery house, and a scurrying horde of rats ran through the ruins.

Through the broken-down doors of the chapel rain had blown in for years. The statues of the Virgin Mary and the Founding Father, their paint capriciously smeared, reflected a wretched and ridiculous sadness. Twisted brambles and thistles with their fine, grayish flowers were growing all over the place.

Once I jumped in surprise when I discovered a billy goat with a magnificent set of horns, stinking of semen, watching me from among the five rotten crosses in the cemetery. He stood there with an expression of satanic pride. I was about to stone him, but I was afraid he might charge me. And so I got out of there, trekking far up the mountain. When I returned he had gone. And the pond had a disquieting sheen on its brackish waters, where wide aquatic plants poked through soft masses of algae, moving imperceptibly every now and then, as if an underground force were pulling on them. The cavernous croaking of the frogs seemed to fill the pond, and depending on how the light fell in its turbid depths, the shadows of long, slimy slugs appeared to slither by.

I had known for a long time that Llàtzer de Vadell had lived at La Trapa. He was almost certainly the cousin of Felip the leper and therefore the second uncle of Françesc Joan. His return to the town must have occurred just after 1832, judging from the sales deed to the land that had been turned over to an administrator by the Trappist monks. Llàtzer paid very little for it. And his arrival as well as his person have remained curiously alive in the townspeople's memory. However, I'm not sure people didn't confuse his arrival with that of the Trappists. There are too many details common to the description of both events. But even though it didn't really happen that way, the coincidence of the facts in both cases is evident: they both appeared suddenly; after having bought the estate, they in turn converted it to either a cloistered or legendary place; and both of them completely disappeared afterward.

In any case, they say the three wagons entered by way of the Pont dels Dos Ulls one muggy summer afternoon, drawn by bluish mules and roan Percherons. A frothy lather, like beaten egg white, began to build up on the hides of the beasts. A grim haze slowly spread out, choking the valley; dirty black clouds piled up out to sea. The leaves hung withered on the almond trees and the earth exhaled a hot dizzying vapor.

Soon it would be dusk and the townspeople sat in their doorways, fanning themselves and slaking their thirst from clay jugs. In the stables, overheated animals bellowed from thirst with the submissiveness of those already defeated by irrational suffering. Excited sea gulls swooped overhead, squawking loudly and frenetically, fleeing the coast in fear of the storm about to break if the atmosphere got any heavier. A carefully closed tarpaulin covered each of the wagons. Some strapping young black men with kinky hair sat on the bench seats. Sweat covered their brows, but they didn't seem to notice. Their gaze was fixed farther down the street, like zombies removed from immediate reality, driving the wagons mechanically, obeying telepathic dictates from elsewhere.

The wagons stopped in front of the town hall and a short man without a shirt got out. He was well-muscled, his skin deeply bronzed from the sun; his head was round and bulky, bald and shiny on top, as if it had been varnished. His eyes were black and furious, disdain obvious in the curl of his lip. Imperiously he demanded to see the mayor. When the official appeared, the bald man, without even greeting him, showed him some papers, declared that his name was Llàtzer de Vadell and La Trapa was his, and that from this moment on nobody could set foot on a millimeter of the two hundred fifty acres. Then he got back up on the wagon.

Meanwhile, some men had drawn close to the wagons, and they heard something like mumbling from within, muffled metallic sounds and stifled snorts, as if something alive were pulsing under the canvas. The heat seemed denser near the wagons.

I don't know what the townspeople might have known about Llàtzer back then. Many of them, of course, would have known him as children or as adolescents, before he went abroad forty or fifty years earlier, although I haven't been able to find his birth certificate. I don't even know who his father was. What is absolutely certain is that from the very moment of his return, a legend of sorts began to form around him, narrated, without any reference to its source, by Father Ensenyat of the House of Joanillo in his *History of the Barony*. I shall transcribe here the brief text he included in the appendix of the second volume, titled *Notable Personages of Andratch*, that he wrote at least half a century after the death of Llàtzer, which occurred just about the time the priest was born. What I mean to say, in any case, is that the details the author was able to gather were relatively fresh, whether real or invented, and were told to him by witnesses still living at the time. And, in short, they are no more fantastic than the events that determined the final catastropic outcome.

Father Ensenyat of the House of Joanillo tells this story: "Llàtzer de Vadell was also a son of the town who, before retiring to La Trapa— where he ended his days, but here is not the appropriate place to relate that mournful event—led a very adventurous life in accord with a pattern that unfortunately attracted too many of our fathers and grandfathers who, instead of accepting with Christian resignation what God has bestowed upon us in our beautiful valley, roamed the world, often in more misery than pleasure.

"It is known that de Vadell lived at an oasis, to the south of the Red Sea, and that his house was a sort of fortress, with great pumpkin-colored walls surrounding it, always under the lash of sandstorms, which is what happens in the deserts. In those places one eats bread and dates, drinks water, and chews sand, we have been told by people who have experienced it. Practicing the Muslim belief, which is false and idolatrous,

Llàtzer de Vadell had seven or eight wives and children and servants, and everybody obeyed him in silence because he was an easily angered man who went around with a whip in his hand.

"His business was the slave trade, both blacks and Arabs, which he bought from the soldiers and minor kings of the African interior. He transported them overland on foot, with them in leg irons, causing many of them to die on the road, and he sold them at the sad but famous market on the island of Gadugú, situated in the Dahlak archipelago just off the coast of Masawwá—where the pearl fishers come from—in Eritrea."

In fact, everything in the story is too archetypal: polygamy, the slave trade, descriptions of the simoom wind, geographical references to a slave market. As for more specific details about Llàtzer de Vadell, there was nothing. But this is the only written record about him I can find.

It's a story nobody in Andratch could have known on that hot summer afternoon when the three clattering wagons slowly rumbled off down the road to S'Arracó, climbing toward the foothills of the Sierra de Tramontana. Some of the townspeople followed them from a distance on foot and by burro. The afternoon faded, and the clouds moved inland from the sea. The wagons stopped at the spring Dels Morers beneath the peak of En Farineta. The spring lay sheltered at the bottom of a myrtle patch, where they say King Jaume the Conqueror ate myrtle berries and drank cool water before ordering the decapitation of a woman who had had carnal knowledge of dog.

When I was a child, mulberry trees grew around the spring, and my playmates and I would walk out there and eat our after-school snack. High above us hung a thick canopy of foliage, and a layer of mulberries covered the ground, most of them split open, making for a dirty mushy mess; it was clotted with bees dazed from the heat and satiated from sucking on that mass of fruit saturating the air with its cloying bitter sweetness. From their vantage point under the shade of the mulberry trees, under the overpowering mystery of twilight overtaking the arid countryside, the townspeople observed how the wagons suddenly went crazy with activity. The tarps fell to the ground and human beings, enormous bundles, and animal forms all poured out of the naked wagons and milled about in disorder.

Then a tongue of fire shot up. The brilliant flames caught the wagons afire and consumed them in a roar of crackling sparks. And in the light of that reddish glare a knot of people with their bundles and animals began the precipitous climb up the forgotten path of the monks. Clouds covered the peaks by now, and began settling into the valley.

From that moment on I have only three details left that could help explain the story of Llàtzer de Vadell without having found any direct descriptions of him. The only things I could track down were reflections of his actions, consequences of his life. I think it's even possible that nobody from Andratch ever saw him again after that first hazy twilight encounter.

The first detail has to do with the house. I had heard of the strange building that Llàtzer had constructed on the mountain at La Trapa. However, I thought there was nothing left of it, or that it was perhaps just part of the imagination of the townspeople, even though some of them described it as if they had really seen it. And it was on that disturbing afternoon of my encounter with the billy goat in the Trappist cemetery when I had run off up the hill to get away from him, that I unexpectedly came upon the house.

Brilliantly white Doric columns held up several unequal floors in a row. The windows were without shutters and the doorways partially bricked up. There were gilt cornices and small and useless oriental roofs on flat walls, and the stairs lead up to empty space. Everything was apparently unfinished, or perhaps finished at a remote moment, but since then had receded backward in time toward decay, abandoned to the ways of the wind. It stood now as a decrepit and absurd vestige of lost splendor, with only one specific objective—to ramble like a vine, a crippled, unplanned pile of wood and ashlars, the chaotic sum of various pieces of a house, a hunchbacked image of a Babylonian ziggurat.

The second detail is an apparently simple, though violent, court case. It began when a woman by the name of Encarnació Bonmatí, whose age isn't recorded, but who used to live in the part of town called Creu dels Ullastres and "practiced carnal commerce with free dedication," knocked at the door of the town constable the night of February 27, 1838. She told him that there was a "young man who was dead or very nearly so" in her house. The police came and found a man who was very brown, stoutly built, and had kinky hair. On his back was an open, running sore. The doctor said, "It's undeniable that he has been repeatedly beaten, which has made his internal organs burst in his abdomen and kill him."

What follows is the interrogation of Encarnació Bonmatí as it was written down:

JUDGE: How and when did you know the deceased?

ENCARNACIÓ BONMATÍ: I had never seen him before. He appeared at my door and in broken Majorcan dialect he told me that he was from La Trapa and that he wanted to rest with me.

J: Are you aware of the immorality of this business you're in?

E.B.: I was abandoned by my husband, I have two children to feed and I haven't been able to find any other way to make a living, as everybody in town knows—none better than yourself, Your Honor—and nobody can say that I've ever hurt anybody.

J: Good, let's get on with it. Did you cohabit with the youth in question?

E.B.: No. We lay down on the cot and I couldn't see his face very well, because there wasn't much oil in the lamp, and he got on top of me, but he didn't touch me anymore because right away he broke out crying and talking.

J: What did he say?

E.B.: Many, many things which I wouldn't be able to tell you because they were very confusing and sometimes I didn't understand him very well, but I think what he was trying to say was that he wanted to marry a girl named Massa or something like that, but that *their* father didn't want her to, because he wanted her for himself.

J: The father of whom?

E.B.: Of the boy and the girl.

J: You mean they were brother and sister and they wanted to get married?

E.B.: That's what I understood, Judge.

J: And what did you understand when he said the father wanted her for himself?

E.B.: The same thing. That he wanted her as a wife.

J: None of this makes any sense and it's an abomination just to think it.

E.B.: That's the way I feel too, but that's what I understood him to say.

J: Can you remember his exact words?

E.B.: No. He was a man who spoke really mixed up and like a foreigner and he said he had always obeyed his father but he couldn't let him take her too, because later they would be miserable like the rest of them, with those hunchbacks always locked up—just listening to them drove him crazy—and he had told his father so, and then his father had him whipped and they took her away, and he said that he had escaped, and that it was a crime, and that he wanted to be free, and she also cried out desperately . . . and that's what he said and kept on repeating.

J: None of this makes sense, but it will be investigated. Tell me now, how did he die?

E.B.: Well, he kept on talking and I kept on getting more and more scared and suddenly he threw himself between my thighs and I felt his face in the hair that we have there in the middle of the thighs and I told him to get out of there, that that was a vice and I didn't want to, and he stayed there without moving but without doing anything with his mouth either, and I got scared again and I moved him off me. He didn't move or say anything. And I thought he was dead. That's why I reported it.

The record closed with an extremely laconic report from the constable, according to whom Llàtzer de Vadell had been cited to come and identify the body of the deceased and answer the questions that had arisen from the prostitute's declaration. But Vadell didn't appear, claiming he was sick. Instead, two children of his appeared, showing some papers "written in Moorish by the King of Egypt" that "proved" the deceased was not the son of Llàtzer, but his "slave." Because of his having robbed "many times and not having his head clear," they whipped him just as "the Lord of La Trapa has a right to do," and that whatever he or Encarnació Bonmatí had said, "we don't know what it could mean because nothing like that had ever happened at La Trapa." The judge accepted the declarations and closed the case.

The capriciousness of the legal process is evident. Did they bribe the judge? It's not hard to imagine that, especially since Encarnació Bonmatí was cited again before the judge and warned to retract her statement "because nothing in her statement is true, as has later been proven," The woman, however, refused to do so.

Seven months later she was accused of having robbed "two sacks of chick peas from the storehouse of Marià Gasparoto." They found them hidden in the bake oven behind Encarnació's house. The charges had been made by Gasparoto, based on the fact that "Bonmatí had been around my storehouse and had looked frequently in my direction these last few days." She denied everything again, although they made her spend "six days locked up and she has received whippings for her crudeness and lack of respect for authority." They condemned her to "walk the length of main street twice on six consecutive Sundays after the eleven o'clock mass, which is the solemn office mass, with both of the loaded sacks on her shoulders, without being able to rest except when the constable should say so, and thus purge through public opprobrium her criminal conduct."

We don't find anything else about her until a month later. There is a brief report in which the judge certified "the body of a woman, which was found at noon on Sunday by the constable in the well of her house, where she had hanged herself and whose name was Encarnació Bonmatí."

After that, nothing more appeared about her, at least in the records. But it's easy, very easy to imagine, hour by hour, each step backward that she took—that they forced her to take—the prostitute Encarnació Bonmatí in the year of grace eighteen hundred thirty something. . . . Or must we leave to one side the people and consider only time? Because the only thing that really exists is its blind ticking, above and beyond ambitions, beyond the flesh, beyond feelings . . . all of them immaterial phenomena, and for just that reason carriers of the stupid, invented illusion of eternity. If nothing we think or say has any limits, what does have limits is what we do: birth and death are limits. We are no more than a circumstantial meeting in time, the passing of one more cog on the wheel of time.

Every Sunday Encarnació Bonmatí would begin her staggering walk, bent over by the weight of the sacks of chick peas on her back, feeling her weakened body begin to give way, her panting lungs wheezing like a runaway bellows. Her two children, their eyes wide with apprehension, perhaps walked together in silence behind her, watching her; or they would turn around in order to see how the other passersby would laugh at the thief; or they waited for her at home, sitting in silence, because their mother had told them not to move. The Sunday church-goers coming out of mass would have observed how that hunchback of shame, all sweaty and out of breath, ashen from exhaustion, lurched from one end of town to the other.

The constable found her one Sunday an hour after they should have started out. He grew tired of waiting and must have gone to her house to look for her, but he didn't find her anywhere and suspected she might have run away, until he noticed the taut rope in the well, and so he leaned over to take a look. The body of Encarnació Bonmatí, with her neck twisted violently to one side, swung slowly back and forth, reflected in the calm silvery water below. She hadn't been able to bear the ridicule, the condemnation that degraded her before the town and destroyed her spirit.

Just one more detail remains unsettled. It showed up seven years after the fire when a list of creditors to La Trapa was made. Marià Gasparoto headed the list as the supplier who had had the longest and most substantial relationship with Llàtzer de Vadell. . . .

It was noon again, but this time in the spring. The most noticeable thing was the odor, a vague, irritating smell that made people wrinkle their noses; animals sniffed uneasily. Then came the ashes. At first it looked like powder, but then the sparks came floating down through an atmosphere that grew ever thicker and hotter, until from Andratch they saw how a dense dark column of smoke had begun to rise above the mountains of La Trapa, rings of smoke that grew larger and spread out wider and wider, becoming a cloud blotting out the sun like a sinister foreboding. The sun's circle became intensely red and opaque behind the phantasmagorical rise of the smoky pall.

A brigade of men was quickly organized to cut a firebreak. With hoes, axes, mattocks, and ropes, they set out for the old winding hairpin trail of the monks. The higher they climbed, the harder the air got to breathe. It felt like an invisible and all-powerful force pressing on the men's shoulders, pushing them down.

When they made it to the top of the first hill, Puig d'En Farineta, they saw the flames: radiantly red, they curled and crackled toward the sky like horrible claws grappling with the unknown. The mistral wind stirred weakly but steadily. The air became unbreathable and the men felt their bodies begin to boil, and they drank water all the time. The fire leapt voraciously forward like a locomotive. Some more details come from the Royal Society of Friends of the Country. During those years they had made a study of forest fires. Thousands of pines were being burned. Dramatically silhouetted, black against the flames, they would explode without warning, throwing off a shower of burning pine cones that in turn burst open like shots. Soon a live oak or some brush would catch fire with a great crackling roar, shooting up huge tongues of flame, sometimes yellow, sometimes orange; the pine resin fried, becoming furious balls of frothing flame.

The fire had started near the pond in the opposite direction of the house. Working their way around the flames, the men from Andratch were able to get nearer the house, fearing all the time that the wind might shift and cut off their escape. When they got to the buildings, they found or saw something . . . what was it?

The best information still comes from Encarnació Bonmatí: "Her father wanted her for himself. They would become wretches like the rest of them with their deformities, always locked up; just listening to them made him go crazy." Later, in the very precise, condensed description by the Royal Society of Friends of the Country, they state that "the fire seemed to have been set on purpose, since half-burned pine torches had been found near what had been the monastery of the monks," and added, "due to causes unrelated to the fire, there were four dead bodies found, among them the owner of the property."

Finally, there is the petition of the town council of Andratch to the Sisters of Charity and to the Foundling Home in Palma, requesting that they "take charge of five and seven cripples, respectively, who have been abandoned by their family and who fled under as yet unclear circumstances during a fire. The children were found in a very agitated state and dressed in rags. We don't know what their names are, and doubt whether they belong to our Christian religion. Only a few of them can speak, and not always intelligibly. Their ages are difficult to judge, and we have divided them up into two groups: those who appeared to be the youngest and those who looked the oldest. Two more had been killed by gunshots. It's probable that they all lived together in a large cellar with barred openings, where bedsprings were found amid foul-smelling, offensive dirt, and the skin of the cripples seemed to have had very little contact with the sun. . . ."

Were those monsters locked up? . . . the mongoloid, shockingly surreal, like a toad; the blind one who drooled; the one with the heavy body and limbs like those of a newborn baby, tender and sticky; the cinnamon-colored girl, almost transparent and insensitive to everything; the mute with the huge mouth. So did they escape, setting fire to everything, killing Llàtzer de Vadell? Were they repelled by gunfire from the other inhabitants of La Trapa, who probably then fled by sea? Or was the rebellion started by the healthy children, with the fire and the breakout of the cripples both starting accidentally? It's impossible to know any more. The deformed ones—in and of themselves a veritable teratology—were most probably found crazy or wandering around in a stupor, as the night filled with stars.

Were they Llàtzer's children that he had had with his own daughters or granddaughters? Were they the product of brother and sister breeding together? The immense institutions of charity in Palma, with their fenced and dusty parks and tall discolored banana trees, their vast cold halls of murky gloom, swallowed them all up.

The fire lasted for five days. I watched one like it once from the sea, the tongues of flame curling up and over the rocks. It was at night and the dance of the flames reflected high into the sky, a solitary and brilliant madness, as if it had nothing to do with the rest of the world, with us human beings. Suddenly the blackened silhouette of a pine turned into a ball of flame, broke free, and flew off into space like a shooting star and then fell back, leaving a tumultuous trail of sparks behind it—an errant star, its inertia suddenly lost. When the burning branches hit, they threw off a crackling rainbow of embers against the calm dark sea.

*E*ncarnació Bonmatí reminds me of Isabel, who always fascinated me. She was the daughter of Cèlia, a second cousin in our family. I would watch her, observe her with my mouth hanging open. I spied on her, and if I had dared, I would have accosted her and entered her house; but that wasn't likely, because she was a prostitute, and so we had nothing to do with each other. At Son Vadell, instead of living by warm embraces, we lived by cold rejections.

Isabel lived in a small house at the edge of the road leading from Son Vadell to town. Every evening she would sit in her rocking chair, waiting. Outside, the sounds of the growing darkness floated in the air, like the moans of a shapeless beast: the owl hooted, imitating the flutelike tone of a wind instrument; the breeze stirred the tree branches with deep softness; a horse whinnied in the distance, like a frightened cry for help; a sheet of rain clattered nervously against the window panes. . . . Isabel would doze off, muffled up in her heavy red quilted housecoat in the blue-and-yellow-striped rocker, wrapped in the sweet turbid lightheadedness caused by the fumes from the tepid coals in the brazier.

At her side she always had a big black coffeepot; every once in a while she would pour herself a cup of coffee. She must have felt her whole body impregnated with that spicy odor. The two cats snoozing on the rug raised their muzzles and sniffed about indifferently. The heat, like a thick halo, filled the room.

She got up and lazily began to rearrange the wax flowers in the two porcelain vases shaped like torches she had on the sideboard; she fluffed up the dresses of the two celluloid dolls sprawled with their legs spread wide on the sofa covered with a purple cretonne flowered print; she went over to the corner table and turned on the radio. She smiled with satisfaction as she listened to the string of commercials and well-worn songs. She sank down into the rocker again to wait. A shiver of contentment ran through her abundant flesh; a dreamy smile appeared on her sensuous lips.

Isabel would normally get up by mid-afternoon and make lunch: raw, blood-red meat, egg yolks, fruit, and red wine, all of them elements still in their natural state, from the last heartbeat of the beast to the flow of the sap from the tree or the vine. Finally satiated, she walked around heavily, her cheeks flushed, almost surely fighting the drowsy urge to go back to bed.

So she would go outside. The weak afternoon sun, like a febrile swooning benediction, cast mauve tones on the walls of the square house, its heavy ashlars worn by time. It had been the Andratch town jail a century or two before. It was surrounded by a bed of prickly pears, between whose thick stalks Isabel would walk the cats. She then went down the stairs to the old underground cells, some of them with rusty chains and leg irons still fastened to the walls. She kept rabbits and a goat down there. She would milk the goat while the rabbits shied off into a corner, wary of the cats. Isabel drank most of the warm milk in slow swallows and then poured the rest into a clay bowl for the cats, who lapped it up methodically, looking around now and then with complete serenity. Isabel then put the halter on the goat and took her out to graze.

The last light of day waned, tinged with melancholy. A heavy solitude hung in the air, the announcement of a storm from up the valley. A few lights in town, sadly wan and lost, vaguely outlined the black mass of her house and the gloomy grandeur of the church. Isabel walked along the side of the ditch, humid from the settling dew, the goat munching the dark heavy grass with rhythmic rapacity.

A swift long-legged hare plunged into the brush. The hoopoe, adorned with its rich plumage, mute as a sea horse, stood guard in its carob tree. From the neighboring live oak came the diffuse rustling of the breeze, passing like a halting, dying breath that reminded me of the deep nasal death rattle of that monstrous whale I saw on the beach as a child, brought in from nowhere by the waves, beached there, shining intensely, as if it were something from outer space.

Isabel soon returned to the house, already feeling the chill in the evening air. She put the goat back in the cellar; the cats were waiting for her in the doorway. I would often watch her from a distance, lying in the prickly pear patch, where I had gotten in through a hole in the fence. From there I could see the whole room through the back window. How many times did I lay there and masturbate? My eyes would hurt from staring so long at the light from the windows. Because it was warm inside the house, Isabel would undress, leaving on only her black lace panties and bra. She carefully made up her big dilated eyes and her luxurious lips. Her soft white and obese body, her generous thighs and breasts, her puffy infantile face like that of a child who had aged prematurely and listlessly became for me a hallucinating and disturbing exhibition of carnal power.

She slipped on her bathrobe and sat down to wait. A wait that could be an hour or two, until a man's knock at the door would draw her out of her tedious slumber. Isabel tried to clear her drowsy head. She touched up her stiff permanent and, with an almost majestic walk, went to the door. A man would then come in whom I could seldom see: neither the door nor the bedroom fell within my field of vision.

I stayed a little longer in the cactus patch. Night had overtaken everything by then. Sometimes I would break into a muffled sobbing, feeling immensely abandoned, without knowing by whom or why. Perhaps in this way I established contact for the first time in my life with absolute loneliness; not the kind where something good is lost, but the kind where nothing is ever received.

I remember Isabel; I remember her room with portentous exactitude. I can see myself hiding and watching her while she let the goat graze. It's so clear in my memory, as if everything had just happened a few hours ago. It's possible that everything I didn't do, didn't say, or didn't even think about doing with her (which would have meant overcoming custom, timidity, and the morality of Son Vadell) became a mental desire for love that grew stronger the fewer obstacles and confrontations it had to endure, and which I carry with me unharmed, like an ever-fresh, eternal predisposition that is basically this: something readily available, isolated there, existing of and for itself alone.

*I*sabel's father had died in a time out of memory's reach for me. I used to see her mother, Cèlia, around her house when I was a child, but I don't remember when she died. We didn't call her "aunt," since we weren't speaking to her because of her daughter or maybe even before that.

She was a crippled-up old lady who walked slowly, leaning on a cane. She had abundant white hair and always dressed in black, always carrying a little basket woven of palm fronds covered with a checkered kerchief. When she was out walking, you could hear the regular click-clack of her cane on the ground; then it would stop, and after a moment resume. If you came up to the place where she had stopped, you'd find a crumpled piece of aluminum foil on the ground: inside the basket she carried foil-wrapped coconut cookies, caramels, chocolates. . . . Sometimes, when we met face to face, she would run her hand through my hair and give me a sweet, and I would throw it on the ground and run away. She would stand there looking after me, smiling, her cheeks sunken in from sucking on her candy, the halo of her white hair outlined against the light.

I never saw her set foot in Son Vadell, but two things of hers remained there, things that neither she nor anyone else would remember, but which unexpectedly connected me to the Cèlia of more than forty years ago. One of them was her photograph, hanging like all the rest on one of the walls in one of the endless rooms in that labyrinthine house. The other thing was a letter from 1902, perhaps from the same time as the photo, since the girl in it was about eighteen, the age Cèlia would have been at the time.

In it she's wearing a bluish or grayish dress, probably floor length—the photo cuts her off at the shins, so I can't be sure. The collar of the dress is white and tightly buttoned. A wide belt prodigiously girds her waist, dividing her body in two voluminous parts: one, her torso and breasts; the other, her hips and thighs. And the face that emerges from among a thick jumble of curls is sweet and delicate, a timid beauty.

The letter was written from Perpignan, and from the sound of it there surely was other correspondence before and after it. The contents were basically a request for her hand in marriage, and possibly that's why it wound up at Son Vadell, since judging from its content my grandfather Jacint was Cèlia's guardian, and he would be the one who would have had to approve or deny the marriage proposal.

I found it in the drawer of the writing desk where all the deeds from all the centuries of Son Vadell were rolled up in brown paper. They describe the properties, and we are declared their owners, properties nobody remembers had constituted a specific place and name in their day. The letter begins *"Ma belle et chérie Cèlia,"* and continues:

> During the short time we were able to spend together, your father got to know me and appreciate me, and I got to know him as well, helping him with all my heart to find his papers, from the defiles of Vianc to our cathedral . . . it was a pleasure, for you were there and I looked at you often. . . . I understand, however, that his death requires that you consult your cousin and guardian, who naturally wants to know where I come from. When we were alone here, I think I told you in passing that M and Mme Gouget, who have been so kind to me, and who have already signed over their dry-goods shop to me, were not my biological parents, but they took me in when I was seven years old and a war orphan.
>
> But now I want to explain more things to you, many more, beginning with the cries of terror with which I react when faced with anything that surprises me, as insignificant as it might seem, and the trembling withdrawal within myself that often occurs, and all that from when I was a child, and even as a youth and sometimes even today when I'm in my room at night with the light out. Or if I'm afraid something might hurt me—as I now feel, dear Cèlia—an avalanche of panic descends on me, at the mere thought that your guardian might oppose our project. This fear haunts me as if a frightened animal were inside me, always ready to jump out and escape. . . .
>
> My father was deported to New Caledonia. And I found out a few years ago that he died ten months after his arrival there in 1873. The cave-in of a tunnel in the nickel mines of Pin Pin buried him alive. The courts of Paris, the ones run by that abominable man Thiers—whom I don't know if you've heard about or not—had condemned him to forced labor in perpetuity, after keeping him locked up for many weeks (I don't know how many) in a barge anchored on the Seine, along with hundreds of other prisoners.
>
> You may ask "prisoner of what?" Of the Commune, that's what. But I swear to you that neither of my parents nor any of the rest of them was a revolutionary. They only believed that God, love, and equality could have been a reality among themselves.
>
> I remember my father. He was thin, feverishly waving a long musket

on a barricade of sandbags in Rue Saint Jacques. He was one among many others: one of them had a drum and he beat it madly, and another one raised an enormous red flag with difficulty, waving it back and forth in an arc. And a compact mass of soldiers advanced towards them with fixed bayonets. A desperate joy shone in my father's wild eyes. His hair seemed to stand on end as if it were in flames. Afterward there were shots, smoke, shouting, I don't know what. . . .

I also remember him from before the Commune, his silhouette on the driver's seat of a stagecoach, his stovepipe hat and cassock—maybe red—the reins in his hands, smiling and looking toward a door, maybe the one to the place where we lived. Was I in that doorway? Was he looking at me? Was he happy with me? Was he a coachman? The only thing I can add is that when he got out of the barge he was syphilitic, with a huge open sore on his neck, oozing pus. He hardly spoke; he hardly understood anything at the trial. The courtroom had round, opaquely white oil lamps, and there were a lot of other men with my father—a lot of them—standing in the dark prisoner area, listening to the sentences being read out by a military officer.

Out of the great confusion and bewilderment that overcomes me when I try to remember, only a few scenes come to me clearly. One is of my mother running, dragging me along by the hand, up the steep streets of Montmartre. There were a lot of us who were fleeing. Then I have the impression that I was falling down into a deep gulley. . . . After that, I found myself lying down with a man on top of me, an old man who stank horribly, who held my body and tried to cover my mouth and my eyes. We were hiding in a high niche in the Père Lachaise Cemetery.

And there in front of us were my mother and many others, men and women squeezed together, with dirty, torn clothing, surrounded by a crowd of soldiers, officers, and very elegant ladies and gentlemen. A lady with a lilac-colored dress and an enormous necklace hit my mother in the head with the tip of her umbrella. I saw her hair bun come undone, her splendid long hair falling down about her shoulders, as the sharp, deafening reports of rifle shots began.

When the smoke had cleared, my mother wasn't there; nobody was there, only a pile of bleeding corpses. And the ladies, the gentlemen, and the generals were all laughing, and they went around sticking their umbrellas, their swords and their bayonets into the noses, the eyes, and other orifices of the piled-up corpses. And there I was with that stinking old man, lying atop a rotten coffin with the bones inside crumbling to dust . . . the boards, the bones, everything crumbled apart every time we moved.

After that . . . well that's enough. On the other hand, I don't know how I wound up in Perpignan, or how the Gougets took me in. All I

know is that I love you, Cèlia, and that I pray to God that everything
can be arranged with your cousin and guardian.

I embrace you with all my soul,
Michel Tulard

But it must have been only the intention to embrace that was consum-
mated, because Cèlia married a man from town named Borràs. And
neither Grandmother Brigida nor Uncle Dionís ever hinted at the existence of Michel Tulard. He had disappeared from their memory, or they
had never heard of him . . . another human being sunken into obscurity,
at least for us. And if I mention him now, it's because of the reference he
had made to Cèlia's father, and the trip they had taken from Perpignan
to some place or places on the Viaur River. . . .

*T*hat man was Bartomeu de Vadell. There were very few traces left of
him or of his life. He had a soap factory in town, a pretty rudimentary
one I suspect; his huge cauldrons gently boiled along, the bursting
bubbles crassly engulfing their own suffocating mess. "He was a well-
traveled man," they used to say of him. And that fact in its time was
remarkable, because if it were not to emigrate seeking work, practically
nobody ever left Andratch.

No doubt quite a few of his trips—and maybe all of them—were to
France. I found proof of another trip, I suppose from before the one
Michel Tulard mentioned, that took him farther up into France, to the
Tours region. I don't know about the other trips, but in this case
Bartomeu carried a diary with him in which he wrote down what he did,
but without dates. Or at least part of what he did, because it seems that
all the activities he wrote down formed a framework that in reality served
to enclose other interests that are barely mentioned. It's a notebook with
brown oilcloth covers. He wrote in a relaxed hand with very small, sharp
letters, the lines looking like rows of little lances. In fact, at times I had to
use a magnifying glass to read them. This is what he wrote:

> The water in the Loire is muddy and apathetic, and every once in a
> while small islands appear in the middle of it covered with tall dense trees
> that look rather gloomy. The shoreline is low, trees abound, and the
> greenness is both intense and sweet. They say that a long time ago the

whole region was a forest. That poet from the region, to whom I was introduced by Françon the architect, was Pierre de Ronsard. He sang longingly of the deep forest after it had been cut over several times:

Lofty forest, towering home of woodland owl,
no longer will the lonely stag, the graceful roe
graze beneath your shade, and your verdant cowl
will no longer brake the summer blaze of Helios.

Now, everything is planted to grapes and traveling by train through the vineyards is pleasant. I like the speed of the train. I imagine myself seated in the carriage like a hero of I don't know what. You see the grapevines rising and descending with the gently rolling hills, and when a little breeze stirs they look like small, trembling bundles.

✢I✦

We visited the castle of Chenonceaux. Jean Marie Françon has been studying the south façade of it for a long time, making drawings of the elegant renaissance gallery and the bridge, an airy, daring work linking the banks of the Cher. No doubt Françon will write a very detailed book, but it will take him years to sketch all the castles of the Touraine. . . .

Meanwhile, I walked about in the extensive park surrounding Chenanceaux, and Yvette kept reminding me of that extraordinary lady, Diane de Poitiers, who lived here and whose clear beauty, like a challenge to promises, remained graven in a mirror . . . Yvette smiled as she spoke, and I kept looking at her out of the corner of my eye. . . .

✢I✦

The wine cellar Au Relais de l'Escargot is like a deep dungeon, and the walls are made of a soft stone that crumbles when you scratch it. There are barrels of red wine from Chinon, and white wine from Vouvray. The owner, André Brieux, is a little old man, a strange mixture of a body that is skeletal and at the same time fat. The skin on his head is fine and tightly stretched over his skull, but from his neck a fat spongy double chin hangs, as if all the fat from his head had run down into it. And his bulging eyes, with those erratic streaks of anger, reminded me of a woodpecker.

The tavern is just before you get to Nevers-le-Duc. The wall around it is high, thick, and covered with dark and shiny ivy, which gives the appearance of hiding something disgustingly ugly. In the courtyard, there are two chestnut trees almost swallowed up by the ivy climbing their trunks and branches, barely letting any sunlight through.

It's pleasant at this time of summer, and above all at dusk, to feel how cool it is inside the tavern. On our return from some of the castles,

— 104 —

during these days while we're staying in Nevers-le-Duc, we stop off at Au Relais de l'Escargot. André never opens his mouth, but serves us large portions of snails. The shells are a pale green with siena stripes, and have been seasoned with butter and aromatic herbs. They're exquisite.

✦I✦

The plain widens, and in the distance the spiked towers of the cathedral of Tours gradually appear. . . .

✦I✦

I feel I'm wasting a lot of time here with Françon and his wife. Of course, in the cathedral of Tours I didn't have anything better to do. But maybe I should go back to Majorca. . . . The problem is, when I'm near Yvette, I feel a lively stimulation that I haven't felt for a long time, since the first year I was in love with Sebastiana. It's a vague feeling of happiness that women sometimes awaken in me. Yvette is slightly pudgy, but she exudes joviality; she walks firmly with her back straight. And there's something secret and incomprehensible about her: her eyes always seem to say more than what her lips speak. . . .

But Yvette is Françon's wife. . . .

✦I✦

The owner of the hostel in Nevers has asked us harshly if we had become fans "chez Brieux," as she says. We answered that the snails were very good there. And suddenly she burst out in a tirade against André, telling us that almost nobody in town will have anything to do with him, that he has spent years in prison, that during the war he collaborated with the Germans, helping to drive the Emperor Napoleon III from power, and that many French patriots were executed as a result . . . sparks were flying from her eyes.

✦I✦

We have been visiting Amboise. The Loire caresses its magnificent walls. Jean Marie has explored every tower. They are round and have a spiral ramp, so that a carriage may be driven up inside. Yvette and I left him so we could visit the secret little chapel of Saint Hubert, and see the supposed tomb of Leonardo da Vinci, who died here where he had come to do some work. In silence, and emotionally, I took Yvette's hand. . . .

✦I✦

We stopped near a garden to rest. There was a man in a body cast seated in front of the house. He told us how he had wanted to make a

— 105 —

small cistern, and how he dug a big square hole. Then he fell in it and landed on a crowbar. When they got him out his back was broken. He had been in bed for weeks and he was only able to get up two days ago. He showed us the hole.

When he had the accident, many roots still had not been trimmed back inside the hole. Thick roots and thin roots, from grapevines, grass, sunflowers, cherry, and chestnut trees, a little forest of filaments hanging in the air, some intensely red and velvety, and others a cool yellow. And then it rained, forming puddles in the bottom of the hole. Soon, as if in a fantastic unreal dream, the roots began to move cautiously. Each day the man saw from the window how little by little they had moved closer to the muddy bottom, burrowing into it, and at the same time creating more little fragile roots, clear-colored and sickly looking . . . blind and aberrant tentacles, burrowing and absorbing the water.

That made me think of all the notes I took in the archives of Tours, and of J.C. and of that. . . .

+‡+

Unexpectedly, Françon and Yvette have had to go to Chartres because Jean Marie's brother is very ill and the family thinks he will die. I should also leave; however . . . I go every morning and afternoon to Au Relais de l'Escargot, and I drink a cold *pichet*. I think of the hours I've spent here beside Yvette. I regret never having told her anything about the beauty of her eyes, about the darkness that was falling and seemed to caress us. One of Ronsard's sonnets ends like this:

> By then I'll be a ghost, long since dead,
> Buried in the shade of the myrtle overhead,
> And you'll be an old crone crouching at the fire
>
> Regretting my lost love and your cold scorning.
> Live now, if you believe me, don't wait till morning;
> Come out and cut the roses from your brier.

But I didn't do it; I didn't cut any roses.

+‡+

The silence weighs on me. I've been reading another book that the Françons lent me, the *Histoire de la France* by Michelet. I tried to strike up a conversation with old André, but he only answered with grunts.

I was irritated, for reasons that had nothing to do with him, so I told him that the townspeople didn't like him. He just shrugged his shoulders. Then I read to him, with emphasis, a sentence from the book: "The national legend of France is an immense trail of light, never interrupted, a true Milky Way to which the world always turns its eyes." He listened carefully. And I asked him if his life agreed with that description.

I expected a snort, but instead his face became transfigured, all twisted up in a crazy grimace. And then he broke out in a horse laugh that wouldn't stop. It was glorious laughter, echoing through every corner of the courtyard, tangling itself in the branches of the chestnut trees, crashing like flint against the exultant sunshine outside.

And here it ended. All the rest of the pages of the diary had been torn out.

I found the notebook among the infinite piles of papers that I inherited from the vicar. Bartomeu de Vadell was a spirit who seemed sensitive though timid, with a liking for culture. Yes, but what caught my attention were not his personal characteristics, nor the literary qualities he might have had, but the intriguing note about the well and the roots, along with the initials J.C. What was Bartomeu de Vadell, soapmaker, doing there? He was surprisingly more cultured than the majority of his fellow townspeople, having traveled through the Roussillon, Armagnac, and the Tours region. What was he looking for in the archives of the Tours cathedral? And by whom and for what reason were the last pages torn from his diary?

Father Vadell had kept other papers with the symmetrical handwriting of Bartomeu in an orderly folder. It seemed to be the résumé of a subject he had researched, Jean Carrier. Could that be J.C.? The soapmaker wrote this about him:

> The name Jean Carrier appeared for the first time in 1406, as one of the rebels who participated in the revolt of Tolosa against Archbishop Vital, who was allied to Rome, with Carrier proposing to raise Pierre Rabat, who was loyal to Avignon, to the miter.
>
> He was famous as a good polemicist, well informed about the Western Schism, always in defense of Benedict XIII, Pope Luna, and they say that he came to be one of the most serious scholars on the subject. In the year 1415, Benedict XIII named him his collector and vicar general in Armagnac. But five years later the Roman pope, Martin V, tried Jean IV of Armagnac as a heretic and ordered the expulsion of the Avignon Schismatics (who were hiding in his territory), since his was

practically the only group that was still faithful to Luna. In one of the edicts preserved in Tours, the name Carrier appears among the heretics cited by Martin V.

But Carrier did not obey. Instead, he sought refuge in the castle of Touraine, located on the top of one of the cliffs in the rough gorges of the Viaur River. There Carrier wrote a treatise against the meddling of Urban VI, the first Roman pope after the Avignon period. Then the Nuncio of Martin V, Geraud de Brie, laid siege to the castle of Touraine, which they then started calling Peniscolette, a reminder that Pope Luna held court in Peñíscola.

In June of 1423, Carrier learned that Benedict XIII had died, but before doing so, had named Carrier cardinal of Saint Stephen. Carrier then fled from the Touraine, and after crossing several states, he arrived in Peñíscola at the beginning of winter. There he discovered that a new pope had been elected, Clement VIII, the former canon of Valencia, a wealthy woman- izer. Carrier held his tongue and investigated further, discovering that bribes had been paid in the papal election. And in November of 1425, at six in the morning, Carrier held a mass of the Holy Spirit in the chapel at Peñíscola, with a notary public and witnesses present. He declared the election of Clement VIII to be null and void, denounced Martin V as a false pope, renewed all the anathemas issued by Pope Luna and, rising up alone before the Sacred College, stated that he had named a new Holy Father, who was the only true pope, and whose name was to remain a secret. Immediately afterward, he fled by means of a rope down the cliffs to the sea and away by ship in the early morning fog.

He returned to Armagnac. He exhorted Jean IV, a man to be feared, to abandon his obedience to Peñíscola, now also schismatic, and to continue rejecting Rome as well. In exchange, he requested that Jean IV declare himself secretly loyal to the hidden pope, whose name was Benedict XIV. And in 1428, he set himself up in the castle of Jalenques, in the territory of the Count de Rouverges, a supporter of Jean IV of Armagnac. Carrier—his Roman enemies later said in the trial convened for him—had established himself as Jean IV's lieutenant, adding that he lived an unbridled, wild life together with his partisans, acting like the lord of the noose and sabre, supporting the banditry in the area.

It is said that the secret Pope Benedict XIV died, and that he must have been Bernard Garnier, Sacristan of Rodez, who before expiring named Carrier as the new pope. He also took the name Benedict XIV.

In 1433, Jean Carrier was captured at Puylaurents by the troops of the Count of Foix, lieutenant of Charles VII of France and Languedoc. They imprisoned him and tortured him, but he did not retract his faith. And he died without receiving the Holy Sacraments. Since he had been ex- communicated, he was buried outside the cemetery at the foot of a hill.

It was surprising to discover the oblique resurgence of Pope Luna, unexpectedly through Carrier. In fact, it was a hallucinated contradiction. What I had believed to have been monomania in that senile, celibate, and clerical old vicar Dionís, as far as the Great Schism, the triumph of Rome, and the defeat of Avignon was concerned, was in fact a subconscious inheritance that had become an obsession for another member of the family, that discrete and unknown Bartomeu de Vadell.

*F*ather Dionís had burned enormous quantities of papers before he died, leaving piles of empty boxes and file folders scattered everywhere. The last time I went to Andratch, that autumn when I had to take care of my inheritance, I found something like a black snowstorm in the vicarage. There were little flecks of ash everywhere from the documents and books the priest had burned in the fireplace and the stove. The finely broken-up, elusive pieces of paper ash were spread over everything. Between the air that stirred up every time a door was opened and the wind that filtered through the poorly closed shutters, the fragile particles danced around everywhere. Just walking about or putting a hand on a table was enough to create great black smears, especially on the floor and other flat surfaces.

The paper by Bartomeu on Jean Carrier was one of the documents that attracted my attention as I was going through the piles of papers that hadn't been burned. Without the work by Bartomeu I probably wouldn't have paid any attention, as I went through the vicar's file cards, to a card that said:

Mariona de Vadell, 17??–1765
Inquis.—folder 132
Visions—Carr. folder 87

The reference to "visions" seemed clear. And was "Carr." a reference to Jean Carrier? As for the other abbreviation, it was frequently repeated all through his card file: "Inquis.", which meant the Inquisition. I looked for the file folders mentioned on the card, but they weren't on the shelves. I was about to forget the matter when it occurred to me to examine the file folders the priest had emptied. The folders were there, numbers 132 and 87, but they were empty.

On the other hand, 1765 was the year the last two Inquisitions were held in Majorca, after seventy-four years without any. That was a time when sane opinion certainly couldn't justify the burnings anymore, anywhere, under any circumstance. In fact they were a sort of echo from Madrid, a show of power by the ultras, and afterward, of the revolt against Esquilache and Carlos III's Italianate reformers. What the organizers hadn't realized in time was that the unfavorable reaction would be so violent. It even motivated the decisive expulsion of the Jesuits, who had to leave a few months later. It was proven, in effect, that from the connivance between the Company of Jesus and the nobles who favored Ensenada had come the impulse for and support of those two inquisitorial burnings of 1765.

In the archives of the National Library in Madrid I untied a large packet of documents nobody had ever opened. They came from the Monastery of Santo Domingo, the headquarters for the Inquisition in Palma, destroyed in the 1820s by the Liberal Triennium. There must have been a couple of hundred documents: depositions, inventories of confiscated goods, sermons, etc., all from the Inquisition of 1765. To reproduce them all here in order to give a sketch of Mariona de Vadell would be fatiguing. To summarize it in order to reconstruct that frightening ceremony would be more instructive.

The bonfire stakes were set up between the solid walls of the Cuarentena and the walls of Bellver Castle. The sea was so still that afternoon it looked like a plate of glass, and from the thick pine woods of Bellver Castle came the dry and subtle aroma of spring. Those barely insinuated mountain fragrances had the capricious lightness of a flight of dragonflies. Palma was visible far away on the plain, as if etched in drypoint, its earth-colored walls and tile roofs and bell towers resplendent in the sun like a celestial apparition.

The previous Inquisition, the first of the two, had been held in the city in a meadow at the end of the market facing the port. However, the smoke from the burnings, saturated as it was with grease, had invaded all the streets, and for several days the curtains and luxurious tapestries in the noble houses stank of singed flesh. By moving the operation out to the Cuarentena, a recurrence of this danger was avoided.

The burning pit was enormous: it measured twenty-five feet on each side; the prisoners were tied and their chains anchored to the seats; the stakes still oozed resin, for they had just been cut at Bellver. They had piled bundles of pine branches on the ground around the stakes so that the blaze would catch quickly, and wild olive logs were added to keep the flame intense enough to make hot coals. The dais of the Inquisitor had a canopy of red velvet with the coats of arms of the king and the pope embroidered on it. But the highest one was that of the viceroy, made of carmine damask. Huge pennants with horrible devils painted on them— horned devils, hairy devils, and goatlike devils with their tails intertwined—were hung all around, a lugubrious counterpoint to the monumental crosses of myrtle and olive outlining the square.

All the bells in Palma were ringing in raptures of joy as the procession started out and advanced slowly through the hills of Santa Caterina, So n'Armadans, and the steep rise of S'Aigo Dolça. It was headed by the Inquisitor mounted on a palfrey covered with a long violet cape. In the large cages mounted atop carts drawn by yokes of oxen, the condemned were piled up: bundles of dirty, ragged people with only their bony hands visible, clutching the cage bars. Their hair was matted and clotted with filth, and their eyes shone like ripe carbuncles, reflecting frightened defeat and collapse. Near the vehicles, between the confusion of prayers and dissonant songs, an escort guard of friars and priests tripped over each other in their excitement as they waved green crosses and purple pennants.

Hundreds of people on foot, on horseback, on mules, in cabriolets, swarmed around the procession, insulting the prisoners, creating a din of laughter and foul language. And behind them all, a voluminous reddish dust arose, billowing up toward the clear blue sky, toward the bay and the sleepy sea.

Father Pere Roig from the Monastery of Santo Domingo said mass. Under the awnings on the main reviewing platform the nobility greeted one another according to protocol, while the Moorish slaves—mixed with the odd Christian slave—refreshed the air by waving large plumed fans. A multitude was struggling near the stakes, pushing and shoving to get a place atop the wagons and the dais. Flocks of peddlers hawked scapularies and medals, flutes, and straw hats. In improvised stalls people were frying sardines, selling vegetable tarts, water, and anís. A bloated yellow Jesuit was giving a sermon in a eunuch-like singsong voice: "The Devil may oblige Judas to deliver up the Divine Lamb according to that verse '*Cum Diabolus iam misisset in cort, ut traderet cum,*' from John 13:2, because the persistent abomination of the Jews and the anathemic and infernal heresy. . . ."

The Official of the Holy Tribunal read the list of sentences hoarsely:

Isabel Pomar, sixty-one years old, widow of Françesc Bonnin, reconciled and captured for the second time as a relapsed Judaizer. Confiscation of property, as a heretic and apostate. . . .

Miguel Martí de l'Arpa, businessman, fifty years old, reconciled and imprisoned for the second time as a relapsed Judaizer. Confiscation of property as a heretic and apostate, convicted and confessed, remanded with merits to the secular authorities. . . .

Margarida Alenyar, twenty-three, recidivistic adulteress and blasphemer, condemned to perpetual exile and confiscation of property. . . .

Baldín Boronat Valls, forty-five, silversmith, imprisoned for the second time and without reconciliation as a Judaizer, relapsed, convicted, and condemned to confiscation of property and remanded to the secular authorities to be burned alive. . . .

Joan Ignasi Vitrac, thirty. . . .

Each penitent, wearing a short cape on which the redeeming flames had been drawn, listened to the verdict on his knees, the Inquisitorial Cross clutched in his hands. Sometimes they would cry as they kissed it; others knelt there in a daze. And some would grit their teeth, glaring at the mob and the crosses with barely contained rage. The voice of the official droned on:

Mariona de Vadell, as a heretic and schismatic, without reconciliation, remanded to the secular authorities with the aggravated offense of abominations and irreverence, condemned to the confiscation of property, and burning at the stake. . . .

A kind of shapeless beast was dragged forth by the soldiers. Its head was shaved, and black gashes crisscrossed its face and neck. It was throwing up bloody gobs of vomit. They let go of it and it fell belly first, its cross clattering to the ground. It then fetched forth a deafening lingering howl. The beast tried to get up, but it was impossible: in the Inquisition torture chamber they had broken its elbows and knees. It was Mariona de Vadell. Once her sentence had been read, she was dragged back to where the other prisoners were caged.

The *auto-da-fé* began. The first sentences to be carried out were those of the three remanded *in absentia*, and the four to be burned to the bone standing up. Two of those who had recanted climbed up the wood pyre between a canon and two friars, who made them kiss the green crosses and overwhelmed them with prayers in Latin. By recanting, their sentences had been lowered: instead of being burned alive, they would be first executed and then burned. They were tied to the stake and a chain was put around their necks. One of them started sobbing. The executioner gave the chain a neat, almost invisible twist, and the heads of both men fell to one side, hanging there loosely like fruit on a tree. A burst of applause rose from the mob.

Then they brought out the three who were to be purged alive by means of the sentence of fire. They were two men and a woman—the one with her arms and legs broken and whom they had to carry between four guards like a sack of potatoes. I can't, however, find even one eyewitness account of what happened when they sat them down on the bench seats at the base of the stake, or when the first licks of flame reached them, for not one of the documents mentions those details.

There is another singular book, however, that refers to the *autos-da-fé* from the previous century, those of 1691. It's called *The Triumphant Faith,* published that same year on the presses of Can Guasp. It was written by the Reverend Father Francisco Garau, Qualifier of the Holy Office, ex-professor of prime theology at the College of the Company of Jesus in Barcelona, and Rector of the College of Montisión, also run by the Jesuits in Palma. I suppose it's not presumptuous to imagine a transposition of the facts from one event to the other, even though three-quarters of a century had gone by; after all, they were also men back then, and it was death and torture that would control events—by all the gods and devils—on those piles of wood.

Father Garau explained:

> Let the truth be told that the converts received the noose with serene eyes and they sat down at the stake with calm spirits, whereas the unrepentant ones became furious when they saw the flames come closer, struggling angrily to free themselves from the shackles. A man called Tarongí finally did just that; although once he had freed himself he could not manage to stand upright, and so fell right back into the flames he was trying to escape. And his sister Catalina had claimed earlier that one should throw oneself straight into the fire. But when the flames began to lick at her in earnest, she screamed repeatedly for them to get her out of there, although still refusing to invoke the name of Jesus. Nor was Rafael Valls' stoic insensibility enough for him when the moment came.

There is a huge gap between words and deeds, and where the tongue goes easily the heart does not always follow. While it was only the smoke that reached him, he withstood it like a statue; when the flames rose around him he tried to defend himself by covering his face, writhing and struggling until he was exhausted. He was as fat as a nursing sow, so that the extreme heat cooked his insides even before the flames had left his skin as black as charcoal. His gut burst and his entrails fell out just like Judas'. *Crepuit medius et difusa sunt omnia viscera eius.* Actuum I, 18.

The pall of smoke on that ecstatic evening hung low in the air and spread out horizontally, invading the awnings and the reserved seats on the dais. The ladies coughed and had to unbutton their bodices amid the malicious sniggerings of the gentlemen, while the slaves desperately wagged their fans and the lackeys served sugared water to the guests. The mob sweated furiously, jammed together as they were, so as not to miss a single detail. The smell of roasting flesh was crushing: in the bleachers they splashed cologne on each other from little bottles of Venetian blown glass.

The fire began to die down, so they lit pitch torches to see better. And the excited multitude began to shout, demanding that the eleven panicked, raving penitents huddled in the cages be whipped. They had been able to save their own lives by recanting everything they had ever believed in or done, and in exchange for exile, they were to be imprisoned. The Inquisitor, with magnanimous solemnity, had granted them this new life. But in spite of his promise, those bundles of convulsing human flesh were pulled out of the cages and amid the drunken, rowdy exuberance of the crowd, the whiplashes exploded on them like the thrashings of the wind.

A very detailed and friendly résumé sent by the Majorcan Inquisitors to the Spanish Grand Inquisitor narrates how the festivities concluded:

The above-mentioned prosecutor provided dinner for the whole Inquisitorial Family, and all the other nobles who were not part of it, and on the first floor of the House they put seven tables together, with table cloths thirty feet long with thirty stools each, so that more people could be seated, and then starting with the Lord Inquisitor and the rest in groups of thirty, they began to eat and there were seven tables of thirty each, and the food was very abundant, with free wines, extras of every description, as well as free water, lemonade, cinnamon, and other things.

The declarations of Mariona were found in the dossier, and I suppose recorded with remarkable exactitude, although the transcription appears to have been altered; since her body had been cracked under the gears of

— 114 —

the torture racks and was thrown roughly onto the floor of her cell, probably very little writing ability remained in that woman. . . .

One can only conclude that a carefully trained scribe's hand intervened, probably trained in the rhetoric of the seminaries, the only purpose being to assemble an irrefutable conviction against Mariona de Vadell by making her appear to be enlightened, but at the same time without her appearing to have lost her serenity, nor giving the least indication of her having been tortured. Summing up, it was done in such a way that she could not escape or get free of her troubles with just a light sentence.

Did she have some hypothetical and convincing line of defense they tried to cut off? Or, on the other hand, was her pseudo-prophetic passion already so out of line that the only thing they could have had in mind was to purge her testimony of the chaos it had come from, and restructure it in a clearer way? Whatever the case, we don't know anything more about Mariona de Vadell than what's in that file. The copy I made of it is correct, with the exception of repetitions and stylistic embellishments which I removed:

His body was beaten, full of bruises, and exhausted. He was dead-tired from their hunting him down, from his escape through the woods, up river and down, to the dungeon in the cellar of the Inquisition. He was whipped with a cat-o'-nine-tails tipped with nails, and with glowing sticks they burned his sex organs and they dunked him in huge barrels of ice water and they twisted his bones . . . and he lay wailing on a straw mattress, his body thirsty and full of running sores.

"A cardinal of the schismatic Benedict XIII? A pontiff in hiding, anointed by insanity?" The prelates and the judges laughed and became indignant. "An idiot, a sinner, an animal, and a heretic," they said. And the undisciplined troops, their lances raised, chorused the farce. They had justice before them and they couldn't see it. Virtue was revealed to them and they didn't notice. They spoke with the representative of Jesus Christ on Earth and they didn't recognize him. I'm telling you because I know it to be true! I'm telling you the truth!

The sentence was without appeal. They cut out his tongue first, because they said he had uttered blasphemies; they amputated his hands because they alleged that with them he had practiced the sacrilegious parody of consecration; they obliged him to show his stumps, with the white and sensitive cut nerves, wiggling like little snakes. They decapitated him because they decided he had plotted against the Holy Spirit with his brain. And his open mouth was a dark and scarlet hole, full of sticky saliva, stringy, thick, and red.

"And because he was insubordinate and heretical he was to be buried in an unknown place!" shouted the judges and the pontifical legate.

Three soldiers with helmet and lance are seated on the cart to which they have yoked a pair of oxen. Under a blanket lies a long, narrow protuberance. Into the woods they go. Evening falls. They stop at the foot of a rock that looks like a huge finger sticking up in the air, pointing to heaven. The thick forest of fir, eucalyptus, and strawberry trees is cold. The rock is black, tall, and sharply pointed. They dig the hole and throw the corpse in, wrapped in the blanket. And they fill the grave and pile a lot of rocks on top so the wolves, the hyenas, and the wild boar don't come to dig up his decayed cadaver with their rooting snouts.

"Hey listen, you. If a wolf were to eat this corpse, he'd probably become the pope of the wolves! Ha! Ha! Ha!" And they leave.

And then it got completely dark. Was it sprinkling? The eucalyptus trees give off a sickly, obsessively sultry odor. The shadows come forward cautiously—they are the elected of God. You know their glorious names: Esteban de Van, Odette Vianson, Elías Carenne, the Abbots of Bonnevald and Bonecombe, Juan Fabre, Pedro Michel, Juan Maysett, Guillermo de Nohalac de Jouqueviel, Juan Farald, the Trahiniers: Pedro the father and his children Batista, Pedro Junior, and Juana. For them, the disciples, it was a silent, dark road, trekking through the soft dead leaves as if led through the darkness by a star visible only from within themselves. Everything will remain a secret forever. They are the disciples.

"The elected of God?" spat out the judges during the trials. "What sacrilegious election was that? What infernal deity? You maniacs! Heretics! Disciples of an apostate! Renounce him! Choose between torture and death or a sinecure which will be given you through ecclesiastic magnanimity."

"We recant, Oh Illustrious Ones, we renounce the errors and the deviations from everything that is not the One, Holy, Apostolic, and Roman Church, and Jean Carrier is a vice-ridden devil."

And they leave the trial smiling, turning their backs on the vindictive spirits of Benedict XIII and Jean Carrier. They'll be made canons, and the few who still say they are sons of the faith of the only pope without sin, will be buried in the dungeons of death.

But no! Everything has to start over because death is not the end for the just, and Jesus Christ and Lazarus and the daughter of the centurion say that the story of the coming of God in the flesh and of his faith will be the story of continuous resurrection. What do we know of the latest laws of the Lord? What yardstick measures and rules the existence and the spirit of the disciples sent by Him? Esteban de Van was proof of that. He's a saint! Cardinals, kings, and the very Pope Martin—the triumphant usurper—proclaim him so. Esteban, in the Council of Constance, had preached in favor of peace, without realizing that it's not words but deeds that matter.

A minor friar, he walked the paths of the world with his three knapsacks: his faith, his theology, and his eloquence. And even Pope Martin wanted to hear him in Rome. Esteban de Van preached there about the agony of Christ on Good Friday and Martin cried. A saint! And later they said, "A saint? A lewd beast! A thief who lives together with a nun, Sister Odette, expelled from the Clarissas of Tolosa, and who drags herself around naked and drunk, swearing a blue streak, clinging to the neck of that pig Esteban. And he has become the confessor of Jean IV of Armagnac, the blind prince who doesn't even try to hide his obedience to that crazy Carrier!"

What happened here? What happened was that Esteban de Van was an honest seeker of truth, and she has made him see the light, so he has given up everything to follow Jean Carrier, who is Benedict XIV!

The disciples hold hands as they walk through the dark forest of howling wolves. There it is—the pile of rocks, the tall spirelike stone. Everything is pitch-black and heavily wooded and the shadows pray for the Holy Father buried there. And the wind brings sounds and sighs from all the places in the world where it passes by, and they cry and pray to Him Who Is, through their Holy Father, and the Voice says, "Faith moves mountains, the faith in our truth, and your faith in my mission, and everyone with faith in God."

The Voice is soft . . . nobody says anything, they all clasp each other's hands again: who was it that spoke? And fear reigns.

It's Esteban de Van who murmurs, "Who was it that spoke?" "It is I, Esteban, it is I, and before you believe it, believe in your own beliefs: the Lord has made us guardians of the Truth, the Lord protects us, the Lord guides us. And you, Esteban, are now the pope and your name shall be Benedict XV and before you die you will name another pope and all the secret popes will carry the name of Benedict XV and this will go on for time eternal until we return to the light and then the new imperial pope will again have the name of Benedict XIII. And I, Jean, who am the pope, tell you this."

"I am the Pope. *Emitte Spiritum tuum, et creabúntur; et renovábis fáciem terrae. O quam bonus et suávis est, Dómine, Espíritus tuus in nobis, Veni Sancte Espíritus, reple tuórum corda fidélium: et tui amóris in eis accénde.*"

"I am the Pope. . . ." Jean Carrier sings the mass of the Holy Spirit. A heavy wave crashes against the huge rock at Peñíscola and splashes against the walls. The fog vibrates and dances. The plaza and the chapel of the castle appear and disappear from view. In the dusky light the temple becomes lost, without outline, without dimension in the surrounding murk, oppressing the small group huddled at the foot of the altar.

"*Veni, Sancte Spiritus.* There has been bribery! And every night I've been here, a stinking billy goat has walked the battlements, wailing devilishly at the yellow moon! Clement VIII is a vile sinner, for he bought his own election and plotted in secret with Martin V the Roman usurper to depose the only true Holy See—the ship of Peter that Benedict XIII left us—and to obtain personal gain."

The notary continues taking notes and Carrier continues speaking and the few witnesses, faithful to the memory of Benedict XIII, listen fearfully.

"I am the only cardinal—the others are jackals—and I appoint a pope, whose name I shall not reveal, who will endure to the end of time!"

And he removes the golden cassock and opens the window; the roar of the waves invades the chapel. The rose-colored dawn converts the fog into gold. And Jean Carrier jumps into the void and disappears. And the voice from Jalenques in 1433—the one from the woods that triumphs over death—continues at sea, for Benedict XIII was pope of the seas as well. And by sea he arrived at the Port and at Les Dunes; everyone saw him come, and I am his daughter, Mariona de Vadell, daughter of the *Dauphin* who landed at Port and Les Dunes, and who was crowned by the Faith. I declare myself loyal to Benedict, successor to all the Benedicts.

I walked around for all of an hour on the Paseo de la Castellana in Madrid after I left the National Library, worn out by so many papers that with each passing day tied me more and more to all those dead people, with that collective memory that I myself had become in the flesh. The dead people to whom Grandmother offered her little butterflies every year on the eve of All Saints' Day; dead people who had afterward gathered avidly around Father Dionís. If it weren't for the documents, not even their memory would exist. Those papers and I myself, so very fragile, all of them. And who was Mariona de Vadell, hiding behind that sinkhole of insanity? She arose from there like a visionary provided with a clumsy and fragmentary knowledge of the end of the schism, with an irrational faith in the secret papacy of Carrier. How could a person die for all that, buried as it was by all these centuries past?

I took a drink in the hotel bar, brilliantly lit with florescent lights, full of accents from around the world, and this woman continued to stir inside me, dead for two hundred years, roaring with insane spirituality.

*T*he galley *Dauphin* beaching in Port Vell, and Mariona coming out of it. . . . I saw an immense whale there one time, lying inert on the beach. I wanted to see a lot of things, so I watched and watched the solid round tower rising at Punta de la Ballestería for hours on end. I would watch until my eyes hurt from staring, from wanting to see that troop of arquebusiers from olden times aiming their weapons toward the oncoming Barbary galleys—fear heightening their senses, making them see colors and forms and hear sounds they had never before experienced—their sails bellied out by the wind as they skitter along the coast at the pier of Sa Mola, their bows slicing through the whitecaps, the soldiers firing from high in the tower, their shots bursting amidships at the waterline. The Moorish galley pitches, its pennants falling as first the bridge and then the poop deck disappear beneath the waves, sinking out of sight. The guards at the fort, already smeared with gunpowder, reload the cannon, glorying now in their fury. . . . The ships of the town were anchored, sheltered by the Point, their holds crammed with soap, pigs, pine logs, pickled sardines, and lemons. They were ready to set sail for Naples, Barcelona, even Lisbon and Cuba. . . . In my imagination the past really existed.

In reality they were just some rotten skeletons of ships clinging like ghosts to the stony beach, amid piles of algae and stagnant stinking puddles. The jetty had been broken up by a thousand storms, leaving giant blocks of stone with cement still stuck to them, piled up haphazardly, the water rushing between them, emitting a hollow suffering moan as the waves receded. The smell of saltpeter, tar, rotten fish, and crude oil was ever-present, heavy and dizzying. Only five catboats devoted to boulter and squid fishing were tied up at the surviving bollards, weakly outlined in the fading light, the street lamps giving off a dirty brown color from the burned moths in their globes.

At dusk the sailors used to eat supper around a couple of bonfires. The fantastic black dancing figures that the flames created seemed to shift their shadows on the huge, absurdly piled blocks of stone, lending a mysterious presence to the solitude of the night. The perfume of cognac floated in the air, tingeing it with a caramel friendliness.

The sea was becalmed, disturbed only by the sudden iridescent flashes of flying fish, even sometimes the sharp bluish sailfish. The shoreline was crowded with rushes, a maze of little channels hidden among the tall grasses where eels slithered through. Long-legged birds and cormorants grazed the salt marshes as they flew over; the owls hooted arrogantly. On the embankments of Puig de l'Espart there were caves the fishermen used for storage. The doorways were salt-eaten, and inside were piles of sailing and fishing gear, discarded junk accumulated through the generations, but among which a bent nail, a rusty fishhook, a broken piece of glass or wood was a treasured item for its owner, witness to the cosmic and insignificant needs of an isolated and miserably poor people.

The maritime life of the town, although limited, had come to center on the Port Nou, or new port. The other one, Port Vell, or the old port, a broken down trace of the past, is where I went to live with Grandmother all that time my sisters were waiting to die at Son Vadell. However, I notice the only time I remember Port Vell is at dusk, when it seems flooded with desolation. There were, of course, many other moments I remembered, that resembled a kind of Sunday happiness or eternal spring that would radiate throughout the whole setting when the sun was shining.

In order to think of those radiant hours, I have to make quite an effort. I'm overcome by another sensation, always anguishing and fateful. I remember those stormy nights huddled in my bed: The sea would come crashing down with a deafening roar against the rocks below the windows of the house. It was those slow early dawns, the howling of the wind, the thick blackness of the blows of the waves, making me more and more tense as I felt them imprisoning me. I became mentally exhausted, defenseless against the furor, my brain turned into a hallucinating avalanche of flashbacks. From one moment to the next I had the feeling of being locked in the hold of a ship, the waves thundering on the deck above me, smacks and thuds reverberating on the deck planks. The framing timbers and bulkheads shivered and groaned. The wind blew insanely, and the whistling in the rigging hurt my ears as if an ice pick had pierced them. I was in constant fear of being engulfed by it all, dissolved by the water and devoured by the fish. I gripped the bars on my bedstead and screamed until Grandmother came carrying a lantern, wearing that long wrinkled white nightgown, making me feel as if I were already dead and being visited by an angel, since angels were not young and beautiful, but wan and lean, white and insidiously sweet.

Onofre Capllonc—a relative from a distant branch of the family I never could figure out—lived there in one of the caves at Puig de l'Espart, overshadowed by so much junk inside that it had spilled over to the outside in front of his door, a tangled mess with grass and thistles and an airy agave cactus growing out of it. His age was incalculable, his hair the color of old corn husks, his face pasty-looking and completely white as if it had been rolled in flour. His portentously long yellowed dentures pushed beyond his lips like horse's teeth. When Capllonc spoke or breathed, his teeth dominated his face. They would rattle when he laughed; they shone brightly when he spoke; they were ferocious when he bit into an apple; they stuck out as if he were about to attack. But it was the dynamite that had marked him most dramatically.

Capllonc used to walk the shore alert for signs of fish, knowledgeable as he was of distant coves and abundant fishing spots. He always carried a leather bag full of dynamite with him. He would look at the water, throw some bread crumbs in to attract the fish, and as they rose to the bait he would light the fuse and toss a stick in. The explosion threw up a huge eruption of water, and when it had settled down dozens of dead fish appeared, many of them torn to bits.

But sometimes the dynamite would go off in Onofre's hand or in the air nearby. Then the explosion would be confused with his agonized cries; from out of the cloud of smoke a mystery would seem to materialize in space. When the air cleared, there was Onofre Capllonc, either standing and half silly or sitting on the ground with a bloody red spot on his face, on his hand, or on his thigh. He was already missing an eye, half a knee, and a hand (a piece of the remaining stump had been destroyed by another charge while working for Daniel de Vadell in the truck garden war with my grandfather Jacint). And on his jaw, his chest, and one of his feet he had enormous red scars.

Onofre Capllonc scared me as a child, although when I grew up we became friends, since he had changed by then in my eyes from what he was theoretically supposed to be, an old mutilated cripple about to die. With his bizarre old-fogy skinniness, he seemed beyond defeat or victory, beyond any organic process. My father was a friend of his, and often when he came to see me at the Port and we went out for a walk and met up with Capllonc, he and my father would have a lively conversation.

Perhaps my visceral aversion to him stemmed from that cloudy afternoon with the sardines crackling over the coals of the fire, my father dripping a thin thread of olive oil over them. The heavy, salty smoke rose;

I brought the coals to life by blowing on them with a hollow piece of cane. The sea was unbelievably calm, as if it had become an imaginary, crystalline surface. I looked at it and would see the desert of Tabaida, an endless hard and flat void where Grandmother said the saints like Saint Anthony went to pray and mortify themselves, besieged by temptations and those men who saw lechery, cruelty, and lack of faith swirling all about them.

Onofre Capllonc, wrapped in a capriciously tattered rag of a cape, jumped over bushes and from rock to rock as he advanced along the beach. He appeared through the smoke, hypnotized by the flying sparks. The civil war was spreading, and there were people with little to eat. Probably old Capllonc was one of them.

My father invited him to sit and eat with us, and he told me to pass him the jug of wine. The sardines were hot and we peeled them with shaven sticks of cane. I really enjoyed eating that hot and savory salty fish. I liked to feel my mouth full of wine, swishing it around before swallowing, running my tongue over my salty lips with satisfaction. . . . Then I suddenly noticed what Onofre Capllonc was telling my father:

". . . the *Mignonette* weighed anchor in Southhampton. My father was about twenty-five then, and served on board as a deckhand. He had been fishing near Newfoundland, I don't know exactly where, and when he changed ships he wound up there. The mate's name was Mr. Stephens; Mr. Dudley was the captain and Brooks was the other able-bodied seaman who took care of the kitchen too. They also had a cabin boy whose name was Parker. Well, the fourteenth of May of 1884, they went to sea headed for Australia. Theirs was a fine long yacht, painted all white with a green stripe down its length.

"Fifty-one days out of port, finding themselves fifteen hundred miles from the Cape of Good Hope, they were hit from the south by a high wind with heavy gusting that created violent waves, some with rough crests and some with deep troughs. They tried to maneuver through it, but suddenly the ship started leaking everywhere like a sieve. They launched the lifeboat and abandoned ship, but were able to salvage only a few canned goods as provisions.

"They managed to survive the storm by hanging onto the thwarts for dear life. They wandered lost and adrift in the endless ocean. During a shower they were able to collect a little drinking water, using their raincoats to store it. They rationed the canned goods, alternating them with some fish and sea turtle they were able to catch and had to eat raw. But all their caution was in vain and they ran out of food.

"Parker the cabin boy went crazy with thirst and put his face in the sea and drank his fill. Soon he got very sick with a high fever and then fell unconscious. They stretched him out in the bottom of the boat, where he became delirious. On the twenty-fifth of July, Captain Dudley slit the boy's throat with a kitchen knife, and he and my father and Stephens and Brooks each took turns sucking his veins, which ran like little faucets, and they drank his blood. Then they cut him up in little pieces so that he was easier to chew. . . ."

Onofre Capllonc took another drink and deftly peeled the sardines with his only hand and swallowed them. My father, with a sardine in hand halfway to his mouth, stared at the ground without saying anything. I looked at Capllonc in fascination, not even daring to swallow. The old man continued to talk, his mouth full of fish:

"Desperation forces people into this kind of situation and they had been many days without food. In England they were later tried, and they said that it was my father's and the captain's idea to butcher Parker. Brooks opposed it and Stephens never said a thing, but they both ate and drank the result. On the other hand, the cabin boy was very sick and probably would have died anyway. Furthermore, he had no dependents and all the others did. They also said that Captain Dudley had cried and prayed over him before carving him up with the knife. On the twenty-ninth of July, a German steamer found them. At the trial, the mate and the other sailor didn't receive any sentence at all, but my father and the captain were sentenced to death. Lucky for them, Queen Victoria commuted their sentences to six months in prison. There are always attenuating circumstances. . . ."

Capllonc kept on eating sardines. He was the only one still eating, washing them down with frequent swigs from the wine jug until two scarlet spots appeared on his flour-white cheeks. It was getting dark; Onofre chewed on, his great teeth moving with spectacular omnipotence; his teeth dripped wine, and I stared at the black hole of his missing eye and the stump of his missing arm . . . the cabin boy all chopped up, the sailors drinking his blood, their teeth dripping, the flesh of the boy, the hand and the eye of Capllonc—chewing and drinking, drinking and chewing in the dusky shadows. . . . My father told the story to Grandmother later. . . . Unexpectedly I threw myself at the furtive old fisherman, kicking and punching him, shrieking and crying at the same time.

A long time later from a window in the house, I saw him die. He had gone out with his dynamite toward the far end of Cala Llamp, where it juts out into the sea like a footbridge. To his surprise, he saw a school of fish coming toward him close to the surface, an abundant horde toward the rocky shore—torpedo fish, wrasse, sargos, serranos, and dapples—a turmoil of flashing silver, as if the little beasts were playing among themselves. He quickly whipped out his dynamite. He lit two fuses, raised his arm to throw them, and in that instant five young sharks emerged from the deep, their fins a shiny steely gray as they rabidly attacked and snapped at each other. They stirred up a frothy, bloody foam in the water around them.

The school of rockfish disappeared in a flash. Capllonc stood there petrified, his arm still raised and his mouth agape. The dynamite exploded, a bursting star of smoke and red, below which you could see the waist and the legs of the man, absolutely immobile. When the smoke cleared there was nothing left but guts and legs. His head was completely gone, and his trunk was a twisted mess of flesh and bone.

Our past is an endless trail of destruction. It seems everything we do is only one more contribution to the continuing barbarity of it all. One summer, a North American professor named John F. Worley came to town. He interviewed Uncle Dionís several times and went through his files. He visited the towns along the island coast. He was from Columbia University, where he taught maritime law, and was writing a book on navigational jurisprudence and crime. He sent my uncle a copy of the work when it was published. It's titled Crimes and Laws of the Sea. I have a vivid memory—as if it were now—of how impressed I was when I read in one of the appendices a chronicle from the University of Andratch where we Vadells appeared. That was perhaps the first time I had truly peered into the abyss of the past and had seen people, distant in time, who carried the same name as mine and therefore, due to that absurd connection, everything they had ever been or done reflected back on me. I felt it in my conscience. Soon I came to feel as if I were going through a prodigious process of aging, a monstrous paradox: my body went on just the same, suffering only a slow series of changes, whereas my spirit was being deformed, macerated by the hemorrhaging of a growing, inexorable old age. This is the chronicle I found:

The day before yesterday, which was the seventeenth of November in the year of Grace 1741, the fisherman Quim Bibiloni and his son Naçeri proceeded to save a Genovese sailor between the beach of Les Dunes and El Port, and concerning the abnormal circumstances about which they have here presented themselves today, to give witness before the bailiff of this very noble town council of Andratch in order to express their petitions and prevent possible later complaints.

First: I declare my name to be Quim Bibiloni, son of Galcerà Bibiloni, oakum caulker by trade, who disappeared in the galley *El Vent,* headed for the Algerian coast. I am in my fiftieth year and a widower of Simona Puigserver—may she rest in peace—for whose soul I arranged a perpetual mass at the altar of the Santos Angeles Custodios. I have one living son and five deceased sons, for whom I pray that they may also have peace and rest. My trade is fishing, and I am a citizen of this noble town and of the Collet Roig quarter.

I declare that on the morning of the fifteenth we headed for Les Dunes; my son Naçeri, thirteen years of age, and I the deponent, were carrying on our backs bundles of netting with the purpose of casting them in coastal waters. We stopped to eat near the Font del Gos, and we had to fire off three shots from our blunderbusses in order to scare off two masked men who were roving there, without responding to the many greetings which in the name of the Lord we made to them, and whom we knew to be the Calatrán brothers, who were sought by the law. Then the sky grew dark because rapid black clouds and a cold wind were coming in from the sea.

When we arrived at Les Dunes in the afternoon, it so happened that the sea was rough due to that storm which came from the north, and thus we decided not to cast the nets and to wait until the next day, and so we slept in the shanty we have at Na Cargola. During the night we heard the waves grow stronger in the dark, which was pitch-black, and the wind and rain put out our fire several times.

By dawn the sea was throwing up huge black crests and the clouds were low and dirty. My son, the said Naçeri, went out on the point to satisfy his bodily needs, and while squatting down he noticed a ship making zigzags near the reef of Es Geperut. Naçeri called me and had me come see for myself. It was a two-masted ship, but was missing both of them and all her sail as well, which turned and sank from sight and then returned, rising on the back of a wave. We thought we saw a person on deck, and at noon while we ate bread with olive oil and olives and salt fish, the ship disappeared from our view, without our having been able to determine whether from shipwreck or drift into other waters.

The afternoon went by and although we watched the sea, nothing new happened and we still couldn't cast the nets, in spite of the fact that the sea was calming down. That night we made a big bonfire on the beach, so that it could be seen by the ship in case it was still afloat, or lacking that, by its shipwrecked sailors and we took turns watching, my son and I, in case a shipwreck should occur that we could make ours, collecting in this way the profit which the storm had denied us with the nets, for the Lord always works in favor of the poor, and to save in the name of the Lord any crew members who might have need of it.

Well into the morning of the day we mentioned at the beginning of this declaration, when we were getting ready to return to this very noble town, we noticed that the sea was throwing objects up on the beach. We got there quickly and this is what we found: a large rudder, two empty barrels, a hatch with three pieces of wood broken from it, seven-and-a-half dozen cane-backed chairs, which must have been part of the cargo of the ship, a cage with two drowned pigs in it, and a half dozen melons, two of which were in such good condition that we ate them then and there. We took charge of the above-mentioned goods, which we brought to town on a burro lent us by the farmer Marc Satuna on condition that we give him the cage with the drowned pigs, an agreement which we fulfilled. We have these goods available for anyone who might want to buy them at our house in Collet Roig, and we request of this town council that they judge it to be my property now because Naçeri is a minor, which is the customary and legal thing to do in similar circumstances. The rudder is usable for ships of medium draft, though it can be cut down by any cabin boy to fit smaller craft. The boards are made of so-called northern wood and can be used for many and varied purposes and are for sale. The barrels are in good condition and are ideal for holding water, salted fish or meat or anything else, and we have them ready to show to anyone. And the chairs are a gift from God, the quality of which is unquestionable.

And it so happened that on the road with the burro loaded down, at a bend between the beach and the Port, we encountered a man wearing only a doublet, whom we understood to be a survivor of the shipwreck already mentioned. He was covered with cuts and bruises, with blood all over his body, and he kept on falling and walking like a drunk. We laid him down under a pine tree and made a fire to warm him up, and after my son talked to him, we decided that I should go on with the loaded burro in order to get the goods under cover and out of the way of thieves and seek help for the sad survivor, who stayed in the above-mentioned place under the care of my son.

I therefore beg this very noble council to take charge of the survivor indicated above, and I also beg that it give validity to our new acquisitions, consisting of the rudder, a broken hatch, two barrels, seven-and-a-half dozen chairs, and the above-mentioned pig cage we left with the farmer Marc Satuna.

Signed with a cross which is my signature, I give witness as Quim Bibiloni.

Second: This noble council accedes to all the demands of Quim Bibiloni, fisherman of this town, fifty years of age, and with whom we, the constable of this very noble council, and a man with a wagon (the wagon being paid for by this very noble council), personally went to the place indicated between the beach of Les Dunes and the Port. The castaway was picked up and laid comfortably in the wagon and he offered abundant groans, but had a clear head although his body was very sick, and that the said castaway died in the course of the trip and they had to stop the wagon because he could not stand the bone-jarring bumps and before dying, he, in a clear voice and begging our pardon, made the following declaration:

Third: My name is Giambatista Carnesi and I am from Genova, forty-six years old, married in Ostia, and childless. In the port of Ostia I was signed on, being out of work, by the ship owner Sonse to sail his galley *Santa Croce*, loaded with wheat and cane-backed chairs and with a port in Provence as our destination, I don't remember which one, and in the Gulf of Lyon we were battered by a very rough sea and I do not know whether the second lifeboat was able to make it safely ashore or not, because the first one in which I was riding sank, and I believe I am its only survivor. But the shipwreck happened in a very vile way, because on shore there was a light and signals indicating a safe haven, but it turned out not to be so because we ran aground in shallow water and I suspect we were tricked, and I want those men to be punished who make other men die, which is not God's law nor is it brotherhood.

Fourth: Deposition having been taken from Naçeri Bibiloni the above-mentioned son of Quim Bibiloni who took care of the castaway sailor described above, his declarations are transcribed, about which the head official feels he must say that they were told by the boy with many doubts and much nervousness, and many times he retracted something only to say it again, and that was that he and his father had not made any signals of any kind, and that they did not know who could have made them, that they did not make false signals in order to cause ship-wrecks, because they only picked up from the beach and the rocks what the sea cast upon them, which was free, and that farther down the beach were the Vadell brothers, and that they certainly did do things they weren't supposed to do, and that often the Vadells had beaten up Naçeri and his father Quim Bibiloni for shipwreck matters and sharing of the bounty, that the Vadells were abusers and they the Bibiloni were God-fearing and honest and that he, Naçeri was very disturbed by all this.

Fifth: Deposition having been taken again from Quim Bibiloni, this officer found him in bed, bruised all over and with an arm which dangles and very, very excited because he wanted to know why the brothers Andreu and Donat Vadell, together with their henchman Jaume Plana had beaten him up for no reason and without provocation of any kind, because they were evil people who, having land and money, and on top of that wanting to rob the bread from the poor, and that he Quim Bibiloni had only taken what the sea had sent him as goods from God, and that the above-mentioned Vadells and henchman had been going through his—Quim Bibiloni's—storeroom and had taken the rudder and all the cane-backed chairs, saying that this was their work and that they should be the beneficiaries of it, and they only left him the barrels and the broken hatch, and that this was plain robbery as he says, and he blames the Vadells for attracting ships through trickery so that they run aground in the shallows along the coast, and that he Bibiloni had often heard the cries of sailors suddenly shipwrecked in rough seas, with death at their heels, and that the Vadells are not to be trusted. And with boat hooks they jab the sailors who are adrift and try to hang onto the rocks to save themselves, so that in this way they drown and aren't around to complain or make accusations which could hurt the Vadells.

Sixth: The personnel of this very noble council having gone to Son Vadell in person to talk with the brothers Andreu and Donat Vadell, who claim they live in Son Vadell, and Andreu being thirty-one years old and Donat forty-five, and having spoken with the henchman Jaume Plana as well, who is twenty-six, and claims to be from Andratch, and also claims to have nothing to declare, for he is only a hired hand, and that his bosses are the ones who know what to do and why they do it, and then having taken depositions from the Vadell brothers, they say and swear that they did not make any signals or anything like a signal to any ship, and that they do not know anything about ships or shipwrecks, and that on the other hand they do know about Quim Bibiloni who makes bonfires at night during storms to make ships go off course, and that he also tricks them with a green glass lantern he has, and he then picks up the derelicts, letting the sailors die so that there will be no witnesses to tell, and that once they buried three badly wounded men who were still alive under the fig trees at the mouth of the stream Salvet. But not the Vadells, no—that they have only taken things which the sea throws up on the shore, free things all of them, and they know very well that the Bibilonis made a bonfire the other night while it was storming, and that they, the Vadells, the next day found cane-backed chairs and a rudder on the beach when they went down there to get algae for their manure piles, and having left the things there while they loaded algae onto their wagons, then it was that they saw Quim Bibiloni rob the things, and that is why they had gone to get them, and that the Bibilonis were. . . .

And nothing more. The end of the chronicle was lost in some indeterminate moment of the past. The strangest part is that many more things have not fallen through that same crack, sunken as we are in the dying grip of time, life beginning and ending in each one of us. The history of the Vadells and the Bibilonis of two centuries ago, if we remove a part of their anecdotal vicissitudes, was only that: a few shades of meaning, a few more examples of the vain and miserable transgression that strikes at us, the transgression of an abstract and all-powerful absolute that goes unalterably on forever. Father de Vadell repeated that often, recalling the pennant of the lineage, those horses galloping into the night.

*I*t seemed our lives were controlled only by quirks in the weather. . . . What was the house at the Port, if not that? It was a huge house facing the sea, full of wide windows and balconies, and surrounded on all sides by a kind of long and irregular park, filled with dusty, devastated eucalyptus trees that seemed to totter, about to fall over any minute. In Carrier's grave, at least the one which Mariona de Vadell had dug for him in her mind, there were also eucalyptus trees. . . . The house was whitewashed, with parts of the walls blistered by the action of the salts in the masonry, like an infectious corrosion. How did air get into this place? Endless currents and drafts followed one after the other, as if in ghostly pursuit of each other, through the corridors, the rooms, and the stairways. Everywhere the place was awash in light. Even with the blinds shut, light dominated my room, almost bare of furniture, with a blaring whiteness.

Then suddenly the wind would blow a balcony door open and the light would lurch at me, clutch at me. Instead of being an enclosed space, the house seemed an enormously open receptacle for the outdoors. I never felt protected in any corner of that building. Wherever I was in it, it always seemed that a wall was about to crumble, that the outdoors—the sea waves, the eucalyptus branches, the rain, the glare of the sun, the crickets in the summer night—penetrated within, unimpeded and overwhelming.

Grandmother and I moved there at the time my sisters were fast going downhill. And then afterward, when my mother was all alone, we left her in the house at the Port. At that time, without my grandmother's knowledge, I would walk from Son Vadell to the Port, climb up Puig de l'Espart, and, hiding among the rocks, I would watch the house and the park around it.

When the sun started to go down, I often saw my mother there, moving slowly among the big trees, stopping a moment to pick up a eucalyptus seedpod, smell it, and absorb its sharp, nauseous odor like someone drugged. She would sit on the edge of what had been a fountain, its little pool lined with seashells set in cement and rocks painted green; the spigot, far off in a corner, emerged from a mermaid. When the moon was full and rose early, huge and orange over the Garrafa peaks, its radiant clarity would fall on my mother, caressing her, transfiguring her long white dress. I have a print of a modernist poster here in my apartment in Paris. In it there's a girl seated before a bubbling fountain, her dress down to her ankles, and a bouquet of flowers adorning her forehead, the forehead of a smiling face, full of candor and youth. I imagined my mother like that, in a past that I never knew. She was like that then, but not anymore.

At other times, under the devastating twilight of autumn, she would stand there like an absent-minded statue, her gaze fixed in space, surrounded by what had barely been a garden before, and now was a jungle of thistles and nettles. My mother would bend over and gather up a handful of wet and soggy leaves, and then, standing erect with her arm extended, she would scatter them slowly, as if she were officiating at an extremely deliberate ritual.

In its day, that mermaid on the fountain must have been graceful with its scaly tail; but after years and years of water flowing over its contorted and immobile figure, it had by then—when I saw it—become just a stubby semblance of a mermaid, a ruinous, monolithic memory of a long-forgotten act of homage. Through the foliage behind it peered the half-demolished battlements of the Torricó de la Fe, the tower where the miracle of Bishop Marc Maria de Vadell had occurred. From there, with a chalice full of hosts as his only food, he had resisted the bloody siege of the Moors. A neighbor lady who lived alone and dressed in black, with an uncommonly large dropsical abdomen, served as a sort of maid at the house, first with us and later with my mother. She had set up a chicken coop in the tower. The area surrounding that old monument to the faith, to resistance against the Moors, now stank of chicken manure.

I used to watch the house from the Puig de l'Espart, without ever getting near my mother. I could never get it through my head that this human being was really my mother, what with her tragic, wandering eyes, dressed in a worn and wrinkled housecoat, probably pulled out of one of the trunks piled up in the attic, and full of cloth memories that had once adorned and protected the living. She seemed alien to me, someone who was only a vacuous shadow of the person who had really been my mother; her real spirit had evaporated, sunken into the depths of insanity.

In the photographs at Son Vadell and in my memory, the image of that small face with large smiling eyes, her hair put up in a daring coiffure, always with its little thin blue ribbon . . . that image was not at all like the solitary woman of the Port who glided along in grief beneath the eucalyptus trees, and whom I approached only a couple of times, crouching and moving secretively from tree to tree. I was desperately fearful that she might suddenly erupt in an aggressive fury that would destroy me, tear off my skin in strips the way the thin bark of the gigantic and sad eucalyptus trees peeled off, brown and ashen.

But she would pass by without noticing me, absent from all but her perplexing pilgrimage through the deserted majesty of the park, just as when I used to see her in church at the first morning mass—was she crazy, absolutely crazy? It's possible that she was. But I also thought that her lost reason was nothing more than the appearance of another drama. The frightening rages of pain, surprise, and shock had broken in her all the inner defenses which normally guide our lives, like the channels of a fountain which distribute its water through an established network of ditches. Everything about her had been fragmented; everything had leaked away and gotten mixed up and surpassed her body without it being able to affect her now in any way as she wandered about, exhausted.

That's because my real mother, the person with the big eyes and the blue ribbon, no longer lived inside the woman in the park. That woman continued to cry out, suffering out there in space, impelled along by the frenetic avalanches in her spirit. She stood ghostlike on the crest of a wave of terrifying passion that had at one time shaken her and broken her.

One day at the Port when I was a very young child, I observed a scene I was never able to forget, and I don't even know how it ended. A bloody, deafening storm shook the sea, and a castaway wearing a life jacket was being dragged back and forth by the surge of the waves, making it impossible for him to reach shore; but at the same time the life jacket was keeping him from going under.

There was very little furniture in the house at the Port. I remember a baroque and voluminous teardrop lamp that looked like a stupid crystalized flower; in the living room there was a sort of sideboard with a vigorous hunting scene carved on it; in the bedroom, the canopy was sagging over the bed, making it look like a camping tent without its ridge pole; bizarre, bulky individual pieces of furniture stuck out in the general barrenness. But my mother, submerged in her gentle delirium, wouldn't have noticed any of that.

She would wander about, and only one idea seemed to dominate her thinking—the necklaces, rings, earrings, gold coins, and little silver spoons and knives that we had had to turn in to the Franco government for the war effort. Then there were the other pieces, the rest of what we had, which she had sold to pay the doctors and medications for Marteta, Cristina, and Joana. . . .

Grandmother Brigida had bought the emerald necklace in her youth in Vienna one morning when the Empress Elizabeth was driving by in an open carriage, responding to the acclamations from the crowd with a frozen smile, barely raising her gloved hand to wave . . . a wonderful round emerald mounted in silver, boxed in red velvet. The wedding ring had been given to my mother by my grandfather Jacint, her future father-in-law, on a summer night long ago in a blue garden of wisteria. The earrings resembled a bunch of grapes, made with the pretentious gold buttonry of a doublet of wrinkled silk, with embroidered Aztec rhomboids. The grandparents had heard the great-grandparents say it had always lain in the upper drawer of the inlaid nacre dresser, a venerated family relic an anonymous relative had made part of the saga of Son Vadell, as if he knew that his gesture and the object which had motivated it would in the long-run turn out to be more basic than his own name, as far as the property and the roots of Son Vadell were concerned.

These flaming hallucinations accompanied my mother until dawn, shimmering in her head to the point of suffocation, excluding all other awareness. It was the unbalanced dance of her nonexistent jewels, invoked with morbid stubbornness.

She would wander slowly about, as if hypnotized, until she finally became exhausted. Then she would leave for the first mass, perhaps suddenly faced again with the devastating memory of her dead family. Like a drifting scarecrow, she seemed to float along the roads and cross the town, insensitive to the cold winter rains which soaked her, to the chirp of hungry birds at the rising sun in spring and summer.

*T*he heroic deeds of the Torricó de la Fe formed a key part in the annual sermon about the Valorous Dukes that Father Dionís delivered with emphatic hoarseness from the great mahogany pulpit, over which a heavy-breasted white plaster dove always hung, frozen in flight. It was supposed to be the Holy Spirit.

The Moors had attacked and were now breaking down the doors to the church when Bishop Marc Maria de Vadell escaped through a window in the sacristy, carrying with him the chalice full of holy hosts. Pursued by the Moors, he managed to get to the old watchtower, where he locked himself in. The pirates tried in vain to break down the solid oaken door, but it remained intact. The siege lasted for five days. Bishop Marc Maria, with neither food nor water, nibbled away at the holy wafers. With only one longbow, working from the battlements to the loopholes, he staved off the assault of the Moors. When the troops of the viceroy, led by the German General Zeplien, liberated him, he glowed with resplendent health.

One year the celebration of the Valorous Dukes coincided with the pastoral visit of the bishop of Majorca, whose name I forgot. He was still a young man, but looked tired. His eyes would alternate rapidly between lifeless drowsiness and penetrating liveliness. The church was full of flowers, almost all the women in town were singing, and Father Dionís gave the sermon. . . . Afterward, in the rectory, the prelate and my uncle Dionís were drinking a glass of water I had brought them on a silver platter. "Explain to me better the miracle of the Torricó de la Fe, my dear vicar," the prince of the church requested.

The priest moved his bald head, cleared his throat, and spoke while looking at the floor, as if he were meditating aloud, "The Tower, Your Eminence, is bigger than it appears to be from the outside. We can go look at it if you're curious. Perhaps so, perhaps the Lord grasped the arm of Marc Maria de Vadell and allowed him to defend all the loopholes with only one longbow, perhaps so. But I must tell you, Eminence, that tradition and truth are not always one and the same. Did you know that they weren't Moors, but a revolutionary group of farmers from town? Well, the fact is the viceroy appointed a notary public to take depositions from those involved in the deeds. One of the statements affirms that in the tower with the bishop there were three other priests, as well as the head sexton, together with his wife, a daughter, and his daughter-in-law, for the revolutionaries had killed his son in front of the church."

With a wave of his hand, the priest told me to leave. I left, but hid in the shadows of the entryway, listening to them. "The sexton and his family, according to the report, demanded damages because the three women had had to give in to—and I beg your pardon Excellency—the lewd demands of the four fathers. And the Notary also recorded that in the tower there remained five jugs of wine, three slabs of bacon, a sack of almonds, olive oil, as well as empty jugs and the remains of food."

I was scared when I explained all this to Grandmother later, but she still didn't answer me. I don't know whether she heard me or whether she was even paying attention. The only thing that seemed to get through to her in those days was the muffled voice of the Sleeping Woman from Coll de l'Aire. Yes, it's possible that she may have managed by then to have descended into the dark regions where only the voices of the dead howl.

Coll de l'Aire rose in the foothills of Garrafa, a sharp promontory emerging like an aggressive cone beyond the town. I particularly remember one of the many afternoons when I accompanied Grandmother there. The crisp air was splendidly transparent, laced with a tremor that made the sharp profiles of the landscape seem to vibrate. Andratch, the valley, and the mountains resembled the background of a renaissance painting or a Chinese drawing, the miniature details in the distance meticulously drawn.

The cold wind bored into our flesh, almost ripping our skin off. Grandmother led me by the hand, almost dragging me up the hill. I felt as if I were flying over the round and slippery pebbles. On rainy days a dirty noisy torrent coursed down through the gorge. Grandmother would sometimes trip over the nasty pebbles, then growl resentfully at them.

Coll de l'Aire was like a medieval castle built among the rocks, its ten or twelve tall narrow and dreary houses outlined at dusk, the walls either covered with ivy or about to fall in. That motley irregular grouping rose menacingly atop the hill against a pearl-blue sky that day, with the wind out of the north, as if light were bursting forth from inside everything.

A narrow zigzag alley overgrown with a strange, fleshy weed with serrated leaves and flowers with twisted mauve pistils waved lewdly in the wind. The houses were sordid and seemed vacant. On a corner, two dogs were hanging by their necks from a laurel tree branch, swinging stiffly in the wind. A woman passed by, urging on a little herd of goats running here and there. She looked at us suspiciously out of the corner of her eye and disappeared behind a collapsed grape arbor, a mass of tangled vines.

The very narrow house of the Sleeping Woman stood three stories tall. A wide chimney almost covered the façade, exuding shiny black lumps of creosote. We knocked at the door. Grandmother was already anxious to infiltrate this heavy, ambivalent, and absorbing universe. I was feeling a kind of intoxication and my heart was beating rapidly; my brain was nearing exhaustion out of pure anguish.

A tiny little lady with a keen angelic smile opened the door. She whispered something we didn't understand. We were shown into a darkened room where we could barely make out some human forms seated in silence. We stayed there for a while, jammed closely together amid the heavy breathing of the people we couldn't see. Grandmother Brigida mumbled a couple of brief prayers. My eyes hurt from trying to bore through the darkness, until the little woman came back and showed us into another room.

It was small and stuffy, reeking of urine and sweat. The walls were covered with little pictures of saints stuck on with paste. A mother cat was nursing a litter of kittens that were making hungry onslaughts at her teats. A carbide lamp stood on a nightstand, whistling from the gas pressure and emitting a livid rancid flame. A bemused old man was sitting on a low chair.

And the Sleeping Woman was absorbed in her own lethargic wanderings. . . . She was a woman of enormous dimensions, of elephantine proportions. She was still young, her skin ashen, a doughball of soft fat; the lids of her nearsighted blue eyes were grossly swollen, altogether giving the impression that she was semicomatose. She was seated in a dilapidated wicker chair, its intricate fanlike back resembling the tail of a peacock. She raised her arm weakly; she was wearing a stained wrinkled nightgown; only ankles and arms showed, as round as drumsticks. Her large head moved awkwardly, as if her neck didn't work.

The diligent little lady urged us to explain the motive of our visit. Grandmother, who was by then a nervous wreck from overconcentration, explained what she wanted to know—abysmal incursions into the nether world of her dead family—in bursts of short, unfinished sentences mixed with perplexing abstractions, all thoroughly detailed, while she devoured that drowsy mass of flesh with her eyes.

The Sleeping Woman listened to the complicated explanation, breathing heavily, her eyes almost completely closed. A fat tongue coated with a milky slime lolled in the corner of her partially opened mouth. She didn't answer, but with infinite calm—as if that insignificant effort required extraordinary energy—she got up from the chair, sighing faintly, and spread herself out on the bed, where she lay, emitting slow and even breaths.

Time passed. Grandmother and I, sitting on the edge of our chairs, watched that body at rest, waiting . . . until her breathing began to get erratic, brief snorts ending in a muffled, agonizing rattle. Then her whole massive self began to quicken, while from her face, her arms, and her feet, thick dark drops of sweat began to emerge, giving off the faint odor of excrement, as if the drops had had to pass through a layer of rotting flesh in order to escape. The sweat soon soaked her nightgown and her hair.

A beatific smile crossed her face as she began a confused mumbling, making guttural sounds that soon became screams as she squirmed and rolled around, as if she were being beaten. The sheet got wadded up, uncovering a filthy greasy mattress. Her movements revealed vast, pale, and blubbery thighs laced with swollen blue veins. The woman and the old man prayed rapidly, looking down at the floor.

The Sleeping Woman finally woke up. She looked exhausted, her breath barely audible. The little lady and the old man lurched forward to hold her up, helping her over to the armchair. Grandmother devoured her with her gaze, attentively, as if that mound of flesh were about to radiate something climactic and improbable. The little lady offered the Sleeper a glass of *rancio* wine with a beaten egg yolk in it. She drank it calmly, looking apathetically at Grandmother with a remote, waxen gaze.

Then she started making sounds, weaving words together in a syncopated way, as a deaf mute might, with a vagueness that never got specific, slowly melting into thoughtful sighs. When she stopped, the little lady explained the tangle of what she had said in a hushed voice, giving every detail its proper order. And as both of them moved forward through the conversation, the Sleeper's breast began to heave in spectacular agitation, soon becoming a crying fit, a flood of tears that left her distressed and exhausted. The little lady pushed us in the direction of the door. We returned home under a crisp, starry sky. The lights of the town in that black well of night flickered clear and red, like pomegranate flowers. The pebbles on the hill radiated a soft, phosphorescent glow.

I only asked the Sleeper one question in all the times I went up there. She didn't answer me, and probably in her immense and bloated condition didn't even hear what that astonished boy had asked.

It had to do with something I had thought about a lot: "Who was the author of the violet book?" Somebody, possibly in the family, had at some unnamed time written some very curious notes. And the writer used a violet ink that had faded with time, so that now it was barely legible. From among the still-legible entries, I'll transcribe a few here:

> We harvested thirteen sacks of wheat and sixty-six sacks of almonds. A good year. I'm writing it down, sitting here where I am. Well, and so what? Ten years from now it will mean nothing. None of this will be worth anything. It's only useful now. I don't know why I don't cry out. I just keep on sitting here.

✦I✦

> Today the widow Pujol died. I remember her when she got married, laughing as she went up the stairs to the church. She was a tall girl who would sometimes languidly run her hand over her breasts. Her husband died more than twenty years ago. On the way to the burial this afternoon, it upset me to think that since then she had never had a man in bed with her. I would watch her often out of the corner of my eye when

she went shopping or sat sewing at her window. What did she live for then, without a pair of *cojones* between her thighs?

◆I◆

I read a book by Count Polonski published in Amsterdam in 1711. He describes how by mixing the juices and brains of bees and ants, a serum could be obtained capable of converting men into supermen. Great ranches could be set up to breed these creatures on the plains of Hungary, where there is a lot of wheat and wildflowers to maintain them, and then use the serum to feed a group of chosen men who would be stronger and smarter and would then become the masters of the world.

◆I◆

A tree shoot nobody recognizes has grown up in the middle of the town square. I laughed a lot this afternoon.

◆I◆

We buried the cat. It rained softly. It was stiff already. It rained and under the oak tree where we buried it, the ground I dug up—everything—was dripping wet and the fog moved in as nightfall came on. It was just a cat with gray fur and yellow eyes. When nobody can see me, I cry and want to bash my head against the wall. I walk through the rooms, I go out among the trees, always expecting it to appear, meowing. Now I know that death is when you never come back. I hadn't really understood until now. And I don't give a damn about Magdalena, the children, or my mother.

◆I◆

37485968673298567285742369583524876493372 6 . . . one after the other, I could always write numbers.

◆I◆

The missionary said we are like dogs. I looked around at the people sitting in the pews at church. If you listen carefully, everything the priest says is a lie.

◆I◆

An author named Ludovicus Askenasi, in a book published in Bologna in 1602, maintains that a man can kill another man, because if man is part of Nature and Nature kills freely and irresponsibly, then an

— 138 —

assassin should not bear any responsibility for his acts either. On the contrary, he should be respected for obeying God—the same God who created Nature and maintains it just as it is.

⚬⚬⚬

The only thing I want to do is not do what I usually do, and escape. I would have married thirty women, would have lived in a hundred houses, would have traveled half the world . . . how should I know what I would have done? And they've called me twice now to go down to supper. I've eaten every day with my family, in my house . . . always."

The man with the violet ink lived beside other people, but no one knew who he really was. I don't even know who might have found the notebook, or where. It always lay where I had first found it, serving as a base for a wobbly glass bell jar made in Prague with a figure of the Baby Jesus inside, all of which was surrounded by bouquets of cloth flowers.

*G*randmother, on the other hand, asked endless questions of the Sleeper. It was there, through the voice of the enthusiastic little lady, that she found out a lot about our family that she hadn't known before, or didn't remember, or didn't want to know. All kinds of news and rumors filtered into the sticky overheated rooms at Coll de l'Aire, like sewage rushing to the sea through its tortuous underground drainpipes . . . and my grandmother Brígida must have found out about the fatal happenings that led to the destruction of my mother, for on one of her visits she made me stay in the darkened living room, among those unrecognizable silhouettes.

I didn't know anything about all that until my grandmother took to her bed, never again to rise from it, obsessed with the idea that she was about to die and had to confess everything. She constantly made me call Uncle Dionís, who would then come limping up to the house, knowing full well that he himself was teetering on the threshold of eternal silence. The old lady would shamelessly tell him that and other stories, a bedazzled chatterbox the likes of which she had never been all her life. The vicar would deny the stories, I don't know whether because he didn't believe them or because he commiserated with the old lady. In any case, they barely understood each other. A lethal insensitivity had overcome the

— 139 —

priest about anything that had to do with life; on the other hand, she seemed to have acquired a belated and insane sense of conscience when she suddenly found herself faced with the truths about her kin.

It was as if she had turned on a record, with the needle always in the same groove, repeating the same words and music. She saw it all in her imagination and repeated it until she was delirious and exhausted. The vicar would leave after a while, without even saying goodbye. And she would carry on alone, insisting on the same thing time after time. Finally, hoarse and murky-eyed, all she could manage was a cavernous, unintelligible gurgling, lasting for hours on end.

Out of all that, the only thing that flashes through my mind is that one singular episode . . . the one when evening was coming on and it was the beginning of summer and the last of my sisters had just died. Grandmother and I still lived at the Port. My mother, at Son Vadell, had prepared a big picnic basket with apple tarts, nuts, a bottle of Malaga wine, and a skinned rabbit. She had planned to come to see us and spend the night, probably to talk about when we ought to return to Son Vadell, since they had already disinfected and whitewashed the walls.

Old Nicolau Patxot must have picked her up in his carriage. When it arrived at Son Vadell, my mother got in. My father waved goodbye to her from the archway of the courtyard . . . so tall, and in spite of all the disasters, so happy, always halfway between irony and affection.

I want to imagine that it must have been an abundantly serene afternoon, one of those when I would walk around outside Son Vadell all in a rapture, looking at the flower beds surrounding the house, full of tiny flowers of every color, attracting a benign army of insects. While gazing at the petals and caressing them, I was overcome by an effervescent happiness, mysteriously like that mad desire to run that overcomes horses when they hear the short brusque commands of their riders urging them on. I remember my mother always liked flowers, and sometimes she would stop to muse over them, her head slightly tilted, lost in a dreamy melancholy fugue.

Close to the Hermitage, after they had driven through a part of the flatlands, my mother began to feel ill. She had a headache and felt stomach pains. This happened quite often and was probably due to the tension under which she had had to live and still lived. She ordered Patxot to turn the carriage around, because if she were able to lie down in a darkened room she would feel better after a few hours.

When they got to the lemon grove she got out of the carriage, telling Patxot that she would walk the rest of the way home. The jolting of the carriage, the odor of horse sweat and the old man's pipe had made her dizzy.

The first shadows of late afternoon had begun to glide into place. I think of the lemon trees, dark and densely green, birds flitting in and out of the perfumed foliage. They must have become quiet—out of alarm perhaps—when my mother sat down on the mossy bench at the foot of the hill. She may have picked a lemon, its bright yellow gone pale by then, absorbed by the shadows. Then she passed under the archway into the courtyard with little sprigs of grass between the cobbles, into the vestibule with its presumptuously arrogant clock, its panoply, and its chill all vaguely illuminated by the one lonely light bulb.

Then she went upstairs; her husband would be surprised at her return, and she would seek refuge in his arms in bed, neurotically famished as she was by her need for protection, which objectively she didn't lack, but psychologically she cried out for. The feeling of an impending new disaster never left her completely, but hovered in the depths of that black psychic well where so many other disasters had been born. She touched up her hair. Should she wear the shiny blue ribbon? She crossed the corridor and was headed toward the hall when she heard the first weak cries.

She hurried toward them . . . it must be another catastrophe. Her heart beat wildly. What could be happening to Antoni? She followed the sound to the empty bedroom at the end of the corridor. Her stomach pains were back. Barely containing herself, she slowed to a walk. The door was ajar and she saw the whole scene:

Amàlia de Vadell lay there naked, except for her black stockings and high-heeled shoes. She lay splayed out on the sofa; her long hair falling over her full, taut breasts, her hips and thighs a vast glow of flesh. With an inflamed look in her eyes she ordered my father—also naked— standing over her with a belt in his hand, "Hit me! Hit me again!"

And my father let fly with the belt. Amàlia twisted about and let out sharp little cries amid convulsive panting. Red welts appeared on her back and buttocks.

"Hit me!" she cried again, her eyes bloodshot, poised to leap at him, to scratch him. My father lashed her again and again, and the woman dropped to the floor, dragging herself along while the man flailed away behind her. Amàlia was soaked in sweat and crisscrossed with red welts, laughing and crying insanely, while my father stood there crazed with excitement.

Then he threw the belt down and pounced on the bitch, raw flesh and slathered sweat colliding in an animal frenzy, the roar of desire beyond mere possession, reaching a gasping groaning savagery, tangling and binding them. He entered her with a thrust that threw him forward, his teeth sinking furiously into the flesh of her neck.

My mother dropped to the floor, unconscious. When she came to, hours or minutes later, she walked calmly about the house, seeing neither doors nor chairs, for she had already become another person. . . . My father found her at dawn when he came out of the room with Aunt Amàlia. Mother greeted them with an evasive, meaningless smile, humming a little ditty to herself.

A nd how was it that Aunt Amàlia and my father were seen? Maybe one of the maids. . . . It's probable that when my father left us, conjectures and rumors were running rampant, since he left us shortly after that nightmare night at Son Vadell. I remember my father, perhaps now more than at any other time since I've had my memory so sharply honed by this flood of details from the past. . . .

He was wearing a black shirt, with some small stripes on the front of it, a polished leather belt and cross straps, riding boots, and britches. He had joined the Spanish Falange right after the war started. The rigor of the uniform was in sharp contrast to his cordial manner, making him appear to me as if he were always just about to laugh, to run after me, to grab me and lift me high in the air, to make me want to jump into his arms.

I think it was about that time when he armed the falcon. He kept it in a cage in the house, and once in a while he would take it out, covering its ferocious little head with a hood. When he unhooded it out in the field, the rapacious little beast would remain as still as a mummy for a few moments, its tiny cruel eyes looking as if they were about to spit metal sparks. And then it would turn its head proudly and smoothly, taking off suddenly in a straight line up into the sky, becoming an insignificant distant speck floating around, lost in space. When it spotted a ring dove or a flock of sparrows, it would dive like a bolt of lightning and attack, amidst a flurry of shrieks and feathers.

My father smoked cigars, and I had seen him lots of times sitting on a dry embankment for an hour or two, blowing clouds of blue smoke as he watched the methodical labor of a peasant in his field. Or he would sit and watch in fascination the monotonous and feeble trickle of water from the lip of a fountain. And one day I saw him standing on a platform like a god, together with other men dressed in the same kind of black shirt, their arms raised in salute, singing and shouting cheers with resounding voices. . . .

"Bernardet, son of the king, left to seek the Love of the Three Oranges, and he didn't find it, but he went on fooling the giants who ate huge bowls of salad and whole roasted oxen, outwitting snakes with seven heads and lions with a terrible roar, until he reached the wellspring of the three oranges in the hidden garden. And inside each orange there was a young maiden dying of thirst. And he was able to save the last and most beautiful of them all, but first. . . ." This was the tale he was telling me that afternoon when they called him from the roadside. They were dressed in the same Falangist uniform. I only remember the nearsighted one, that sour-faced Albert Balaguer, who later worked in the courthouse. The other two were Italians. There was a steady stream of boats and planes back and forth from Palma to Italy. We never heard from him again, though he might have gone to Rome. . . . He had fled, he had left what we considered to be our whole world. "When I come back, I'll finish the story," he said as he got up, messing up my hair playfully and carrying off his hooded falcon on the back of his raised hand.

_G_randmother, already bedridden, would describe and describe to herself again, then start over, repeating each of Antoni's, my mother's, and Aunt Amàlia's gestures . . . Amàlia, Amàlia. . . . She would describe what they had told her, plus maybe what she had added about Amàlia, and it's probably true that today I've added my own impressions as well; that is, what I see in my own imagination, giving it at least as many twists and turns as the dying old lady did. But I am more trapped than she was by that foul trap—a trap I can't define, but know is there. . . .

Amàlia ran her hand over her forehead, trying to think. But trying to analyze herself led to a suffocating confusion, like walking through choking clouds of smoke. Quickly, she walked to her bedroom. She threw the bolt and locked herself in, lit two oil lamps and the five-candle candelabra; it was the time when electricity was still rationed. She closed the curtains to the balcony.

A sharp light filled the room; the large mirror seemed to melt in the quiet, brilliant euphoria of blinding whiteness. She drew near it and peered at herself with her eyes wide open. She was still young, still capable of inciting desire in others. . . . But he had left. . . . A sort of hysteria emerged on her face, as if the twisted conscience tormenting her, mincing her to bits, had appeared in the mirror, reflected in her eyes as a point of frenetic delirium, as if it were that force marking those heavy lines on each side of her lips, tightening her skin, pulling the corners of her mouth down. She got so worked up she blew out the candles in frustration.

The oil lamps remained lit, casting deathly halos in the quiet, dim light. The bedroom acquired a mood of intimacy, as soft as plush. Amàlia slowly undressed: she dropped her skirt, unbuttoned her blouse, undid her hair, and let it fall loose. She went back to the mirror and looked at herself again, carefully, caressed by the licking shadows. Her thighs were two sleek columns of splendid flesh; her panties hinted at that hidden, most desirable of fleshes; held in by her bra, her breasts became two turgid tips swelling to her slow caress. Amàlia ran her hands slowly over her whole body again and again, as a sweet feeling of faintness made her swoon.

In the room next-door she heard her husband making his chirping grunting sounds as his wheelchair bumped against the walls and the door. Ferran Salines was almost completely paralyzed. He couldn't speak or move his legs or his body. He could only move his waist, his neck, and his upper arms a bit. He was, however, an unusually active beast. He ate and drank greedily as the maid fed him and held the glass to his lips. He would drink a glass of wine and two or three of water. They had to limit him or he would keep on until he burst. When he saw the table had been set he began to bellow, to roll his eyes, to wriggle around in his wheelchair, into which he barely fit since he had become so fat.

Salines had always been a tall, stocky man. A few years after their marriage, he and his wife went to spend the Christmas holidays at Son

Calafat, his father's place, the last one at the edge of Andratch, lying at the foot of the tall Tramontana Mountains. Old Colonel Salines, who lived in Palma and always swelled with satisfaction at their arrival, was waiting for them with the fireplaces roaring, with lambs ready to be popped into the oven, with a large table filled with pastries, jams, liqueurs, and fritters. He laughed and hugged them and the next morning when they got up everything was white: an unusually heavy snow had fallen.

The heavy whiteness bent the trees with its weight, covered the grass and the hills and all the roof tiles of Son Calafat. Everything seemed to disappear under the weight of the snow, at the same time creating a fantastically singular reality, silent to the point of irritation. Soon everything froze under a tentative misty sun. And it snowed again. On New Year's Day, restless from their long confinement, the two men and Amàlia set out on a long walk.

They trekked along the edge of the pine forest at En Caliu, which meandered up the mountain to the deserted gorges of Evangèlica, where unknown voices wandered, protected by the peaks of Galatzó and S'Esclop. The colonel ceremoniously held the arm of his daughter-in-law. Amàlia, wrapped in her soft thick Astrakhan coat, laughed at the old man's jokes. Ferran playfully knocked snow off the pine boughs with a long stick, making the snow rain down on them.

"It was during the Northern Campaign, with the snow freezing in the gorges, that my up-until-then unbeatable troops were routed by their falls, their very unmilitary slipping and sliding around . . . ," elaborated the old man. Amàlia laughed more and more each time, snuggling up in the warmth of her coat. Then two nervous and hungry gray shapes, in sullen silence, appeared from amid the pristine whiteness and threw themselves upon the surprised hikers.

Amàlia cried out as she was scraped by that mass of rough and burning fur rushing by. She fell flat on her face in the snow and rolled blindly away. When she was able to see again, she observed in mute stupor the heavy vapor clouds of panting breath spewing from the throats of two enormous mastiffs, their eyes glazed and full of fire, as they dragged the bodies of Ferran and his father into the woods, leaving bloody trails behind them. Amàlia felt herself suffocating; she fainted, overcome by a burst of fear, a maelstrom beyond pain.

When she came to, she staggered back toward Son Calafat reeling like a drunk. Three farmhands came out to meet her, heard her story, and set out with shotguns for the pine forest at En Caliu. They followed the trail through the brush, great chunks of snow falling on them as they pushed through the branches and came to a clearing. There the two dogs were, observing them with opaque eyes from behind a pile of bloody clothes and guts strewn about. The hired hands aimed and fired. One of the animals dropped in its tracks, vomiting black gobs of blood, and the other limped into the woods and escaped.

They were wild mastiffs, driven down from the high crags by hunger after the snowstorm. The colonel was all torn apart, but Ferran's life was saved, even though he was crippled. And Amàlia noticed how the intelligence of the man had survived intact. She saw an infinitely deep sadness reflected in his eyes during the first few days. Then it began to fade, at the same time that he was overcome by a stultified, silent mood that soon came to dominate him. He became distant and obtuse, and only perked up—with violent shrewdness—when faced with food or when he gazed at his wife. . . .

Amàlia came to ignore the cripple, beyond seeing to it that they washed him and took care of him. Sometimes she would keep him company, smiling at him once in a while, as she thought about other things. She had set him up in the room next to hers. And she didn't pay any attention to his shrieks and groans when he looked at her furiously, imploringly, as a stiff protuberance rose between his thighs. She thought about that now, framed between the two oil lamps, looking at herself as if she were an apparition, listening to the sounds of Ferran in the other room.

Suddenly she opened the door to his room. Wearing only her bra and panties, she moved closer to him. Her husband grunted and wriggled when he saw her, as though he were being macerated. It seemed as if his eyes were going to pop out of his head. A white froth appeared at the corners of his lips. She carried him over to the bed, undressed him, and laid him on his back. The cripple writhed and sucked in his breath fitfully, his penis rising, red and turgid.

Amàlia looked at him in irritation as she finished undressing. Then she slid on top of the cripple and began to rub her sex against his as his face got more and more contorted by the moment. And as he bellowed between spasms, she felt that shaft of flesh spew its hot liquid into her.

*I*t's strange how frequently hunting dogs have served as primordial elements in the family. Jaume Vadell had them before he went to work as a watchman on Dragonera. Another relative, Antoni Vadell, must have been his grandson who was alive around 1725. He had the same name as my father and lived with the same animals; he was a trapper. In the *Flower of Andratch Romances,* Dr. Bonaventura Montmeló transcribes a couplet probably dedicated to Antoni:

> In all the woods and glens, this trapper-hunter,
> of all the rest, he knows the beasts the better.

However, since he inherited Son Capovara, it's strange that a Vadell should devote himself to hunting as a profession, that is if the couplet is telling the truth. Perhaps hunting was just a great hobby for him. Or it might have been a question of a relative, and not one of the owners of the Vadell estate.

As a child, I knew some of the last of the independent trappers and hunters, one of whom was Pau el Marter, the only one from Andratch, the one who came to town so often. . . .

In the middle of the town hall square, strung up, stinking, and stiff, hung the dead bodies of several stone martens, a couple of sables, an eagle, some kites, a few weasels, and wildcats. A weak and tepid sun hovered overhead. Swarms of fat, black bottle flies with green stripes buzzed about. Some dogs were sniffing the air and backing away, yelping, their tails between their legs.

Pau el Marter stood there with his arms crossed over his barrel chest, watching the constable cut half an ear off each animal and the beaks off the birds with a pair of pruning shears. He held the animals with his foot, and with his free hand he held his nose, disgusted by the smell. A group of people stood around at a safe distance watching the show. I was among them, keeping an eye on Marter's huge dark gray dog that showed its teeth when it growled. It was tied to a pine tree in front of the town hall.

With traps and nets and his shotgun, Marter hunted and trapped vermin and birds of prey. He came to town only to collect the bounties or to buy supplies. When he was among people he acted surly toward them. A rustic odor emanated from his large muscular body, from his sun- and wind-burned face, from his corduroy clothes, and his thick, scratched-up boots. He smelled of sap and earth, of aromatic herbs and animal sweat.

He lived in the mountains in huts he had made from stones and logs or in caves he closed off with piles of brush. He had these shelters scattered around in different places where he could be dry and protected along his trap line. He carried a frying pan, a cooking pot, wine, and food in an old oilcloth sack; a can of kerosene and a lantern were tied together with a rope; his blanket was tied atop the rest of his pack.

The woods and the animals weren't exactly work for him, but a very real extension of his being, of his life. He knew every tree, every bush, and all the phases of their existence. He knew whether a piece of vegetation was fatigued, or about to burst forth with new life, by the color of its leaves, the humidity, or the strength of the wind. Marter would feel at ease or in trouble, depending on the condition of the trees in a pine or oak forest.

He didn't pursue animals: he lived alongside them, sharing their open, agile cleverness. He breathed the same air and took refuge in almost the same lairs when it was stormy. He walked the same valleys and trails as they did. He respected the terrain and the dictates of the seasons just as the birds and beasts did. And, since he himself was the strongest link in the food chain, he killed the weakest of the lot. Within that world, absorbed by cosmic forces, alone with his dog among the crags and peaks, Pau had become just one more powerful element—like a bear or a feline hunter might be—in the indestructible magma of nature, tied directly to primordial matter itself.

When he had finished, the constable paid Marter, who then tied the carcasses together with a wire, made up a bundle, and headed for the shed he had rented at the last house on the road to Son Vadell, almost beside Isabel Borràs' house. There the fetid smell was overwhelming, with all the hides strung out under a porch to dry. He had already gutted them in the mountains. . . . Antoni Vadell must have been something like Pau Marter.

Or maybe he had done something else. In 1730 there was an Antoni Vadell who was jailed, without mention of his profession, for having killed fugitive slaves. Andratch was just the right kind of place for anybody wanting to hide out, with its extensive mountain tracts surrounded by the most deserted, precipitous, and rough coastline on the island. Runaway Moorish slaves would wind up there from other parts of the island. They would pick their way along trails through the uninhabited hills and gorges to the mountains facing the sea. Their hope was that a Moorish galley would heave into sight, so that they could signal it and be picked up by their countrymen. In most cases, the slaves had robbed their masters of jewelry and money before they escaped.

Whoever captured a slave was supposed to turn him over to the law so that the slave might be returned to his owner. But Antoni Vadell, who knew the countryside well, would be on the lookout for Berber and Turkish pirate attacks during high season, in the spring and summer. When he found a slave he would rob and kill him and throw his body off the nearest cliff. "Guilty of having been seen killing two black men and a woman—they don't know what color she was because he threw her down a well—and robbing them of a lady's gold necklace set with precious stones, and a bag of gold coins and three rings. It was unknown where the murder victims were from. One of them had a huge lump on his back full of pus." That's how the charges against Vadell read.

The story about the trapper recorded by Dr. Montmeló has survived intact. To reproduce it here in its entirety would be excessive and perhaps boring. What is of interest, however, is the plot the couplets weave, since in them the character of that austere and magnificent hunter is described. Is it a survival of medieval superstition related to the dance of death? Or is it simply a question of superimposed appearances of the Virgin, of which there were so many, with profane additions and a changed ending?

It's easy to imagine the scene the story describes—a torrent rushing down a bed of steeply falling rock between sharp high peaks, polished by the crashing force of the water, as if its borders had been crystallized, frozen by a sacred disaster of nature. Along the shadowy course of the torrent, the unpruned acacias—a weary tangle of branches and leaves and strong sharp thorns—created tunnels where not a ray of sunlight entered. They were like caverns come alive through the somber shadowy exuberance of green foliage and light. Those caves seemed to descend to mythical depths, then expand to the very edges of space

The trapper lay asleep near the coals of his campfire, wrapped in his blanket, immersed in the vibrations from the dizzying stridency of the roaring torrent nearby. Suddenly he awoke, his mastiff barking menacingly. Antoni opened his eyes sleepily, perceiving the roiling waters, the humid darkness under the acacias, and with a jerk sat up. On the bank before him stood the silhouette of a young girl, marvelously dressed in white, who disappeared instantly. Antoni el Marter blinked. No, there was nothing there. Was he going crazy? He went back to sleep in a gruff mood.

Two days later, on a moonlit night the dog's barking woke him up again, for the young girl had reappeared with her radiantly white dress, loaded with flounces and veils and lace cuffs, looking for all the world like a bride. And she smiled silently at him, cavorting through elegant dance steps on the opposite bank. The trapper watched incredulously with his pupils dilated, until she disappeared.

He hardly slept for several nights, but the enigmatic apparition didn't appear again. Antoni didn't understand. The cave, the torrent, the hills, the trees had lost their serenity for him. He searched everywhere for her, slightly terrified as he investigated. He must have thought, without knowing whether he was satisfied, intrigued, or deceived, that she would never come back. . . .

He awoke with a start the next night, under the impression that a snake was crawling through his hair, but it was her fingers instead, caressing him. Antoni tried to grab her, but she jumped backward, light as a feather, running toward a dense thicket. Bewildered and full of foreboding, Marter ran after her. He saw her glide between the pines and carob trees, faintly outlined beneath the starry sky, as if she were floating. It was a silent tenacious chase: she slipped ghostlike through the trees, he splashed through the water, getting tangled in the thicket. He felt as if he were living a relentless black-and-white nightmare.

Until he finally caught her. Sweaty and out of breath, he grabbed her by the shoulders in front of a wild plum tree with small red fruit. With her back to him, her long hair brushed against his face, her veils still in motion, softly, like the wings of a butterfly just landing. The trapper twirled her around to face him in the light of the quarter moon.

It was an old hag, dressed in soiled torn rags out of which hung a pair of flaccid wrinkled dugs; her legs were hairy and scrawny. Antoni retreated in confusion; the old crone smiled: only two snaggled, blackened teeth showed in her mouth. And she extended her arms toward him. . . .

The other hunter, Pau el Marter, died at just about the same time as my last sister did. I was feeling depressed during those days, as if I had been hopelessly smashed against a wall, at the same time sensing a subconscious, barely noticeable feeling of liberation. That's probably why I didn't pay too much attention to what was said about Pau. After nobody had seen him for three or four weeks, some lumberjacks found him in the exact same stream where I had situated my relative, Antoni Vadell. The stream was called Sa Coma Freda at its upper end near Coll dels Cairats. His body was wedged between two monumental rocks. He must have fallen, becoming stuck and unconscious there, a prisoner in the crack. As far as crying for help, nobody would have heard him; the gorge was deep.

They found him because there were usually crabs—little tiny critters—in that full-running stream in the winter. But during those days they were catching big white bloated ones. The crab hunters, tempted by their size, tracked them upstream. There they found Pau el Marter's body, also bloated, stinking, and infested with crabs feeding off his decayed flesh. They recognized him from his oilcloth bag lying nearby, intact.

*H*a! ha! ha! for Marter to fall off the cliff! He who was like a piece of the rock himself. . . . I don't know anything about it and your father's the one who could talk to you about that, but he's not here. Why don't you go and see Albert Balaguer, who was a great friend of his? He just might like to swap gossip . . . ," Onofre Capllonc (the one with the dynamite injuries) told me one day.

I had never spoken to Balaguer before. I remembered when he came by Son Vadell dressed as a Falangist, like the rest of them who called on my father to go with them that day. It was afterward, when I began to dig through the records, that I first dealt with him. It was in the courthouse, that dilapidated place he was in charge of, where I scrupulously read many long-forgotten, cold, and clammy folios. Balaguer always sat behind an ancient table that would wobble if you touched it. He was in charge of writing death, birth, and wedding certificates, all of them real, existential deeds. When the documents arrived there to be legally registered by that ravaged accountant, they seemed to turn into pale memories of things long since decayed. He barely answered my greeting with a mumble, and when I asked him where this or that book might be, he limited his response to pointing with his finger, looking at me but not seeing me through those myopic eyes, reduced by his thick lenses to puffy dots like toad's eyes, staring at me in a frozen burlesque of blindness.

Albert Balaguer tottered down the street four times a day, covering the route from his house to the courthouse and back. When I saw him I had the impression that his body might begin to rise slowly at any moment, losing itself in limitless space among the winds, the last torn rag of a scarecrow in autumn, stranded in a field beside the remaining bony twigs of harvest time. He always wore the same wrinkled and tattered black suit, its shoulders laden with dandruff, its baggy knees and elbows shiny from wear. It must have been a suit rescued from some celebration—a wedding or the death of his father—from which even the memory had faded.

However, in that suit resided the only key to what tied the man to the complex circle of life: it at least reflected traces of life, feeble as they might be, traces of the passion and human contacts that had existed in the ancient ceremony where the suit, new and clean and pressed, had been worn for the first time. The traces of life in the sunken shoulders of Balaguer, in his watery gaze, in his terrified stuttering speech, had all disappeared.

In the treasury of yesterday's images lying in my memory, only one remains of Albert Balaguer's parents. I must have been very young when I once saw them seated at mass. His father was large, with a reddish beard and moustache, who breathed heavily, with a top hat in his lap. His mother was busty and well-girdled, with her hair piled up as if she were wearing a turban. Her gaze was immobile and waxen, her mouth rounded as if cast in a permanent state of surprise. And in an unlikely way—for all this must have happened years before I was born—I include an adolescent Albert in the picture, a wan pastiche of solitude, his huge transparent ears, his mother always at his side. . . .

The first time he responded to my presence it was as if he really hadn't at all. While I was thumbing through a report on the property put up for sale under Mendizábel's Alienation Act of 1836, I distractedly chatted with him about my father, referring to what Capllonc had said about Marter. He stopped writing and sat there, paralyzed and cringing, as if he feared a heart attack. I can't be sure he heard me, and even less that he was answering me when he started to talk. It sounded as if he were talking to himself, answering a question that had hung eternally before him—or that he was chatting with someone whom I couldn't see, giving them the explanation:

"Pictures of saints covered the walls and a sort of dim, deathly light filled that room I never left, since I always had a cold, and when I blew my nose I always got a nosebleed. On my neck and in my crotch I got lumps and a kind of eczema. My mother used to smother me like a brood hen in the hot, stale air of that room. She curled my hair; she peeled the fruit I was supposed to eat; she bundled me up and fed me lots of medicines as if they would fatten me up. What they did was impregnate my flesh with an odor, a chemical stench, to the point where I smelled like medicine instead of like a person. I felt happy, however, in that situation of spoiled eternal convalescence. Curled up within myself, I lived on the edge of the real world with which I only had furtive sensory contacts, as if I were a kind of jellyfish.

"Until my father burst in like an explosion . . . oh, Balaguer the notary, oh . . . so big and ruddy, with that stinking cigar. . . . The door opened and he shouted that he wanted me to go out in the sun and play. But my mother hugged me and stopped him. He angrily slammed the door on his way out. And then there was that boy whom my mother got to come up to keep me company and play with me. . . . The boy would sit on the bed and imitate riding a horse, or he would move around, playing with a ball. His thick thighs . . . I would stare at them, the rosy brightness of his soft tight skin, the fullness of his movements. One day I timidly caressed his thighs and he sat there, impassive. Little by little, as we were left alone, I would throw myself on top of him, touching him all over with agitated delight. I can still feel the touch of him—it electrified my fingertips.

"And that's the way we were that afternoon, with our pants down, feeling sweeter than honey, our hands on each other's engorging pricks, getting hotter by the minute, as if a hidden fire were coming to life. And then my father suddenly burst in, panting like a big ox, shouting convulsively as he started to thrash me. And if my mother and the maid hadn't come and pulled me away, all black and blue and bloody from his thrashing fists, he might have killed me.

"And I imagined doing the same to him, during the several weeks I spent under the blankets and the down comforter as a result of the blows. I would outline the scenes in my mind in great detail, with an enthusiasm that sometimes gave me a high fever; then my mother would have to put cool wet rags on my forehead to bring it down. I would imagine my father as small and skinny, naked and weak and tied up, hanging from a beam in a dark cellar with rats in the corners, stinking puddles all around and myself standing there, tall and barrel-chested, dressed only in a jockstrap, a resplendent being. With a long knife I set about carving out one of his eyes, which burst open, spraying a watery pus all over; and then I applied a red-hot iron to his veins. His flesh burned and his blood coagulated and hardened. And with a whip tipped with nails I beat and lashed him until his body turned into a scrofulous open sore. I lay under the covers in the fetal position, all curled up and hot, until I swear I began to smell the odor of his blood mixed with sweat, like the aroma of a pastry that has gone bad, like the ones that were left over in the pantry after a party, and they went bad and we had to throw them out. As his wailing died away, I drank an amber liqueur from a fine crystal goblet. I coughed, all rolled up in bed, and it seemed as if a fungus were growing down my throat and cutting off my wind; at the same time it excited me, oh orgiastic suffocation. . . ."

I almost threw up. Balaguer gave me the impression of a leech somebody should have stepped on. Disgusted, I left without answering him, in spite of understanding that for whatever motive, from his introverted solitude he needed the charity of somebody to hear him confess, something that he'd probably wanted to do for years without being able to. And just then circumstances had been right for him to spill his guts out to me.

The next couple of times I went to the courthouse we didn't speak to each other. And on the third occasion, mumbling awkwardly, he invited me to his house.

Can Balaguer was a big rambling place that appeared abandoned. The door was always locked, and more than half the windows were bricked up. Albert opened the door with a huge key that squeaked shrilly in the lock. "I just live in the dining room," he said as he entered it and began to turn on the lights. It seems he had marshalled all the lights from all over the house into that one room—floor lamps, table lamps, chandelier—and he had connected them to extension cords crisscrossing the floor; bursts of brilliant white light followed one after the other.

I had to shield my eyes from it while Balaguer moved around, bewildered by all that light, as if he were drunk, at the same time telling me, "You see? This doesn't look like the courthouse nor the town. It's like another world. And it's mine. Don't you believe that above the clouds on a dark day there's light like this, right under the sun?" And moving over to an old sideboard, he picked up a bottle of wine, some slices of ham, half a loaf of bread, and an overripe melon. He began eating by starting with the melon and tearing it apart with his fingers, eagerly swallowing the yellowing pulp. His mouth and chin dripped melon juice.

An overpowering decadence hung in the air. Dirty pots and plates were everywhere, some with an inch of delicate, spring-green mold on them. Other plates were covered with rotten leftovers, out of which little white worms wriggled. Empty wine bottles were piled up all over the place. Some of them had tipped over and dripped on the floor. Little fruit flies were stuck in the sticky drippings. On the table stood a tub with murky water in it, two grubby towels, and several small worn bars of soap. Wrinkled laundry hung on the backs of the chairs. A single bed was pushed up against one wall with stinking dirty brown sheets wadded up in a bundle on top of it. Beside the bed he had stacked a pile of paperback novels, many of them with torn bindings. Pictures of cowboys waving Colts or of girls with angelic faces gazing up at dark handsome men with wavy hair. A reeking stench of sewer gas saturated the room.

And Albert Balaguer kept on eating and gazing at me with a wandering look, shut off in his own muddled and mute soliloquy. His expression would swing from biting irony to a series of nasal guffaws, and then shift to a tone of exorbitant cunning. His eyes, magnified by his thick-lensed glasses, acquired an increasingly clownish air. He drank in gluttonous swallows, one after the other.

Then, all that fire became verbalized in a voice half-mocking, half-suspicious: "Of course, or do you think that he who does it doesn't pay for it? The Reds found ways of getting away, and my father, who didn't have to die, did. When we signed up for the war we all went because we wanted to get away from here, get away from ourselves, and we didn't know where to go. When he died, there was nothing left in the house, not a penny. And I was only trying to survive. So what if it had to be the courthouse! O.K., so what? It doesn't matter, and I still came out ahead. If I had lost, I still would have had to pay for it.

"They escaped up through the mountains. We went to look for them and they weren't there. They said we didn't know where to find them. Mountain trails, animal tracks, the hiding places . . . and Antoni, your father, went up the mountain in his short pants and blue shirt. . . . He ruffled my hair, oh yes . . . his thighs, so full, moved miraculously . . . one day they made you swallow it. A dozen . . . no, no, hell no! We spied on Marter, Antoni and I and two others, in spite of the fact that he was smarter than we were. After we spent a night hiding in the brush waiting for them to go by in the dark, with my head resting on his thighs, it was him that appeared. Alone. So what! Alone, but the bastards probably had already escaped wherever they could. Alone.

"And some of us jumped him, I among them. He who does it pays for it. The crab trail, ha, ha, ha! It will never be known; nobody knows, nobody ever told. And I was there alone with Antoni—I don't know where he is now—only we could have told. He was my friend, always the two of us together in that dark room where we played that the chair was a horse . . . and he went away. From me, from everybody. And I couldn't believe it. He ran his hand over my neck. 'We'll see each other tomorrow,' he said. And never again.

"Can you sing? Bah, it doesn't matter; go on, get out! I'm drinking, see? D'ya want some? And I'll drink some more. Under the lights. And I'll turn on the radio. They sing and chatter on, and I keep turning it up louder and louder. Every day. And I'll lie down and read. Oh, any old book, any one at all. And I'll open it to a trip to the Orient or to a girl in love or to a gully in California. And I'll drink and listen to music and voices and I'll go crazy from all the light and I'll be in California. Or he'll come back. An archangel will come, and if I start to get it up, I'll unbutton my pants and. . . ."

I didn't want to hear any more of that stuff so I left in a hurry, without knowing whether to kick the hell out of him or not; I was running by now, maybe more afraid of myself than of him.

Because he stayed there—maybe he's there even now—and left me here with . . . no, there are bridges even I won't cross, and I want to remain strong by stopping before I start. "Let it be the Sleeping Woman who takes the step to the other side. I listen to her, but I won't do it," my grandmother used to say to me, repeating it to herself again and again.

As for the death of Grandmother, the first and most disturbing effect I remember was a unique sense of estrangement. The last rain of spring fell that day, and, as though the weather were obeying a fierce command from beyond, the sun burst forth with all its blistering summer ardor. Changes appeared in the leaves on the same trees and plants. Some of them began to languish in the sudden intense summer heat, while others remained lustrous and graceful.

I observed that curious contrast from the vicarage, where I spent a few weeks with Uncle Dionís before I left. He was also living in an increasingly crazy reality that was breaking up into scattered pieces of various and contradictory sizes.

While I was waiting for Grandmother to die at Son Vadell, I sat in the hall downstairs, not daring to start up the inane magic of the music box with its little drum. I went up to her room and watched her wasting away, tucked under her comforter, finally freed, indifferent to her shriveling body. I knew then that from the great beyond her death would pursue me absolutely and forever, like a crushing drumbeat.

We buried her in a coffin stuck into a niche in one of the long cemetery corridors, decorated with banal crosses and baroque plaster wreaths, as though they were the luxurious foundations of a palace, yesterday superb and today dissolved to nothing. Orange trees grew along the narrow rows of niches. They had grown too big; their branches had spread out, pushing against the niche stones, then bending around them and growing straight up. Sometimes the climbing rose bushes would intertwine with the tree trunks, and up in the tangled foliage both rose and orange blossoms would bloom side by side.

I used to look out on the cemetery from the balcony of the vicarage with its wrought-iron railing and dirty windows. The withering might of the summer sun fell on everything the day after her funeral, turning the cemetery into a rosy, joyful, explicit, and absolute show of nature. I gazed out there, without feeling anything calling me from the tomb. I had to force my imagination to recall something of Grandmother, of her corpse rotting out there before me. The bright and broiling sun had overcome time and my affections.

Once I left town, I never saw Father Dionís again. And my memory of him is not pleasant. The vicar was an atherosclerotic, a swamp of ancient flesh. As his circulation slowed, he would forget things and remain transfixed, as if paralyzed. One day, as he was coming out of one of those trances, his skin bled white; he said, "I remain like this, and I see a barbarous pile of naked corpses, mute and rotting, being attacked by angels dressed in red armor waving coiled green snakes with poisonous whistles."

And there he sat, frozen, staring at the room with repugnance in his eye, as though what he had imagined had been a virulent liquid washing through the office in a great wave, receding now into the corners, ready to return and rise again like an invading sea. His mouth hung open, overcome by nausea. He looked like he was about to vomit up the last of his life, but then he calmed down and staggered over to his bed. Only there did he really feel comfortable, surrounded by the artificial heat of six hotwater bottles. His body could not even manufacture the heat necessary to keep him going.

The vicar was obsessed by the cold throughout those last weeks. One evening he interrupted himself in the middle of supper, stuttering that maybe it wasn't true that the center of the earth was an incandescent ball of fire and that life came from fire. On the contrary, he saw the sun, the heat, and the fire as a titanic effort to conquer the ice and all that moisture that exists at the beginning and the end of everything. If the sun were to disappear from its regular course—a dead body, a dug well, the top of a hill—all would be surrounded, whether on high or deep below, by an icy atmosphere that would destroy all possible forms of life.

Perhaps driven by the certainty that he was the embodiment of fear itself, just before passing on to a state of absolute ice, the vicar was indirectly trying to confess to me . . . a confession about others, however. I wasn't even able to guess until much later, after following a tortuous spiraling course, that the confession pointed to something much further beyond. . . .

He nattered on and on, his unintelligible babblings always coming back to the Valorous Dukes. "Why has the celebration of their holiday been canceled these last few years?" I asked him, out of respect for that dark mania that seemed to consume him. And then he suddenly began to explain, thoughtfully and without pause, as if a blockage of many years had been removed:

"The duke and duchess . . . I've never been sure that they were dukes. First I have to tell you that he, the Duke of Pantaleu, didn't know or didn't know how to speak a single word of Catalan. And nobody seemed to know what his native tongue was, in spite of the fact that in the documents every once in a while you find a kind of phonetic transcription of things he said.

"I'm not sure, but I think it could have been Greek. Like *aporon*, for example, which if it were Greek would be written α-πορος, which means "without a path," more or less. At another place I think I read *pararreo,* which could maybe be "flow or run," or in Greek παρα-ρρεω. And if he said, among other things, εχνροζ or *exiros* before dying, it could be that he was trying to tell Elionor de Vadell to be "strong, firm." Because Elionor and Marc Maria de Vadell the bishop, were always the intermediaries between him and the rest of the people. Intermediaries or just translators, because I cannot imagine the duke dominated by the other two. I don't know . . . and does Pantaleu mean "five islands," or is it a trick, inspired by the name of the little isle of Pantaleu beside Dragonera, out there in front of Sant Telm, and also the name of the oldest quarter of Andratch?

"Marc Maria de Vadell was the older brother of Lau, the owner of Son Vadell at the time. Both of them were the sons of Donat Vadell, implicated in the drowning of the sailors the North American professor had studied. Elionor was the eldest of the three, and in 1756, when she arrived in town married to the duke and accompanied by Marc Maria, she was forty-four years old. She must have been born in 1712. Her father, Donat, who in 1737 was forty-five, must have been born in 1692 . . . but it was around 1708 that Escolàstic de Capovara died, leaving Onofre Vadell as his heir. And as far as we know, he had no brothers. Nor did they ever find his unfortunate sister, Margarideta. Nor any relatives of the galley slave Jaume Vadell. What I mean is, if you study it in detail, it gets complicated and none of the dates match up right. Where do Marc Maria, Elionor, and her father come from, all of them unavoidably contemporaries of Onofre Vadell?

"Ugh . . . one or the other of them has to be a fake. Or the lot of them. Or whatever happened was different from what can be reconstructed by history itself. Or the dates are wrong. Which inevitably brings you to this point: however it may have been, the roots of our tree dance and dangle in thin air.

"Years ago, I sought an explanation for things, believing that one ought to be guided by ideas, held to a line of inquiry. . . . But now it's only the facts I'm interested in. All the rest is like a sea or a fire, something all-encompassing or nothing. But let's stop here, in 1756, when those three people landed in the Port of Andratch from a boat named the *Dauphin*.

"Marc Maria was then just forty years old, according to the Canonical Registry in the See of Palma, where he was in charge of the Holy Charity. And among the portraits hanging on the walls of the Episcopal Palace, there's one that well could be his own. Under it is written, "The Most

Illustrious Canon of the Holy Charity," and it was paid for in 1741, one of the three years in which our ancestor occupied the post. But, of course, had it really been painted then? There were frequent cases of endless debts, of court cases, because the Curia never paid painters, master masons, chandlers, or even the priests themselves. . . .

"Let's accept the fact then that it was a portrait of him. His forehead was narrow and simian, composed of two huge wrinkles, in spite of how young he was at the time. He had angry eyes and thick, sensual lips. He seemed to be a proudly stubborn man . . . who knows how he got the position of canon priest? I don't know that either. Maybe by examination, though there's no proof of it. Because I don't understand what influence the Vadells could have had in order to get him the position otherwise. Then there's the possibility that while he was still in seminary or when he had just started out as a priest, he had made some influential friendships . . . I don't know. It upsets me to have to wander blindly from one question to the next, among so many unknowns. A thorn pricks away at your insides, calling out for attention, for its removal. And you pull it free, but there's nothing there except tricky, slippery hints. And let me tell you something: I never *will* clear it up. I'm going to die soon. When I think about it, I'd like to cut my own throat; it's so absurd, so horrible. I'll go to my grave without having found a single one of the proofs I've been looking for.

"I don't know if I'll be in a state of perpetual sacrilege, or if I've sinned against the Holy Spirit. I can't, I just can't answer that because I just don't know—and I suspect that I really don't care anymore. I'm tired and I can see how I'm falling to pieces. And why does my soul have to be immortal? Soul, faith, supernatural life, I believed in the Dogma, and deeply so. But now, seeing how this life is ending for me, and knowing what I know, chaos is the only thing that frightens me. And what must have happened to Marc Maria de Vadell? The 'de' he added when he returned, just as he and the duke resurrected the insignia of the Capovara, the three golden horses galloping through the black background. Did he find unknown papers referring to the end of the Schism of the West as he rummaged through the archives of the cathedral? The end that was finally accepted by Rome, I mean.

"I imagine him walking through the great naves of the See, eagerly reading by candlelight in those little Gothic cells. Because you should know that the canon of the Cathedral of Valencia, who was named Pope Clement VIII in Peñíscola at the death of Pedro de Luna, was later named Bishop of Majorca. His real name was Gil Sancho Muñoz. He abdicated all his supposed rights to the pontifical crown, either voluntarily or under pressure; he withdrew all the excommunications and condemnations that Benedict XIII had dictated against Martin V, and as a reward for that they named him as our bishop.

"But did he really believe that Luna was a fake and Martin of Rome the legitimate pope? I don't know that either. But the fact remains that Marc Maria embarked in 1743, leaving his post as head of charities in what could only be described as a hurry, since the post remained vacant for several months afterward. And he must have left with his sister Elionor, because he returned with her after having presumably experienced the same things. Elionor wasn't married then, and must have taken care of her brother the priest as his housekeeper. If not, there was no logical reason for her to leave Andratch.

"Well, we were at the point where Marc Maria was about to leave. And if I were to think that Vadell was sent off on some secret mission by that Clement VIII-Muñoz, it's because in 1760, three years after his return, a grave and serious accusation was presented against him by the vicar-general and by the Inquisition. He was accused of authoring a book in Latin titled *Introito ad Anima Dei,* which defended heretical positions. But they couldn't prove that the Benedictus Johannes who signed his name to it was really him. Now concentrate on the name Benedicto Juan or Benedict XIII and that cardinal whose name was Jean, Juan Carrier. . . . And Vadell embarked and disembarked several times in Marseilles, frequently traveling the Rhone coasts near Avignon in the course of thirteen years, back and forth from one place to another without knowing why. The crew of the *Dauphin* were all from Marseilles, for example.

"The book has not survived, but it's possible to get an idea of its contents through the church's trial records. He seems to have been inspired by a confused mixture of Manichean theology, and he spoke of the impossibility of man escaping from Evil, for the enemies of the Soul are not the Devil, the World and the Flesh as the doctrine teaches, because the Devil has nothing to do with that. The World and the Flesh are two of the three parts that make up man and the third is the Soul. But since two parts weigh more than one, man cannot avoid his own fall. Thus the

— 161 —

Kingdom of God, the Soul, will not triumph here on Earth until the World and the Flesh are eliminated. And only a conscientious generation full of Divine Grace will achieve that miracle by sterilizing both men and women, and in that way destroying society: cities, money, honors, everything. Human beings would then return to a pure nomadic state, freely wandering over the newly purified earthly paradise. Then the end of the world would come immediately, through which God, in the final judgment, would have in all those beings the only clean souls ever, and with them could build a new creation.

"And the one who would appear in the Final Days wouldn't be Satan or the antichrist—for they would have no reason to exist, sin having been plucked out of mankind, but would be a hitherto unknown messenger of Jesus Christ, who is always invisibly at our side, and who would be elected pope and chief of all nations and would reign in the new creation . . . a *hidden* pope, it says literally in one of the documents.

"One of the transcribed texts says, 'Human beings are like the man who, on a rainy night, walks through the dark and splashes through muddy ditches and feels the wings of a soft, warm, unknown bird rub against him, but keeps on getting drenched and splattered with mud. I don't know. . . .'

"Later they accused him again, after listening to him in the closed church, swearing and uttering unspecified oaths against the pope. The accusers, all citizens of Andratch, didn't know how to report such blasphemies. That occurred in 1762. At any rate, a broader investigation of Marc Maria de Vadell was begun.

"Was he really a bishop? Remember, he had returned to Andratch in 1756. And six years later, at the time of the trial, he showed a papal bull, an appointment, etc., of let's say a domestic prelate, emanating directly from Pope Benedict XIV, who died in 1758. But when Vadell returned, he announced himself as Bishop of San Juan de Acre, stating that the Holy Father had appointed him to a mission as a *secret* emissary, and that's not reason enough, the secret part, and the pope was also Benedict XIV, just as Carrier had called himself. Anyway, he was sent to Palestine to negotiate with the Emir Daher el Omán—whom he found in San Juan de Acre—for the return of the Holy Sepulchre to the Christians. Did it really happen that way? Everything about Marc Maria was left hanging in midair, without being able to prove anything with clarity, in spite of the comings and goings of episcopal judges and inquisitors. They went through his library, where they found some strange books indeed, all referring to the same thing: the New Man . . . crazy things about raising ants and bees in Hungary and using them to feed a new race of supermen, and others dealing with Nature, God, and Darkness and whether they are one and the same or not. After Marc Maria died, these hallucinations flowered anew through Mariona de Vadell, who had problems with the Inquisition over matters that are not germane here."

In order to realize that the dauphin about which Mariona spoke was in reality the ship *Dauphin* of Marc Maria de Vadell, I had to wait until after the vicar had died. That day he explained to me the shaky story of the bishop. Although he wanted to, it hurt him to suggest the rest of what worried him to the point of such great anxiety. I observed him as he struggled with this, convinced that he was losing his mind. One time he made me sit through a long harangue on why we had to work, if by doing so we only obtained food to feed the body, which was as obscene as defecating.

"But the rebellion," he continued, "destroyed everything: investigative reports, the aleatory dukedom, everything. It happened in 1765. One of the arguments in favor of Marc Maria before the Ecclesiastic Court was that his accusers were in debt to his sister Elionor. It seems that the duke and duchess had a lot of money, and the day after they landed they began to remodel Son Farriol, to buy land, to give out loans at draconian interest rates, and to organize a sort of private army at their service under the command of an oriental freedman—Greek or Turk?—whom they called Captain Dako. And all that in close alliance with Bishop de Vadell.

"There weren't really any Moorish pirate attacks as in the sermon of the Feast of the Valorous Duke. Either tradition or special interests have gradually suppressed the truth. What really happened was that the peasants—more than half the town—wrung dry by continual extortion, driven to a feudal vassalage before the duke, either under threat from Dako's troops or because their hands were tied by so much debt, finally rebelled in anger.

"A whole mob, a human wave of hungry and agitated men advanced across the stubbled fields brandishing spears, scythes, sickles, and flaming torches. Marc Maria de Vadell was saying mass when they told him of the advancing mob singing songs of death. He held out in the church at first, then later escaped. And when the trial of the peasants was over, and right after Elionor had taken justice into her own hands, the bishop disappeared out of fear. The *Dauphin* weighed anchor in the Port, and Marc Maria evaporated from the map forever. And when the peasants assaulted Son Farriol they demolished the place and set fire to the furnishings. Dako and his men were decapitated, the walls were knocked down with sledge hammers, and all the domestic livestock was killed. Then they nailed the duke to the front door.

"They held him up to the door, then took spikes and nailed his hands, and then spread his legs and nailed his feet to the oaken door. The Duke squirmed and screamed out a stream of words that nobody understood, and the peasants laughed and dragged Elionor de Vadell outside, her splendid dress embroidered with rubies and silk thread from China already partly ripped off her.

"It was the same dress she wore that day in the Tower of the Faith, without any of the rips repaired. She had bribed General Zeplien's lieutenant commanding the king's troops who put down the rebellion, and made him bring from prison all the peasants who had been charged with participating in the assault, and who were supposed to be taken to court in Palma. She ordered them lined up in front of the tower. Elionor, laced up in a girdle, her crotch all torn and raw, had set herself up on the battlements, on a stretcher luxuriously upholstered in damask. Ninety-seven prisoners were lined up before her.

"And Elionor, gaunt from age and wear, was urged on by the stinging memory of when that mob of crazy, dirty bearded men tumultuously invaded her bedroom; they brandished pitchforks and billhooks and greased her dry lips with lard so they could all rape her, one after the other, again and again. Elionor directed her vengeance majestically: with a blow of the sword each prisoner was castrated, and while they rolled around on the ground either howling or dying, the rest of the townspeople gathered there were commanded to eat the testicles she had harvested and cooked up in a great cauldron of boiling oil. . . ."

It was I who fled now, so as not to throw up, sick of that conceited old man who had lost touch with reality. And I told him so, harshly. And he broke down and cried. And it was as if he were crying for himself alone, absent from his surroundings, asking himself what the relationship was between who he was now—a shaking body and a mind at times turned to mush—and who he had been as a child, as a youth, as well as the mature man he had become.

"To run after a rabbit through the hills, to read the Evangelists with goose pimples of pleasure, to feel the coolness of summer evenings, to suffer carnal desire and substitute for it the mystical joy of victorious celibacy . . . what I have been, I am no longer. All of that happened, but not to the person I am now, but to a Dionís who has nothing to do with me. . . .

"The only thing that I feel is really mine, clutched close to me, is an image of the future, that of the hearse going up the linden tree hill. And I leave behind me, unfinished, just like all those who have gone before me, what someday perhaps you or someone else will reconstruct."

Bishop of San Juan de Acre. . . . I was in Acre some years ago to give a lecture on the very subject of the Inquisition and the Jews of Majorca. My book *The Majorcan Jews: Seven Centuries of Racism* had sold well in the Jewish community. The meeting had been organized by the Students and Young Workers Association, the *Hanoar Haoved Vehalomed,* which had its meeting room beside the Mesquita of Ahmed Pachá el-Jazzar. I liked to go there and let the temple melt in my mind, seated in its garden before the fountain of ablutions, and walk around its walls, their forceful geometry casting reflections on the sea, the minarets piercing the sky. I lunched on grilled fish in a silent corner near the sea, under a fig tree growing out of that colossal wall. And I had traveled to the Dead Sea, intimate, pale, and quiet with those great flocks of crows circling in the sky.

I lost myself in the Arab market. In my mind, the Knights Templar and Teutonic horsemen were galloping through it, led by princes and bishops and Saint Louis, King of France, conquering inch by inch the light sands of Palestine, inflicting defeat upon the infidel of the crescent moon and prostrating themselves fervently before the sign of the cross.

And I went down in the crypt of Saint John, to the subterranean galleries of the Crusaders. Lewd internal greed had enthroned Balduino IV, the leprous monarch; the Grand Master of the Templars, Jacques de

Molnay, was burned at the stake for sodomy and satanic dealings with the East; it happened right here beside these weeping willows, at this bend in the gray Seine, a little farther down from my apartment in the Bûcherie. . . . The kingdom of Jerusalem was drawn and quartered.

When I returned to the hotel one day in the late afternoon with the press clippings praising my lecture, the concierge handed me a package; I opened it and inside was a cluster of three oranges. For a moment, I didn't make the connection. Then my head suddenly felt as if it would explode—"The Love of the Three Oranges!" and there was only one person with whom I was connected by that illusive and secret bond.

I was driven absolutely mad thinking about my father, and I asked the concierge who had delivered the package. He didn't know. His companion had received it, but his shift had finished at six; I hurried to his house. He said the person who delivered the package was a sailor wearing a hat that had *Spátha* written on it. I ran down to the small port of Acre. There were only a few fishing boats and yachts in port. But a policemen told me I should go to the big docks at Haifa on the other side of the bay, where ships from all over the world were anchored.

That afternoon is graven in my memory. . . . The light was fading to dusk, as if a tender breath were rising from the sleepy sea, looking like a sheet of glass. It was Saturday and the port of Haifa was a field of solitude, like a landscape in a dream, with giant cranes pointing into the opaline sky, rose-tinted to the west. As I moved slowly along in the taxi reading the names of each ship, the water at the dock's edge began to sparkle with the reflections of the first lights appearing like flowers on the hump of Mount Carmel.

Down at the far end of the bay, the tall conical masses of the refinery streamed smoke, and to the north the walls of Acre, where I had to return, were vaguely outlined in the twilight.

Suddenly the cab driver pointed with his index finger to a ship that said *Spátha* in white letters on its extremely long black hull; it was slowly, carefully pulling away from the dock, the noise of its engines barely audible, entering the silky sleeping waters to starboard. Two sailors were coiling hawsers on deck. And leaning against the bridge under a feeble bulb, the heavy silhouette of an officer was visible, his face hidden by the bill of his cap.

I jumped out of the taxi and shouted at the ship, waving my arms desperately. I don't remember what I said, probably "Father!" "Antoni de Vadell!" "Love of the Three Oranges!" I don't know. The officer shouted something back at me that I didn't understand. The *Spátha* drew farther away from the dock, the sound of its engines growing louder.

All I had before me as I stood there was a steel ship of about five or six hundred tons, the hull low in the water from its heavy cargo, a sturdy poop deck, the bow riding proud and high. The next day I went to the Port Authority Office and discovered that the whole crew of the *Spátha* had Greek names.

Everything is winding down. The last day I was in Andratch, a spectral emptiness seemed to have overpowered everything. Autumn dominated the town with the ashen barreness of its chill air. The trees looked like charcoal sketches, most of them already naked. Others still retained some of their sumptuous coppery leaves. The church was outlined as if it were one solid rock, as if for centuries no voice nor gesture had ever resonated within it.

I went by Son Vadell again. I sat in the courtyard on the edge of the well. The chain was rusty, and from deep down in the dark hole, vague guttural noises arose. There probably wasn't any water left. The sturdy barren tower looked as if it were going to plummet into the courtyard. And from their hiding places amid the ivy, whole squadrons of bats rose on the wing, and like splashes of shadow they darted about with electrifying and labyrinthine speed, dispersing and fading with everything else into the spectral light of the dying afternoon. . . .

I wake up in my apartment on Bûcherie Square and take a few stiff, halting steps. It seems like a resurrection, as if I were just emerging from the grave. I'm reminded of a verse by Thomson:

I have seen ghosts who were like men
and men who were like ghosts, gliding about. . . .

Deep in thought and a bit on edge after such a flood of apparitions, my mind is groggy; I feel washed out from fatigue. At the same time my nerves, my whole body feels as if it were rebelling; I feel my tendons painfully tensed.

I haven't even had lunch. And then suddenly I remember Zaida. I look at the time and realize that I have thirty minutes to get to Le Drugstore at Saint-Germaine-des-Prés. I had invited her to dinner. Hunger, the imperative demands from the world of survival, are what push me down the road of life—yes, my life—and it draws me away from this neurotic, secular annihilation surrounding me. . . . It's already eight o'clock. I'll have to hurry, and so I try to shave with a few quick swipes of the razor. In the mirror I see my dark, sunken eyes. A sudden giddiness makes me waver.

But the image of Zaida draws me, returns me to myself. I wash my armpits and spray on some deodorant. This morning, after paying the man with the reddish goatee at the bookstore for *The Contribution to the Relations of the Order of Mercy with the Slave Markets of North Africa and Redemptions Carried Out by It,* I turned around and bumped clumsily into someone: a girl, who fell over backward into a table full of books and posters, knocking the whole mess down, and her along with it. I apologized, helped her up, and then together we picked up all the books and set the table in order again.

Meanwhile, we chatted. She's from Tunis and is studying history at the Sorbonne. She looked at the book by Father Santaló. It interested her right away, because she's also doing her master's thesis on piracy, but the opposite from my work: she's studying the incursions and captives taken by the Christians on the Maghreb Coast. "Some of my relatives were slaves in Majorca and Catalonia," she says. I tell her about mine, carried down the Mediterranean into the Moorish hinterland. And then we laugh: our times are not the times of Jaume Vadell the galley slave. I offer to lend her the book after I've finished reading it. And then I notice how thick her lips are, what a splendid copper-colored complexion she has. That's when I suggested Le Drugstore for dinner.

I head down the stairs with their deeply worn wooden treads creaking, nearly collapsing. The past should be laid to rest, for it *really is dead.* I want to distance myself from my town, my family, and that whole procession of ghosts. We'll have dinner, and then for dessert I'll ask for two of those colorful baroque ice creams laced with whiskey. I want to feel an ample breath of joy as I look into Zaida's eyes . . . yes, joy, as I feel a lush desire rising in me, slowly filling her as well.

And a desire to forget all that rot and decay. I don't know whether it really exists or whether it's just me who is impaled upon it. . . . But I *do* know that with willpower I can get rid of it. Just as I did in Andratch on the last trip at the office of the notary, who, after reading me Uncle Dionís' will, handed me an envelope the vicar had also left for me. Under my name it said, "They will give you this after I'm dead, because it contains another inheritance, this one occult, which you should receive in private and make your own as I did these many years ago, and. . . ." I instinctively tore up the envelope without reading it. I lit the pieces with a match. The tiny flame loosened the thick, tentacular grip that the word *occult,* like a magic formula for darkness, seemed to evoke in me.

I walk on, my umbrella tilted into the rain, which has let up a little; the street lights seem to float, vague and dull in the night. I glimpse Notre Dame out of the corner of my eye, the gargoyles disgorging their streams of water . . . the same gargoyles that were here when Jaume Vadell roasted sea urchins on Dragonera . . . and they'll still be here even after the cocks have stopped crowing for Zaida and for me.

For a moment it feels as if I'm looking at myself from outside my skin—a man with an umbrella walking down the Quai Saint-Michel on a dusky autumn evening . . . amounting to nothing much, really. Just another fleeting, perhaps vague and grotesque presence. Yes, but with something already overcoming all the phantoms of my past: it's the real me, and I'm heading for Zaida's eyes and lips and thighs.